ALEYTYS . . .

hated Company worlds . . . planets owned and ruled solely by the inbred elite descendants of those who had first found and exploited them. Company worlds were like slave plantations in too many ways. Everything for the owners and crumbs for everyone else.

But on one such set of linked worlds, the owners were running scared. A kidnapper of superhuman cunning had already collected ransom on their class kinsmen. And their own security agencies had proved helpless. So they had finally called on Star Hunters—and Star Hunters had called on Aleytys of the Diadem. . . .

JO CLAYTON

has also written:

DIADEM FROM THE STARS

LAMARCHOS

IRSUD

MAEVE

STAR HUNTERS

THE NOWHERE HUNT

MOONGATHER

MOONSCATTER

GHOSTHUNT

Jo Clayton

DAW Books, Inc.
Donald A. Wollheim, Publisher
1633 Broadway, New York, N.Y. 10019

FIRST PRINTING, MAY 1983

1 2 3 4 5 6 7 8 9

 DAW TRADEMARK REGISTERED
U.S. PAT. OFF. MARCA
REGISTRADA, HECHO EN U.S.A.

PRINTED IN U.S.A.

THE HUNT PROPOSED

"How's the ship working out?" Head's bright blue eyes moved over Aleytys, amused and assessing. "You're looking fit." She leaned back in her chair, her hands resting lightly on the wide arms, not fiddling with the fax sheets piled neatly on the desk in front of her.

She's cooler than usual, Aleytys thought. Why? Aloud, she said, "Grey tells me I'm worse than a silvercoat with a sickly cub." She smiled. "He was getting a bit testy when you called him for his Hunt. He said to me, we're together maybe two months of any year and he wants my attention on him, not on some stupid ship."

"I take it you're satisfied with its performance." Head was growing visibly impatient with these chatty exchanges.

"Hah!" Aleytys chuckled. "Sly, that's you. My fuel bills. Madar!"

"Then you're ready for a new Hunt." Head straightened, the chair hummed forward. She bent over the desk, her eyes fixed on Aleytys.

"Ready enough. Depends." Aleytys eyed the fax sheets warily. "You're in an odd mood. Should I worry?"

"Mmm, there are things you're not going to like, but they've got little to do with the Hunt itself—that's relatively straightforward. Cazar Company wants you to chase down a ghost who's been oozing through their security and walking off with clients of theirs. By the way, you mind having a trainee along?"

"Me? You're joking."

"No." Head shifted away from Aleytys, a faint flush staining her cheeks. Aleytys waited.

"My daughter." Head stared at her hand for a moment, closed it into a fist. "She finished her classes at University a few months ago." She separated four sheets from the others,

5

pushed them across the desk toward Aleytys. "Her report summaries. I want . . . no." She shook her head, with a rueful smile. "If she finds out I finagled this, she'll kill me. She wants to make her own way. Read the reports. Favor to me. Think about taking her—up to you, Lee. Has nothing to do with this Hunt." She began fiddling with the sheets, let the silence stretch between them. Finally she lifted a hand in a quick impatient gesture. "Lee, take her with you and look after her a little. And, damn it, don't let her know what you're doing."

"That'd be a good trick." Aleytys wrinkled her nose. "She knows you too well, I suspect." She folded the sheets into a small square packet and put them in her shoulder bag. "Ghost?"

"The Hunt." Head slid open the cover over the sensor plate and touched one of the squares. "This first bit is background, what makes the Cazar so nervous."

The wall screen lit as Head's fingers moved through a short sequence. A star map appeared, showing a section of one of the spiral arms thickly populated with stars. The focus altered until five suns filled the oblong screen, arranged in a ragged oval, highlighted so they stood out starkly against the dusting of stars behind them. "The Aghir suns, so called because their Lords descend from the five sons of a pirate—" Head grinned—"though they'd object vociferously to the term, a bloody old pirate called Aghir Tam. Less than a light-year apart in a heavy drift area, each with a minimum of three planets, each of those rich in heavy metals. Not good for the health and long life of anyone unfortunate enough to live unprotected on the surface on any of those worlds though they have oxygen atmospheres and near one-normal gravity. The present Aghir tejed are sixth-generation survivors. Suspicious, careful, almost prescient in their ability to sniff out danger. Vindictive grudge-holders. Makes them chancy guests." Her blue eyes fixed on Aleytys. A silver-grey brow rose and her mouth curled into a tight smile. "They use contract labor," she said and nodded at the disgusted hiss from Aleytys. "Morally scabby, but there's nothing you can do about it, Lee. Out of every batch imported there were a number who couldn't take the mines and ran away into the wild. Most of them died in a few days but some lived, not only lived but took women from the villages and bred. In five hundred years that could add up to a lot of people in spite of the appalling conditions they lived in and the constant threat from the hired guards of the tej. These people have started fighting back. Within the past ten years they've gotten organized somehow, all five worlds. Looks like one of the tejed imported a leader. The rebels have taken to raiding the metal shipments and supply shipments. They've gotten translight transmitters somewhere, energy weapons, other things, apparently have managed to get in touch with an enterprising smuggler."

Head chuckled. "No, Lee, I'm not going to ask you to hunt the smuggler. Point of all this is, the tejed have tried dealing with their local problems themselves, but there's just too much land to patrol, not enough ships to set up a search for the smuggler. About three years ago, one of the tejed, Kalyen-tej of Liros, started pressing for a conference to set up a joint force since they were obviously getting nowhere on their own. Took a lot of shuttling about before he got an agreement to meet, but he did get it. One year ago. Then he had to find a place they'd agree on; they were far too suspicious of each other to meet on any of the Aghir worlds. He found that too. Cazarit." Head broke off and tapped another sequence on the plate. A new star system appeared on the screen. The focus swooped inward past a pair of gas giants and hovered over a world that was water except for a band of large islands circling it like a linked belt. "Cazarit. Where company execs play their favorite games served by programmed people and androids, whose minds are wiped when the exec departs. One island set aside for common folk who come to pretend they're seeing the depths of depravity, or spend a little time skiing or hunting or lying about in the sun. Everyone tagged who sets foot on soil, visitors get a medalion, employees a bit of metal screwed to a shoulderblade. Cazar brags about the security they provide their favored customers."

"Blackmail?"

"They guarantee privacy and mean it."

The focus changed again, hovered over one of the islands. "Battue. Whoever named the islands had to've had a literal sort of mind." The point of view passed over grazing herds, a few prowling predators. Head was silent as the flying eye circled a large structure, a lodge built like a fortress. The screen flickered as if some of the record had been cut out, then the eye circled a mountain whose peak had been lopped off. A squat massive structure occupied the center of the man-made mesa, tall bronze double-doors in each of the five walls, a landing stage beside each of the doors. "The Conference Hall," Head said. "The other was a specially built lodge where one of the tejed will be housed; there are four more scattered about. In about three weeks the tejed with their guards, women, whatever, will be settling into those lodges."

"How long from here to Cazarit?"

"One day short of two weeks," Head said, her face carefully expressionless.

"They waited a long time to panic." Aleytys blinked slowly. "It ccurs to me I still haven't got much idea why they're in a panic. The Aghir tejed are coming to Cazarit. So?"

Head touched the sensor plate. The screen flickered and split into three sections, two men and a Yaln-tie pair. "This is what has its teeth sunk in Cazar. Three snatches in the past year. Each time they tightened security, each time the ghost didn't wiggle a needle but got his man or, in the last case, tie-pair. After the ransom was collected in the same . . . um . . . unobtrusive way, those—" she nodded at the screen— "were picked up wandering about in a haze on some world a long, long way from Cazarit with no idea how they got there. Cazar would like to cancel the Aghir conference, but stirred up such an uproar when they tried it, they had to back off. With this ghost slipping through their security as if it didn't exist and with the Aghir tejed refusing to let the Cazarit people put any men on Battue, refusing to wear the medallion tags, refusing to let Cazarit security check out anyone in their entourage, the Governors of Cazar Company are about to jitter out of their skins. They want you to find their ghost and turn it over to them before the Aghir arrive."

"They don't want much. One week? Madar!" Aleytys grimaced. "Am I also supposed to guarantee nothing happens to the tejed at the Conference? I don't see how. One determined suicidal rebel could take them all out and me with them."

"Cazar wanted that." Head chuckled. "Even Hagan wouldn't go along with that. It's impossible. After some haggling I got the Hunt limited to the ghost. Get him before the snatch if you can, no, be quiet a minute, get him after the snatch if you have to, but get him."

"Head, what in the world. . . . before the snatch? He could be anywhere, anyone, he could be she, who the hell knows? Their security must have spent hundreds and hundreds of hours, days, months on trying to locate him, to get some kind of clue to who or what he was. I'm supposed to stick my finger in that pie and tease him out? Tell me how, I swear I haven't the faintest idea how to start."

Head grinned, her eyes twinkling. "They've promised complete cooperation. Which means whatever you can make it mean."

"Hah! There's another thing. I have to give him up to them if I catch him?" Aleytys moved her shoulders, grimaced. "I won't do it. I wouldn't give a slime mold into the hands of Company security." She shook her head. "It's not my kind of Hunt. I'm no analyst. How does he pick his targets? How does he take them? How does he slide through alarm systems and past the eyes of guards. . . ." Her voice trailed off; she blinked again. "I knew once. . . . no, too strained a coincidence. Never mind. What makes them think he's still operating? If he's smart enough to fool them three times, he's smart enough to stop when he's ahead. Luck is bound to turn sour sooner or later."

Head tapped her fingers on the top of the desk waiting for Aleytys to run down. "You finished? Good. They're snatching at straws. Ever heard of a scarecrow? Yes? Well then, that's you. The power of the word. Exaggerated stories about you that get more grandiose the farther they spread. The hearings on the Haestavadda Hunt took six months. You saw how many visitors trailed through the hearing rooms. That was over a year ago, word's had time to travel far. Your name alone. . . ." Head smiled, "nowadays your name alone lets us double and sometimes triple our fee." She sobered. "Doesn't make my job any easier. Bruised egos for my Hunters and disgruntled clients when they can't boast of hiring you."

"I take it I'm still on probation." When Head nodded, Aleytys pressed her lips tightly together and stared past her at the wall. After a minute, she said quietly, "I have to thank you for the ship, my friend. I'll take this Hunt. I don't want to but I will. It's the last I'll take under these circumstances.

Either I belong here or I get out. You can put that to them more tactfully if you want, but I mean it."

"I know."

"Damn, I hate this kind of thing. By the way, when Grey and I were out testing the new ship, we had a long-distance escort. RMoahl hounds."

Head nodded again. "They're still sending periodic demands that you be turned over to them. They want their property."

"So I can expect to be followed whenever I venture out of Wolff space."

"Did they crowd you?"

"No, not really. Just hung on and followed."

"They won't. Not after what you did to those Tikh 'asfour ships. The chief arbiter turned pale when you got to that part and offered to demonstrate if they didn't believe you. Very naughty for you, Lee." A corner of Head's mouth twitched up into a half-smile. "But effective. Well, now, back to the business at hand. On Cazarit you'll be dealing with people who got where they are by the ruthless use of power. To cap this, the kind of people they deal with have accumulated enormous wealth and power also, usually by means that won't stand light. Cazar Governors can promise all they want, it will be Cazar local execs who have to do the performing. They'll give you just as much as you can force from them, even if, in the end, that undercuts their own positions. The nature of the beast, get it now, tomorrow I may be dead. Use whatever means you have to pry what you need out of them, your reputation gives you a bit of added leverage. Our fee, by the way, has been set on an ascending scale according to what you accomplish. We get paid something if you just show up and sit around. More, if you pick up information but nothing happens. Most, if you actually catch the ghost."

Aleytys sighed. "This whole thing stinks. The sooner the rebels kick the tejed out of their holds, the better, far as I'm concerned. And any being clever enough to bleed the Companies has me cheering for him. I know I said I'd take the Hunt, but, dammit Head, I can't turn the ghost over to them if I luck out and catch him, her or it. Couldn't live with myself after. Do this for me, will you? Screw out of Cazar Governors an agreement that says I decide what to do with the ghost." She smiled, her lips trembling a little. "At least you

got me a ship, my friend, thanks for that, whatever happens."
She stood, tapped the side of her shoulder bag. "I'll read
these. And I'd like to talk to Tamris, send her to my house
when you've got the agreement—or not got it as the case
may be. If I think we can get along, I'll take her with me. If
I go." She passed her hand back over her hair, sighed. "Might
as well have one friendly face around."

Head walked with her to the door. "Don't count too much
on friendly, I'm afraid she's going to resent Mother manipulating her again."

Aleytys laughed, touched Head's shoulder. "Why wasn't I
born to a quiet life?"

"Because you'd die of boredom before the year was out."

LILIT

In a little over two weeks I am going to kill my father.

Ink like black velvet, thin lines, forceful strokes, a powerful contrast to the delicate ivory of the paper. Lilit smiled at what she'd written, liking the dramatic flow of the script, the drama of the words. She brushed her hair out of her eyes, flipped the mass of it back off her shoulders, dipped the ancient pen into the ink Acthon had made for her of gum and lampblack.

I can't remember when I started to hate my father. Not fear him, no. That I sucked in with my mother's milk. Milk. That was all I ever got from her and that grudged since I was her seventh daughter when she desperately needed a son. She was not quite twenty-five when I was born and making heroic efforts to hold my father's interest, or so I was told much later. In her disappointment she came close to killing me. My sisters made sure I learned that once I was old enough to understand what it meant. I think they were as angry at me as she was—because I turned out to be a girl, I mean. A brother would have given them status. I never really knew my mother, can't remember much about her though I was nearly two when she died trying to have another baby. The child died too, but no one mourned it—another daughter.

Tapping the end of the pen against her chin, Lilit gazed at what she'd written. She laid the pen down in the tight crease between the pages of the book, pushed her chair back and walked across the room, the fur on the bottom of her long black gown brushing softly against her ankles, the silk of the gown sliding agreeably across her bare skin. Feeling a little like one of the ghosts that haunted her as her unshod feet moved over the thick rug with not a whisper of sound, she crossed to the window and pushed the gauzy drape aside. Holding back her thigh-length sweep of black hair, she settled herself on the windowseat and pressed her face against the glass looking out hungrily past the flicker of the force dome that protected the Hold from the dangerous free air of Liros II. The sun hung low in the west, its light nearly swallowed by the heavy clouds. Colors were more subdued than usual, the rough red firebush lying like velour on rolling hills that swept to the jagged bleak line of the Draghastils, crossed by lines of chalouri that were black in the distance and a rich deep purple up closer, their fleshy stalks and hair-fine foliage hanging limp. The air out there seemed to hang still. Nothing moved—even inside the Hold she could feel the stillness, the sense of waiting became almost unbearable, though that perhaps drew something from her mood.

She looked past the outer wall at the settlement across the sluggish river. Children were running about, in and out of the squat houses built of crumbling mud bricks and the lamina of dirt-lily pads, a dark grey-brown, darker and drabber than ever in the half-light. Some women were gathered at the well. They stood talking, their water jars held on the well coping with one hand while the other gestured with staccato impatience. What was the point, her father had said when she asked him why he didn't give the village folk a pump and water in their homes. The water in the well was limited, he said, but it was less contaminated with poisons than that in the river. A pump and plumbing would have made them careless, they'd soon exhaust the well and have to turn to the river. This way, having to carry every drop, they were forced to conserve. It made sense in an unhuman sort of way, like much of what her father said and did. A few old men sat on benches outside the houses, some of them bent over chess-boards set between them, others were talking or staring out toward the mountains. She counted them. Nine. Two gone, sick or dead, since she'd counted them last. In the distance she could see a line of men trudging back from the small cleared fields where they fought the poisonous vegetation and the stingy soil to wring from it the crops they needed to supplement the basic provided by her father. At the well, one woman dragged a bit of cloth across her face; she glared up at the Hold, picked up her jar and stalked off, the others

watching her a moment then closing in again and talking intensely.

Lilit passed the back of her hand across her forehead, the
medallion on a thin gold chain about her wrist tickling her
face. She fingered the smooth oval, feeling the indentations of
the incised crest. Tagged and ready for sale, she thought. She
made a fist. Enjoy the bride gift I bring you, toad, she
thought. The world outside the Hold stretched to the horizon,
plum and magenta, garnet and vermilion, a mosaic of bands,
stripes and spots. Lightning danced through the clouds and
the mountains were beginning to glow as the sun sank away,
shining an eerie bluewhite in the almost-night. This isn't a
place made for man, she thought. She'd never, not once, been
outside the Hold; her life had been spent in the halls and
walls of the Hold, in a small patch of lush roof garden filled
with off-world plants that died after a year or two no matter
how carefully they were tended. Nineteen years, she thought.
She laughed, a harsh, bitter sound that pleased her as she
stood aside and listened to herself. "To protect my breeding
capacity. No malformed grandsons or granddaughters to em-
barrass Kalyen-tej."

She watched the storm roll closer for a few minutes then
slipped from the seat and stood with bare feet sunk ankle deep
in the moss-green rug. Her lips pressed together, she contemplated the contrast the room made with the settlement. Lacy
curtains, heavy dark furniture. A wide comfortable bed with
clean sheets changed every second day. A bathroom through
a hand-rubbed wooden door in the wall by the head of the
bed, clean towels, all the hot or cold water she wanted at the
touch of her finger. And this was only a room in the woman-
side, high up in the womantower, isolated, a place where she
could brood and be forgotten. "Until he needs a bait to catch
a sly toad," she murmured. Though the room was cool and
supplied with air purified and kept fresh by the great conditioners in the ground beneath the Hold, she felt stifled. She
lifted the hair off the nape of her neck, closed her eyes.
Abruptly she pulled her hands down, went swiftly back to the
writing table. She stared at the pages, smoothed them slowly
while she stared into the shadows gathering in the corners of
the room. She dipped the pen in the ink and wrote:

It's foolish to be writing these things down. I know that.

Insanity. Dangerous to myself and the people I'm going to be naming. From what I've read in the books I stole from Father's library, most murderers seem to want people to understand why they did what they did. It seems I share that compulsion. I want someone to understand why my father has to die—no, that's not honest. At least let me have that luxury here—being honest with myself and with whoever reads this. Luxury, yes it is. I can remember being honest, really honest, only tiny bits of time before this—when I was alone or with Metis—and not even much of the time with her—so—so I'm going to kill my father and the rest of them, the Aghir tejed. This won't come again, this chance that brings them under one roof.

Why?

You who read this don't need telling why the tejed need killing—

Why me?

Because I'm the one who can make sure it goes right.

Because—

Acthon came to see me one night last year, the way I showed him, through the walls—

She stretched, set the pen down beside the book and stared at the flickers of lightning outside the force dome.

She felt a tug. In her dream it was a tiktik running along her arm, six six-toed feet cool and pattering on her flesh. Another tug. It was Jantig, her next older sister, hissing at her, pulling her arm. Dimly she knew this was wrong. Jantig had been married off two years before to a merchant of the Cladin Group. More hissing, an urgency in it, her name, a slap on her cheek. She came groaning from uneasy sleep to see Acthon bending over her. She felt to make sure the narrow straps of her nightgown were where they should be, pushed the quilts back and sat up. She rubbed her eyes, tried to get her weary, aching head in some kind of order. "What is it?"

Acthon sat on the bed facing her. "You know that conference he's trying to set up?" He never spoke Kalyen-tej's name unless he was forced into it.

She let her hands drop to rest on her thighs. "Well?" His face, a younger version of Kalyen's, held a brooding angry look. Sometimes she wondered why she didn't hate him for his face, but there was no question of that, behind the face he was utterly different from her father. He was Gyoll's son far more than he was Kalyen's.

"He was talking to Aretas tonight. Got him to agree."

"So? You knew he would, one way or another." Her hands closed slowly into fists. She leaned toward him. "Why are you here now?"

"Lanten-tej wants a sweetener. His last wife killed herself a few months ago."

"Me?"

"You got it. Lanten wants the wedding held before the conference opens; *he* held out for after, he doesn't trust Aretas farther than he could throw him, but had to give in finally, Aretas wouldn't be budged."

She sat silent, so cold inside she couldn't move, couldn't think.

"You want out?" He bent toward her, tapped her silk-covered knee. "I can take you to Elf in the Wild."

She sucked in a long unsteady breath, exploded it out. "Let me think." She pulled her knuckles across her forehead. "I can't think. What's Aretas like? You went with Father when he was shuttling about on the first round of talks."

"You remember Grandfather?"

"No. I've heard things."

"Magnify what you heard, add a body like a bloated toad."

"My bridegroom. Go away for now, brother, I have to think and I can't with you here." She pushed her hair back, smiled at Acthon, who slid off the bed and stood beside it looking gravely down at her. "Come back tomorrow night if you can." He nodded and turned to go. "And thanks, brother," she called softly.

She set down quickly what her brother had told her. A year ago, that night, a night when she paced the room struggling with impossible choices until the sky outside began to pale. She pressed a new page down and began writing more slowly, dipping deep into the past.

Hate—yes—I don't know when it was born in me, but I know when it began to burn me. That came when he took Metis. My Metis. I've loved one person in my nineteen years.

*One. When my mother died, my father left orders I was to
have a nursegirl from the village. He named her. Metis.
Aiela's daughter. And Gyoll's daughter. Someone brought her
to the Hold and left her in the nursery. She was, I think, about
seven at the time, Acthon's half-sister. Her youngest sister
was two, exactly as old as I was, born the same day, almost
the same hour. Metis was greatly fond of her, it was this perhaps that caught at her imagination and broke through her
bitter resentment and let her see me as the miserable little rat
I was instead of the pampered daughter of the family that
oppressed her people.*

*Men are cheaper and easier to replace than machines and
at times self-replicating. And trapped here. Most of Liros II
vegetation and animal life is poisonous so we keep a rope
about their necks, or so Father thinks; the others too. I suppose. Or they'd do more about it than they have. Metis told
me that her people have found out how to cook muddogs and
some other things so they can eat them. It's enough to let
them live in the Wild—I'm getting away from what I meant
to say. It's easier, I think, to go on about things that don't
really matter.*

*Metis. Her heart always betrayed her. She came to me in-
tending to do the job—that and only that—but I was a
scrawny, sad little thing, nothing like she expected though she
was simmering with resentment when she measured the difference between her home and the Hold nursery.*

*The first things I remember for myself are soft arms and a
husky voice that comforted me when demons came at night
wearing my father's face. I trotted around after her, she told
me, like a tiktik after its dam, all black hair and black eyes
and skinny arms and legs like sticks. I knew she was my
friend not just my nursegirl the day she smuggled me in a
tiktik baby when she came back from her freeday. Not because she gave me something but because of what she risked
to bring it to me. It was a tiny thing with prickly black fur
and beady black eyes, a pointed black nose that was cold and
wet, a nose that sniffed nervously about and poked into everything. And it had long skinny legs like mine, but (not like
mine) covered with a fine red fur, six legs, each paw with six
delicate fingers. When it ran about, it used all the legs, but it
could sit up and use its front paws with formidable dexterity.
I was entranced by it from the moment it wrapped its tiny*

red fingers about one of mine. Metis made me take care of it
by myself, clean up after it, I think she was trying to teach
me how to love something other than myself. When it was especially content it made a tiny cooing and its whole body vi-
brated with the sound. When it bit off bites of something, its
small square teeth made the sound that gave it its name. In
the wild it lived in large herds and the tiktik of their feeding,
Metis said, could fill an afternoon.

For some time we managed to keep the tiktik a secret, but
one day I was careless. I'd been playing with it in the unused
storeroom where we kept it. In the hall outside, just down a
bit, two of my older sisters got into a hair-pulling fight. I ran
to watch the fun, forgetting to make sure the latch clicked
home. Of course the tiktik got out, and, of course, another of
my sisters found it, started tormenting it—that being her
nature—and got herself bitten. Her screams brought the attendants and me—in time to see the tiktik's terror as it raced
about, in time to see an attendant snatch it up and dash its
brains out against the wall.

What followed might not have happened if Metis had been
with me but that was her freeday and she was home. I started
crying over the tiktik's body. That was a mistake, but what
did I know, a four-year-old baby? I should have known, I'd
had all too many lessons in the need to keep quiet, to keep
my feelings hidden from the others, but I'd never really loved
anything before, never had anything that was mine alone. It
was mine and it was dead, that's all I knew. Mine and dead.

My stepmother heard the furor and came. She was a quiet
woman, a rather nice woman, I know that now, though I
hated and feared her then. She'd already given my father the
son my own mother had died trying to produce. At that
time she was newly pregnant with my second half-brother
(legitimate, that is) and suffering with him. She might have
tried easing her misery by passing it on to those around her,
but she didn't. My sisters and I knew, all of us, that we lived
here on sufferance, worthless, unwanted. You'd think we'd
draw together, make common cause against our father and
the system that made us worthless, but that didn't happen.
I'm digressing again, this is harder than I thought.

My stepmother discovered easily enough how the tiktik had
got into the Hold. I told her. I had a strong sense that what I
was doing was wrong, was a betrayal, but at four-going-on-

five, one oftimes does not really understand all the consequences of one's acts and adults are formidable adversaries.

The attendants brought Metis to the nursery. My stepmother sent my sisters away, her ice-blue gaze silencing their protests, but she kept me there to watch. In her stern way she was being kind. She was teaching me my place and she was protecting both Metis and me. Something had to be done, something fairly drastic, or word of this escapade might have reached my father. Metis could have been whipped bloody with the spansir and taken from me, might have been killed for endangering a tej's daughter—even a worthless daughter was worth more than the child of a contract laborer, that was what my father called them always though others of the tejed weren't so delicate in their pronouncements.

My stepmother forced me to stand in front of her. Her long slender hands were firm on my shoulders. Metis was cuffed to the wall and her blouse was torn away. A serviteur was instructed and given the clisor. Her neck and shoulders were rigid. I couldn't see her face. I didn't want to. My stepmother spoke, holding me tight against her legs. "Girl, you brought an animal of the Wild into this house. Your life would be forfeit if I thought you'd done this with malice, but I believe it was only thoughtlessness, a misguided attempt to amuse your charge. You will receive fifteen strokes of the clisor and be sent to your family in disgrace for one week. At the end of that time present yourself at the postern gate to resume your duties here. Do you understand what I am saying?"

With my stepmother's hands so tight on my shoulders they hurt, I waited in agony for my friend's answer, for it seemed to me that Metis could be lost forever in the space of a word not spoken. For what seemed an eternity Metis's back and shoulders held rigid, then she sighed and said, "Yes, Taejin, I understand."

Though some of the ice melted within me, I still had bad enough ahead of me. My stepmother held me, would not let me turn away. I think I felt on my own body every blow of that whip. The clisor. Its five broad soft strips of leather hurt but they wouldn't tear flesh. Again, in her way, my stepmother was being kind. The spansir had five tails also, but these were braided, knotted about small spurs, with metal *points on the tips. Fifteen strokes of the spansir would have killed my friend.*

Metis was stubbornly silent for the first few strokes, but in the end she screamed as the leather beat again and again in the same place. My body jerked with hers. I tried to turn away and bury my face in my stepmother's long skirt, stop up my ears with my fists, but she wouldn't let me, she made me watch. I learned a lot more than the simple lesson of obedience she intended to teach me. I learned in a way I have never forgotten that a single thoughtless act could have terrible consequences and that—bad as it is to endure punishment yourself—it is infinitely more terrible to be the careless cause of suffering for someone you love.

The attendants took Metis down and led her away. My stepmother marched me back to the nursery and left me there—left me to the attention of my sisters. Well—let that pass. I can understand them better now, though to understand it not to forgive. I will not speak of forgiving my stepmother, she deserves better than that, but the system that forced her to act as she did—that I can neither forgive nor forget.

Metis came back and life went along much as usual. She sat in on my lessons, learned more than I did. She could already read and write, her father taught her, and her mind was quick and sure. She had a terrible hunger for knowledge, more than I ever had or ever will have. The first books I sneaked out of my father's library, I took for her though I was soon fetching them for myself as well, so powerful was her influence over me. Neither of us found much meat in the things females were allowed to learn.

When I was six and Metis was eleven, we moved away from the nursery into the tower room. Stepmother worked that for us, it made the nursery that much more peaceful. Selas, her youngest son, was sickly and Metis and I were at the center of most of the noisier fusses. It was better when we were alone, easier for her when we were gone.

I had a lot more in common with the tiktik than the way I looked. I poked my long nose into everything. Many nights I couldn't sleep and went roaming through the halls. I found my way to my father's library, as I mentioned before, and spent long hours looking through it. I even found a way into the walls. Those walls that looked so massive were fake, honeycombed with passages that must have been bored by one or more of my ancestors. They went everywhere with plenty of peepholes. I loved the dark silence between the walls and spent as much time as I could there, though Metis didn't like it and was afraid I'd get lost and starve. Yes, I spent as much time as I could there, locating all the exits, mapping the maze in my head. I don't think my father knew about the passages, I never saw any sign he did.

I loved spying on people, watching them when they didn't know they were being watched. It was a kind of power and gave me intense satisfaction. This is one of the things I never spoke about to Metis. I know without having to think it that this would disgust her. I was very careful in my explorations, having learned my lesson most thoroughly. I could not take chances with the skin of my friend; she certainly would have been blamed for my mischief. For the same reason I became a model girlchild, modest and quiet, industrious and obedient. I wanted no one to think that Metis was bad for me. Actually, she should have been sent home when I reached my eighth year, because I was starting my serious schooling—not books, but the arts of pleasing a man and running a home for whatever husband my father would select for me. Because my father said nothing, she stayed. I despised those lessons, but I have my share of vanity, more than my share Metis used to say. I have good bones. I'm not pretty, but I like my face. I can be elegant. I like my skin to be smooth and fair. I like the sliding feel of silk against bare skin. I like the gold chains that call attention to the delicacy of my wrist and ankle. I like having hair that is a night-black fall so long I can sit on it.

And I hate the thought of dying.

And I hate the thought of lying under that toad of a man and letting him do what he wants with me.

Though my father is more intent on crushing the rebellion than on seeing me wed, he is a devious man and never so pleased as when he can make one act serve many ends. He is pleased enough with my looks and with the docility I've exhibited these many years. All my other sisters are married now, Jantig was the last. I've been holding my breath the past three years, but with Stepmother dead and not around to remind him he'd got an unwed daughter stuck in the attic, he just forgot about me until this conference began obsessing him.

*Still, I don't really care what he's planning for me, I have
my own plans. In a way I have to keep talking myself into
this, reminding myself how little power I have for changing
my life, how much my death would mean if I took the tejed
with me.*

Lilit read the last words over then put the pen down,
stroked burning eyes, smoothed the tip of her forefinger over
the cool surface of the ivory paper. She shut the book and
began tracing the patterns stamped in the soft leather binding. She'd found the book years ago behind some others in
the library. Lilit the child had been fascinated by a book with
no printing in it, only blank pages. She'd left it where it was
with reluctance; for over a month she fingered it every day
but left it behind when she left. In the end she couldn't resist
it, took it from the library, hid it away in the walls with her
other treasures—and waited with sweaty anxiety to see if her
father missed it. He never said anything. And the book was
obviously old, the heavy paper yellowed at the edges. For a
long while she forgot it and only now found a reason for
using it.

Ouside, the rain struck the force bubble and slid in a grey,
wavery curtain to the ground beyond the walls, lending an
eerie unreality to the view; she kept the curtain draped back
from the window because she liked the effect of moonlight on
the vista, because in a way it seemed to widen the strangling
narrowness of the world she lived in, the room in the tower,
the holes in the walls, the garden on the roof of the tower,
the dining room where she now and then acted as hostess for
her father, a round she knew as well as as she knew the lines
in her palms. She no longer took light with her into the walls,
her feet read the stones for her, she seldom needed to think
where she was or where she wanted to go, she ran through
the holes, a peeping ghost in the walls. The peepholes were
like the window in her tower room, giving her a fleeting contact with a world she'd never touch.

She yawned, finally tired, hoping to sleep, though that was
always a chancy thing for her. It was late, very late, and
there were many things she had to do in the morning. She
picked up the book, held it a moment. A prickle at the back
of her eyes made her shake her head impatiently. There was
no one to talk to now, not since her father took Metis from

her, not since Metis died bearing his child—only these
smooth silent pages. She pushed the chair back and stood,
stretching a little to work out the cramps from sitting so
long. At the wall she pressed on a section of carving. A small
panel clicked open. She set the book in the cavity revealed,
pushed the panel shut, her hands trembling on the wood. She
was never sure how much her father knew about the hidden
places in the Hold, but she did count on his unexpressed but
evident contempt for the female members of his family. What
she'd already written was enough to warrant the strangler's
cord for her and death by spansir beating for those she
named in the book. That was what bothered her most, betraying the others involved in her plans, yes she needed the book
and this talking out of her life, she was saying things she ab-
solutely had to say, things she could tell to no one else. Not
even to Acthon. She clicked the panel shut, slipped out of her
dressing gown, hung it neatly in a closet, slid into bed, the
sheets whispering crisply about her. The bed was empty and
cold, the other body that once shared it with her was gone
three years now and she still was not used to sleeping alone.
At the beginning of each night she stretched out on the right
side of the bed, not in the middle, though her restless turning
carried her into the middle most nights.

*For the past month Father has been insisting I come down
to dine every night with the family. I know why he's doing it,
he wants to be sure I'm really calm about the proposed marriage, to be sure I'm in good health, to be sure I'm properly
submissive. Somewhere he has picked up the notion that I've
gone strange, living alone in my tower room. He can't believe
that even a woman could be content spending her days em-
broidering her wedding robes. I think he's decided I'm a little
stupid. And he's satisfied with that. Though he still calls me
down, he ignores me and spends much of the time lecturing
to my brothers on how they are to conduct themselves when
he's gone and quizzing them. I learn a lot to pass on to
Acthon and Gyoll so it's worth the boredom and the wear
and tear on my stomach.*

*At the table my father confirmed finally the date of our de-
parture then spent much of the meal questioning Ekeser
about handling every possible difficulty that could come up in
his absence. He ignored Selas, anyway Selas was off some-*

*where in the dreamworld where he spent most of his time.
Weak of body, weak of mind—though I don't know about
that last, it was hard to tell, he seldom said anything, but
I've seen him, time after time, defeat Ekeser's malice without speaking a word, simply by seeming not to notice what
was being done to him. I wonder about him whenever I
think of him, but that's not often, he escapes me as easily as
he does the others.*

At the table she watched the play in front of her with little
interest; most of what she heard, she'd heard before and
passed on. She was long over her first amazement at seeing
that her father despised his sons almost as much as he did his
daughters, though he valued them considerably higher. Not
Acthon, he didn't despise him. Sometimes she'd thought he
might go against custom and law—he was after all the ultimate law in the Liros system—and acknowledge Acthon,
make him the heir, but lately she understood that he couldn't
do that. He believed in tradition and law; no matter how
much he might stray beyond their borders in his private life,
in matters concerning the rule of the Liros system, he kept
strictly to the precedent of his forebears. The legitimate line
must be preserved, power must be conserved in the hands of
his family, the family bonds must be kept intact, the line of
the Kalyens guaranteed continuance.

*From the look on Ekeser's face I'd say he'd listened to
identical catechisms at times other than dinner. He's fifteen
now and getting more and more restive, especially since Father won't let him indulge habits here he picked up on trips
to the other worlds of the Aghir.*

*Father ignored me as usual during the meal, except for
those elaborate rituals of respect by which these men honor
women but actually dispose of them, pushing them into a
place were they become meaningless except as walking
wombs, virtually interchangeable and eminently discardable.
Enough of this too; by the gods that don't exist, I miss you,
my sister, my love. There's no one I can say these things to
and vent the venom that threatens to choke me. I hold them
in until I feel like exploding because what's the use—who
would ever listen to me? No one but you, my Metis. No one.*

Father came into my room after dinner tonight; he almost

*never comes up here, so I was caught by surprise. My throat
closed up and I felt frozen. Fortunately I was putting a few
last stitches in the outer robe of my wedding display. If he'd
come a few minutes later, I would have had this book in my
hands. That was the thing that dominated my thoughts as he
looked me over. He spoke and I answered, I don't know
what, but I suppose it was suitable since he made no com-
ment. Fool, fool, I told myself over and over.*

*You look like a scared rat, he said. His face sour, he
walked around me as I stood clutching the robe to my
breasts, not understanding his evil mood. Your appearance is
good enough, he said. He put his hand under my chin and
lifted my head, ignoring my involuntary flinch. I hate it when
he touches me but what can I do? Skinny, he said. No spirit,
he said. He took his hand away and stepped back. Just as
well, he said. You'll get through this better that way. I've a
good idea what passed between you and that girl. (He meant
Metis, why couldn't he say her name to me, he knew her in
every sense of the word, why won't he say her name?) Lanten-tej will school you in other directions, it's only necessary
that you be virgin. The less you struggle, the sooner he'll tire
of you and let you go your own way. Remember that, he
said. The choice is yours, he said. He left me then, walking
out without another word.*

*He doesn't like what he's doing to me, I saw that from the
moment he first told me about the marriage. At least he saw
my sisters wed to fairly decent men. Aretas sticks in his
throat, but he thinks he's working for a greater goal and he'd
swallow worse to achieve it.*

*It was some time before I moved. I stood frozen in the
center of the room, hating my helplessness, hating my father,
hating myself, my stomach churning, my mouth dry, my eyes
burning, my head throbbing.*

*Father coming in like that frightened me but it started me
thinking also. Who am I writing this for? If for myself, then I
intend to see the book burned to ash and scattered to the
winds as I leave. Yet I, the not-yet-murderer, am writing to
explain—who am I explaining to, what am I explaining? Yes,
I want someone to know who I am, yes, that's it, know me,
warts and all, know what I've been doing for years, that,
locked behind these walls though I am, I have reached out
and helped change things in the Wild, in the village. Yes, I'll*

*give the book to Acthon the night before we leave and ask
him not to read it until the rebels have the Hold and have
taken Kiros II for themselves and their children. What they
do with it I don't care, I've listened to Gyoll explain a
hundred times but it never meant much to me. I just know
this is wrong, the way things are now, here, it had to change.
I'd like the people to know that I joined their struggle, joined
it when I was a child, joined it before I even knew there was
a struggle. If I dared leave this Hold, my people, you'd spit
on me if you dared. I want you to know me, to understand
what I'm doing and why. Yes that's it, I want someone, anyone to understand.*

Lilit sat back, nibbling at the end of her pen. The small
lamp over the writing table cast a cone of light down on her,
leaving the rest of the room in shadows, shadows that flickered now and then as lightning flickered in the distance,
whited out momentarily as closer flashes cut through the
murky night outside. "Maudlin," she muttered, sighed, rubbed
the end of the pen holder across her forehead. "I'm begging
them to sympathize with me, as if they owed me something,
but that's nothing close to the truth, I did all of this because I
enjoyed it. Right, my Metis?" She laughed, laid the pen
down, stretched her body, raising her arms as high as she
could, enjoying the stretching of her spine. After a last
stretch and a groan, she relaxed, pushed her hair back off her
face, pulled a leg up and tucked it under the other, swinging
the dangling leg back and forth as she frowned at the book.
"It's hard to say what I want. One's mind goes off in all
directions if one lets it loose." She smiled into the darkness,
seeing Metis standing on the far side of the bed, affection in
her eyes but a scolding frown on her round face, her head
turning slowly back and forth, her shining pale hair catching
the little light of the room. To the ghost Lilit said, "I know,
dear one, discipline myself, no one can do it for me." She
saw a slow smile stretch the full lips then the image melted
and Lilit turned back to the book.

*Facts—this world is called Liros II. My family never gave
it a name and the people in the Wild call it whatever occurs
to them after some particularly frustrating occurrence. Liros.
Our sun. A sore in the sky. The mountains shine in the dark*

on nights when there is no moon. I am not permitted to know what that shining means to the men that work the mines. I am not permitted to know how little protection the protective gear my father provides gives the miners. For my father's men—and this too I am not permitted to know—life is marginally less harsh. On other worlds the tejed don't bother, the miners are sent down in whatever rags they bring with them. My father is generous too as to the shifts his men work. He buys enough of them that he can divide them into three shifts. Three months in the mine, six off. Even so, twice in my lifetime, he has had to go offworld to contract for more laborers as he calls it, I could give it a far harsher name. Naturally, the others of the tejed go far more often to the market.

There are five continents on this world, each with its overseer, the overseer's Hold, his villages and fields. Each overseer receives a percentage of the profit from the ore he gets out of his miners. The rest of the income goes to my father who controls the only landing field and the only starship on the world. He also limits the number of flitters and floats the overseers can use. The advantage of controlling the air is near incalculable on this sparsely settled world with its five small centers of population, no waterships to sail the sullen seas, no reason to fish these waters since the fish the fishers would catch would be poison. Metis tells me that when it is very dark and no rain falls, the seas glow like the mountains; whether that's true or not I couldn't say.

We've been here on Liros II such a short time, only five hundred years. Outside the protection of the Holds many die. Aiela, Acthon and Metis's mother, she died of sheer exhaustion after producing ten children. That's what Metis said, she was simply tired to death. Little Sister wasn't the last, two more were born after her.

The children of Aiela—Acthon (sired by my father), Metis (Gyoll's daughter), Elf. Elf was very small but otherwise apparently normal. They kept her hidden from the death squads, Metis told me, exchanged her for a borndead. She lives in the Wild, eats the plants, fish and beasts of the Wild with impunity. She is tiny; according to Acthon her head wouldn't reach my waist, though she's past twenty-five. Nothing attacks her out there, it's her gift. She serves as go-between for the rebels on this continent, rides the huge flying *predators I see sometimes outside my windows, no tapping into that sort of communication.*

The child after Elf died in the womb, the next two only lived a day or so, both were smothered by the death squad though they would have died anyway. The baby just before Little Sister was a healthy bright boy though he had no arms or legs; him they sent into the Wild and replaced with a borndead from the Wild or Father's guards would have taken him away and smothered him too. They did that with all the radically changed who survived birthing. After Kedarie Little Sister, there were two other babies, born too deformed to live. Aiela died with the birth of the last.

Without realizing it, the Aghir tejed are producing natives for these hostile worlds by exposing the men to the poison earth and making the women into broodmares. By their intransigence and extravagance with life they are creating a population that in a few more generations will rise up and destroy them. While they—we—remain strangers and sojourners of this world, their slaves are making it a home.

But those slaves aren't going to wait.

"Well?" Acthon stepped through the wall panel, clicked it shut, came over to the bed.

"Well enough." Lilit sat cross-legged in the center of the bed. She smoothed her hand over hair she'd brushed until it had the sheen of black glass. The feel of it comforted her as she contemplated what she was going to say to her half-brother. She'd read in one of the books from her father's library that to be continually touching or caressing oneself was a sign of something wrong inside. That had bothered her awhile until she decided that with so much wrongness outside her, a little inside was only a way of mending the balance.

"That isn't. . . ."

"I know. What do you think of doing something at the conference, taking out the tejed with one stroke?"

"We've talked about it. A lot." He spoke slowly, his eyes intent on her. "Hard to plan when we don't know the ground or if we could get one of us into the entourage."

"You already have one." She lifted her head and stared at him.

"Lilit!"

"That's right." She smiled. "Lilit will be there. Think about it. All of them there for Lilit's wedding. I've been thinking. Between Cazarit and Aghir security you'd have a tough time getting anything powerful enough into the Hall, you can't even know when they're all in one spot. That's not something you can handle from a distance. Pre-set devices, too chancy, too easy to detect. You need someone in the Hall to carry the death—whatever you make it—and trigger it when the time is right. Someone who won't be suspected. Someone able to carry the death safely among the skirts of six or seven bulky robes. In a word, me."

He stared at her. "You want to die?"

"No," she said. She laughed. "Think about it, brother. Think about Aretas. Think about death. A handsomer bridegroom than the one my father found me and a kinder one. Isn't that so? I don't want to talk anymore. Tell Gyoll what I said. Go away, please."

She watched him step through the panel, look back at her, then pull the panel shut. She smiled at the ghost that shimmered in the corner, broken planes of light and shadow. "A better bridegroom," she said.

TAMRIS

She tugged her tunic down with hands that shook a little from nervousness and irritation. There was a lump in her throat. She knew her voice would break when she thumbed the announcer, knew it and was disgusted at herself. She swallowed.

"Go see Aleytys," her mother said.

Her mother's voice was mild and unemphatic, but Tamris recognized the tone. This was reason speaking, experience presumed to equal wisdom. She was very fond of her parent but sometimes she felt smothered in silk, resenting her mother's time-honed skills in manipulating others. Head Canyli Heldeen could sometimes be a very difficult parent even while she was being a warm and loving woman.

"If she'll take you on this Hunt," her mother said, "keep her steady, Mari."

She tired not to let her mother's accomplishments overwhelm her, though this was hard now and then. Head had done and been and already left behind what Tamris wanted to do and be. She wanted to stretch herself, to see how far she could reach—above all, she wanted out of her mother's shadow.

"She's been calming down a bit lately," her mother said. "Accepting the compromises of living. Dammit, this is going to disturb that accommodation. I want her steady, I want her ready to work for me. I'm counting on you to keep her on track."

She swallowed again and pressed her thumb firmly against the sensor plate. "Apprentice Hunter Tamris Heldeen," she said and was pleased to find her voice steady enough. "I have an appointment."

The answer came in a pleasant contralto, a recorded message. "Follow the flagged path around the house to the garden at the back. I'm waiting for you there."

Tamris wrinkled her nose. Garden? What's this? She started along the flags, stepping in the center of each to keep the ends of the clipped grass off her carefully polished boots, humming a half-forgotten tune from back-back times, sniffing at the perfume of the doradora blooms on the adoradee vines clinging to the rough-cut stone of the tall narrow house. She whistled a few notes, tentative, dying after just the few as she turned a second corner and saw the flags disappearing into a dense growth of old tolganek trees. Garden, hah. She pushed at her hair (the stiff breeze was snatching at her short crisp curls and stirring them into a tangle) and tugged her tunic down over the outthrust of full breasts that embarrassed her by their jiggling during her unarmed combat training and the other sports she was supposed to master. And they spoiled the line of her tunic when she wanted to look neat and efficient.

Ahead of her, somewhere in the shadow under the trees, she could hear the delicate tinkling of glass wind chimes. Feeling very young and gauche, she moved into the grove. The chimes sounded all around her, near and far, blending into a magical whisper of sound, underlining the pungent smell of the trees and the mold underfoot. After a few turns of the twisting path, she heard above the singing of the chimes, the liquid ripple of harp notes and after a few more steps, a woman's voice singing. She walked slower. Aleytys. She stroked a finger down her short straight nose, then along the curve of a cheek whose plumpness was another curse of her life; children aren't often kind to each other and she'd suffered under names like fat-face and chagali—a small nervous rodent with cheek pouches that doubled the size of its head when stuffed with nuts and seeds. She knew that this particular memory was being called up by another, the memory of the tapes of the various escrow hearings on Helvetia, of a face more attractive than beautiful, mobile and expressive, shifting between disgust, deep interest, flashes of sudden amusement, the wry appreciation of absurdity, indignation and satisfaction. When you're not quite twenty and heading for a make-or-break interview—not quite that bad but almost—it's not easy to step into the sunlight and face a legend in the making.

She could hear two people now, a man's voice, a low rumble that refused to separate into words, then the woman's contralto, no longer singing, but speaking in lazy phrases. Grey? she thought, shook her head. He was still on Hunt, couldn't possibly be back yet. Who? Something to do with the Cazar Hunt?

"Council overrode me," her mother said. "I didn't want her on this one. But, dammit, when Cazar Company appealed to them over my head, they caved in and ordered me to offer it to her. Hagan kept sniping at me as I tried to explain that this wasn't the kind of thing she was good at. They should let me use my Hunters the way I want, after all I know them a helluva lot better than any of those politicians on the council. She's too expensive, he said. Can you believe that? After the fees she's won for us even if you don't count Maeve? Dangerous woman, he said, outsider, not one of us, how could we ever trust her to hold our interests above her own, half-breed Vryhh, you know what Vrya are like. After she's risked her life and her sanity for us, endangered her own son, though I don't say she knew she was doing that when it happened. What are you implying, he said, that you can't trust her? Cazar wants her, not any of the others. Should we lose this fee, funds we need! for what amounts to nothing? They want her name, that's all, they don't give half a damn if she does anything, he said. He went on and on and on, every time I opened my mouth. Aleytys won't go and do nothing. She'll stick her nose in and stir things up if there's no one there to keep her on track. She distrusts and despises the Companies and they want to put that down on one of the most controlled Company worlds I know of. I want you at her elbow, Mari. I know there's no way you can coerce her. I just want you to remind her of what she's supposed to be doing. Do the best you can."

"The best I can, hah." One final time she tugged down her tunic, stepped onto the broad expanse of neatly trimmed lawn. Across it on the far side of the clearing she saw the creek, whose music blended with the notes of the minstrel's harp and the voice of the red-haired woman by a solitary tolganek, its dark limbs arching low over her head as she sat on one massive root, her back against the trunk. A black-haired man lay stretched out on the grass close to her feet, a big man in a worn shipsuit with a scarred face, a short black beard. As Tamris hesitated, Aleytys stopped singing and smiled down at the man, a current of affection passing between them so strong that she felt the warmth of it from where she stood. Definitely not Grey, she thought. Who?

Aleytys looked up, saw Tamris and waved her closer. Tamris took a deep breath and walked toward her, beginning to get a little irritated at having to march up under two pairs of eyes. The harp was set aside and Aleytys's hands were folded loosely in her lap. Her head was back against the rough bark of the tolganek, her long fine redgold hair blew about her face. Even in person she wasn't pretty, but her face was her own in a way Tamris had rarely seen—her mother, Grey, a few of her teachers had that look, the look of having grown into the face from behind so that they were of a piece, strong, powerful and dangerously charming. She was wearing a long loose robe with wide sleeves, its soft material falling into graceful folds over the hills and hollows of her body. Her bare feet rested gold against the green of the grass. Tamris looked away. Her eyes caught the man's amused grey gaze and that was the last thing she needed to touch off her temper. Misgivings forgotten, she stiffened her spine and said crisply, "Apprentice Hunter Tamris Heldeen."

Aleytys smiled. "Find a spot and sit, Hunter. I suppose I should apologize for the informality but the day promised so fine I couldn't bear to stay inside. Besides, I'm not much good at politesse."

Tamris glanced at the man, disturbed by his intrusion in Hunter business. His face was deeply tanned, scarred and worn, his light grey eyes laughing at her. He'd shifted lazily onto his stomach. Looking at him made her uneasy. She folded down quickly and, she hoped, neatly, holding her torso stiffly erect, settled herself as comfortably as she could, her legs crossed, her hands resting on her thighs.

The silence hummed around them. Beyond the tree, the creek brush-sizzled around the scattered boulders and tree roots. A gust of wind blew a veil of red hair across Aleytys's face. Dreamily she reached up and brushed the strands from nose and mouth, tucking them behind her ear. The windchimes tinkled in the distance and overhead a sakar screamed its harsh hunting cry as it soared in overlapping loops across the crystalline blue.

Tamris waited, stubbornly silent, a sinking feeling within that this collaboration wasn't going to work. It was all wrong, nothing like she'd rehearsed with herself. She didn't feel crisp and confident, no, she felt as uncertain as a child suddenly pitched into a party of adults without knowing the rules of the games they were playing. Aleytys wasn't what she'd expected either, oh, her face was familiar enough but this dreamy creature, it seemed impossible that she'd done the things Tamris knew she had, she looked more like she belonged in a harem somewhere disporting herself on silken sheets—Tamris blinked and caught back her wandering mind. That was absurd.

The man chuckled, the sound startling, cutting through the stiffening silence. "Behave yourself, Lee."

Aleytys smiled. "You haven't changed, old growler, body or no." She straightened, stretched, drew her legs up and wrapped her arms around them. "Once more I apologize, Tamris Heldeen. I find I simply can't force myself into a proper state of mind for working. My ugly friend here. . . ." She looked fondly at the man. Tamris blinked, swamped this close to the current of warmth passing between them. "He dropped in for a visit three days ago and I haven't thought about working since." Her lips twitched into a rueful smile. "Especially since this Hunt is . . . well, I can't dig up much enthusiasm for it."

With an incongruously graceful movement the man was on his feet. "Playtime is over, Lee. I'll be moving on."

"No." Aleytys was on her feet, agitated. "Wait." She moved closer to the man, wrapped slim golden fingers about his arm. The fingers were trembling. "Come with me to Cazarit."

"Hunter!" Aghast, Tamris jumped to her feet. Steady her, she thought, how the hell am I supposed to do that? Silently she apologized to her mother. This wasn't make-work for her first outing.

The man stood with arms folded across his broad chest, his eyes fixed on Aleytys's face. He didn't look at all pleased with the invitation. "As what?" he said. "House pet?"

Aleytys looked away, took a step back, took her hands away from him with visible reluctance, pushed at the long fine hair the wind kept blowing across her face. "Would that bother you?"

He snorted. "You have to ask?"

"Obviously." The word trailed off as her face went blank. She stared at him but as far as Tamris could tell she wasn't seeing him. Her eyes, those bright blue-green eyes, were looking inward. She flushed, looked angry, as if some monitor inside her head was calling her to order and she was rebelling against it. Aleytys shook herself, blinked and was back with them.

The man watched the transformation, his pale eyes starting to twinkle. "Harskari being sarcastic?"

"The three of you drive me wild sometimes." She stepped close to him, reached out but stopped her hand a half inch from his sleeve. "Do a thing for me?" For a moment she was gone again, looking over his shoulder toward the mountains rising behind a line of trees. "I think. . . ." Her voice a whisper of sound almost lost in the susurration of the creek and the rustle of the stiff green leaves behind her fiery head. "I think I might have to run when this is over. Might . . . I don't know, there's a shivering under my ribs." She shook herself as if she shook off something clinging to her shoulders. "There's a world called Ibex, Swardheld love, and a city called Yastroo, a man called Kenton Asgard. You know what I'm saying. I need to know if they actually exist, and existing, are still what and where my mother's letter said. Find that world for me, locate Kenton Asgard, just find out if he's alive and where she said, that's all. Come back and tell me. A business proposition. Yes, That's it. A sort of charter. Will you?"

He unfolded his arms with a sharp sudden movement, caught her chin and turned her face up. After a moment, he nodded. "Ship needs overhauling. Here's as good a place as any. You pay for that and for fuel to Ibex and back." He chuckled. "And for filling my hold with tradegoods. No use going out empty."

"Skint! Gouger!" She stepped back, glared at him. "Overhaul that greasebucket, sure, probably fall apart before it left the system otherwise, I'll pay for that. And fuel. Find your own cargo."

He grinned at her. "Think of the centuries of well-honed tact and tracking skill you're getting thrown in gratis."

"Gratis, hah! Pawlicker." She gathered the webbing of hair plastered across eyes and mouth and tucked it behind her ear. "I'll go that if I get a half-share in the profits." She grinned back at him. "All that tact and skill." She shook her head. "Too bad I can't set Karskari on you. Just wait, my hairy friend. When we find her a body, she'll comb your beard."

"Private business, Lee. Remember the audience."

Aleytys blinked. "Madar." She turned to Tamris. "Once again I have to apologize. How do I say politely I forgot you were there?" She came to Tamris, smiling ruefully, her hands outstretched. "You've been very patient with me. You sure you want to go along? It'll probably be educational, but not in the way your mother intended."

Tamris rubbed at her eyes, "I'm not sure even Mom knows what she intends." To her surprise Tamris found she did indeed want to come along on what threatened to be an out-of-control business. There was a subtle flattery in Aleytys's easy acceptance of her and willingness to relax and act natural with her. Tamris knew that for now this was more a tribute to the friendship and trust between Aleytys and her mother, but it was a start. She grinned. "I wouldn't miss it."

Aleytys laughed, touched her cheek, pulled her back to the tree, sat down beside her on one of the huge old roots. "That . . ." she jabbed a thumb at the man, "is what might be termed an entrepreneur—if you care to be polite." She smiled affectionately at him. He raised an eyebrow. "What are you calling yourself now?"

"Quayle, love. Remember?" He dropped to the grass at their feet.

She grimaced. "Too well. I get a half-share?"

"Yes." Grey eyes laughed up at Tamris. "You see how she takes advantage of my fondness of her?" He turned to Aleytys. "Given the overhaul is to my own specs."

"Ay-mi, skinned, I see it now." She sobered, swung around to face Tamris. "You've read the Cazar reports?"

Tamris nodded. "Sketchy."

"Mild word for them." Aleytys moved her shoulders impatiently. "Damn Company worlds." She sniffed. "I tell you, Tamris, I want to stand back and cheer for the ghost." She sighed. "Did Head get that clearance for me?"

Tamris dipped her hand into her sleeve, fished out a folded bit of paper. With a flick of her fingers she tossed it into

Aleytys's lap. "She said she wore her tonsils out for this so you better do a damn good job and keep your temper." Tamris shrugged. "I'm supposed to remind you."

"Conscience at my shoulder." Aleytys shook her head. "A miserable job, you're going to earn your seal, my friend." She raised a brow, turned away and unfolded the note. She smiled. "Good. Long as I keep the ghost from running off with the Aghir." She refolded the paper. "Do my best. It's not my kind of thing."

"So Mom said, but the council overrode her." She drew a fingernail along her cheekbone, narrowed her eyes. "You could refuse the Hunt."

"Can I?"

Tamris rubbed at her nose. "No, I suppose not."

Aleytys looked grim. "That never changes, does it? No matter what I do." She pushed at her hair. "Mmm. You've got backing; you could get sworn as a notary?"

"I suppose. Why?"

"I've got a feeling we'll have to squeeze hard to get the fee out of them. Tamris, I'm going to stir up a lot of hostility. We'll need proof my intentions are honest and my actions pure. Head screwed them down on specifics pretty damn thoroughly, but I don't want it to be just my word against a barrage of them at the hearings. Our word. The verifier won't take me, you must know that. Besides, the sight of the link on your belt should keep them honest. Means no privacy from the moment we set foot on Cazarit. You mind?"

"I suppose not. Never thought about it. I'll have to see Mom to fix that. How come you were never sworn . . . never mind, I'm only occasionally dim. I see you'd have to be bonded and Hagan and Betts would have triple fits." Tamris got to her feet. "I'd better get started on this." She took a few steps, turned. "Only occasionally dim—you haven't said you want me on this with you."

"If you don't mind an atmosphere of confusion and hostility." Aleytys grinned at her. "Come back after you've seen Head and spend the next few days here, we've got some planning to do."

ALEYTYS

Her house. The house on Wolff. The place she was beginning to think of as home though she wasn't fully aware of her commitment to it as yet. Aleytys and Tamris went over their meager reports again and again, argued over the Cazarit world maps, spent the splendid summer days in the garden, the crisp summer evenings before a briskly crackling fire in the library. Three days. Swardheld shuttled between the port facilities where his ship was being worked on and the house. Sometimes he joined them, grinning at Tamris's glares of indignation as he teased Aleytys into wild, farcical, funny word exchanges that left both of them helpless with laughter.

At night Aleytys dreamed and woke sweating, dreamed and thrashed about in her dreaming because she was replaying old and painful events, time-jumbled and fragmented but consistent in that they centered about two ghosts from her past.

She dreamed:

She lay in an open-fronted cell staring at a corridor visible but unreachable beyond a force shield. She turned her back on it.

"Lee."

She swung around. Stavver stood outside. "Miks," she said. She thrust her hands against the yielding floor and shoved herself onto her feet. "Where am I? What happened? How did I get here?"

"Hush, Lee, listen."

She brushed distractedly at hair tumbling over her face. "Get me out of here."

He ran a hand across his eyes. She could see the veins distended at his temple, running in a blue weaving over the back of his thin hand. "Shut up and listen."

An ache began to beat behind her eyes. "What about a few answers?"

The thief glanced nervously over his shoulder. "Lee, I've bought a few minutes with you, not enough to waste like this. You're in the slave pens of I!kwasset."

"Slave pens!"

"Maissa tricked me. When I was out hunting down some friends, she gassed you, hauled you here and sold you, claiming you owed her passage money. When I got back to the port the ship was gone."

"Sharl? My son?"

He rubbed his forehead, gestured helplessly. "She took him with her. I'm sorry, Lee."

"Sorry. . . ."

"He'll be all right, Lee."

"No, Maissa is . . . ay, Madar, get me out of here."

"No way, not out of the slave pens." There was a faint beading of sweat on his forehead though he tried to smile. "Don't you think I'd have you out of here if I could?"

"Would you? Or would you be just as happy to get me off your neck?"

He flattened his palms against the forceshield. "I'd have to." His mouth worked, the pale tip of his tongue flicked across his lips. "You've hooked me hard." He looked over his shoulder, turned back. "My time is almost up. I can't steal you out, Lee. And I haven't got the gold to buy you, you know that. After you're sold, then I can get you away. No owner will have the kind of security they have here. I'll come for you, I swear it."

"No."

"What?"

She stared at him, a long thin man with moonwhite hair tumbling over pale blue eyes, lover and rescuer, though reluctant at both. "Go after Maissa," she said. "By all we've shared, get my son away from that crazy woman."

He jerked away, took two steps down the corridor, wheeled and came back, his face twisted with the pain that radiated through his body. Gasping, he banged his hands against the shield. "Stop it," he cried, "stop it."

Her mouth pinched into a grim line, she waited.

He closed his eyes. The muscles loosened in his face and

neck. "All right, damn you, you win. I'll trace her and get him away from her."

The stiffening went out of her spine; slumping, nearly falling as her knees went weak, she pressed her hands against the transparency near his shoulders. "I'm sorry, Miks, I wish ... ah, man, you know how sick Maissa is."

He stroked his hand outside the shield at the level of her face as if he caressed her, pain in his face as if he did this against his will. "I'll find your son and bring him to you."

"No. Not to me. Madar knows where I'll be. Take him to his father. Vajd the dreamsinger. You'll find him on Jaydugar in a mountain valley called the Kard. Ask for the blind dreamsinger."

A dark-faced guard tapped Stavver on the shoulder and jerked his head toward the exit. He left her without looking back, the long narrow man who moved with the elastic glide of a hunting tars, a sly man and a quick man and a man suffering now under the geas she'd wished on him. Once her lover, now her victim, she watched him walk away and leaned her head against the transparency and, once he had disappeared around a corner, wept.

and woke with tears on her face—
She sat up, dabbed at her face with the corner of the sheet. "Why am I doing this to myself?" Her voice sounded sharp in the darkness, the tremble in it frightening her a little. She reached out to Swardheld for comfort but there was only a cooling space where he'd been. "Harskari, mother," she whispered. "Shadith, my friend, talk to me."

Amber eyes opened in the darkness in her head. "Aleytys."

Violet eyes opened beside the amber. "Lee."

She felt warmth spread through her. Lying back on the bed, she punched the pillow, folded it and tucked it behind her head, stretched out her arms, wriggled around until she was comfortable, smiled into the darkness. "I dreamed about him, my thief."

Harskari said nothing. Shadith's violet eyes blinked slowly as her delicate pointed face materialized about them. "That bothers you?"

Harskari's burnt umber face with its halo of white hair was suddenly beside Shadith's. "Why?"

Aleytys winced. "Because I'm afraid."

"Of what?"

Aleytys laced her hands behind her head. "That Stavver is the ghost I have to track down. When Head told me about the snatches, I wondered. Now I dream. It's his kind of thing, it stinks of him. Haven't I done him enough harm?"

"A feeling and a dream—why couldn't one trigger the other?"

"I know all that, I'm still afraid." She stirred, the sheets whispering about her body. "How can I take the chance it's him?"

Harskari was silent again, a disapproving silence. "Head," she said quietly after a moment of that silence.

The single softly spoken word hit Aleytys like a blow under her ribs that drove the air out of her. It pulled her up from her tumble into excess, her headlong rush to refusing the Hunt and with the refusal casting aside Wolff and all the responsibilities she had there. Again and again Head had acted her friend, her defender, had fought for her against the xenophobia of the council. Was fighting for her now. Had invested a lot of her prestige in winning the concessions Aleytys had asked for. "Damn," she said.

Harskari smiled. "Now, Aleytys, it's not so bad. You've arranged things neatly for yourself, don't think I haven't noticed. It won't hurt your thief if you put a crimp in his plots and you don't have to give him to the Cazar thanks to Head's efforts, so stop fussing. You make your own troubles as always. In any case, is it so likely, out of all the thieves around, that the ghost you've contracted to chase is Stavver?" Harskari's voice was dry and crisp, intended to puncture her gloom. "Despite his healthy ego, is it even likely he was as good a thief as he claimed? Consider how many people there are in this small sector of the galaxy. How many more thieves could there be, must there be?"

"Why isn't that a comfort to me?" Aleytys sighed. "I have a feeling. . . ."

"What feeling?" Swardheld came through the bedroom door, a bottle in one hand and a pair of glasses in another. He knuckled on a light, crossed the room to sit on the bed by her feet. "You've had a busy night. Like sleeping with an itchy octopod." He worked the cork out and poured dark amber wine into one of the glasses. "Here."

Aleytys wriggled up until she was leaning against the polished wood of the bed's head, a pillow tucked behind the curve of her back. She reached for the glass, sipped at the wine while he filled the other, slapped the cork back and set the bottle beside the bed. She closed her eyes, savoring the clean cool taste of the wine. Purple eyes twinkling, Shadith murmured, "Sweet old bear, I miss him." Aleytys chuckled. "Shall I tell him?"

"Tell me what?" The bed swayed and bounced as he stretched out beside her.

"Shadith says she misses you, you sweet old bear."

He looked pained. "We're going to have to find that one a body soon, she's starting to get over-ripe." He scratched at his beard, raised an eyebrow. "What feeling?"

"I've been dreaming about Miks Stavver."

"Ah." He grinned and raised his glass. "Yearning for old lovers?"

"No, you sour old bear, afraid he's my ghost."

"Lots of other thieves about. Met a good few myself the past couple years."

"That's what Harskari said."

"Hah. Two great minds. What more you want?" The bed wobbled as he sat up. "You're finished, give me the glass."

After he filled it and held it out to her again, she took a sip of the wine, held it in her mouth, let it slide down her throat until warmth tingled through her body, shivered as he began stroking warm strong fingers along her thigh, gasped as his fingers thrust into her, spilled the gulp of wine left in the glass, gasped again as he drew himself alongside her and began drinking the trickles of wine from her breasts.

"Forget him." His breath was hot against her, the hairs of moustache and beard tickling gently against her.

Aleytys dreamed:

Sharl kicked his feet and burbled happily in the improvised sling, a strip of batik tied in a knot over her left shoulder, crossing her body so the baby lay snugged against her right hip. In the glow from the orange sun swimming low in Lamarchos's polychromatic sky, the stark drab buildings looked uglier than ever. She glanced up at Stavver walking coldly silent, his only concession to her presence the curtailment of his long stride to match hers. "Still mad at me," she muttered.

(The dreamer stirred, called out, she thought, but only made a soft cawing sound. "Before, it's before," she thought she said, but only got out a series of stutters and mumbles; she fought to break out of the dream but only skipped the sequence forward.) She dreamed:

The sky was suddenly dark, a scatter of stars replacing the swirls of colored dust; the baby was gone from her hip (this bothered her as dreamer but not she who walked in the dream). She stood outside the ugly pile of stone, alone except for a breathing in the darkness.

Less than a shadow, Stavver thumbed a stud on his belt, waking a circle of light that spread out under feet unseen inside the chameleon web that fit tightly over his body, covering all but his hands, thought it could cover them at need, hands that floated like pale creatures until the mooncream on them absorbed enough light and they were reduced to blurs. A hand blur gestured impatiently.

With some trepidation, Akeytys stepped onto the light circle. It shuddered under her bare feet like something alive, sending tremors shivering up her legs. She clasped her arms around the thief. It was strange to feel his thin powerful body pressed against her when she saw nothing within the circle of her arms. Under her entwined fingers she felt silent laughter vibrating in his chest.

Riding the circle, they drifted up across the wall then skimmed along the façade of the building, the ascent stopping when they reached a narrow window sealed with a thick block of something that didn't look like glass to Aleytys. She clung to the thief as he ran a softly buzzing tool in quick swooping sweeps back and forth across the plug. The clear material glowed sickly yellow then began to flow in a messy dribble down the stone—

Aleytys shivered in her sleep, moaned, blinked her eyes open. "Not again," she whispered. Swardheld's arm was heavy across her breasts. Feeling tender yet impatient, she moved it off her, rolled onto her side, turning her back to him. Warm and wrung-out, she slept—and sleeping, dreamed:

Night in the Vadi Kard. The moons are both down or not up yet. She walked slowly along the river Kard, savoring the familiar sounds and smells until she was dizzy with them. She moved to the edge of the water, knelt to look down into it. Mountain river. Singing to her. Laughing and crying at once, she splashed the water onto her face, bent lower and drank. Cold leafy taste. She jumped up and walked on.

The sound of the barbat brought her to a stop, heart beating in her throat. How many times have I heard him play that song? she thought. How many times?

The barbat sang. The music changed to a slow ripple of notes that melted into the song of the river. Aleytys straightened and went on. Regret was futile. She couldn't make the past years unhappen and she couldn't force herself back into the skin of the girl she'd been when she fled the witchburning. She followed the sound and saw Vajd sitting beside the river on a bench built in a circle about the trunk of an ancient horan. As she watched him draw his fingers across the strings, flatten his hand on them to kill the sound, she felt a dizzying surge of desire that muted after a little to a deep affection and aching loneliness. He's older, she thought, smiled at her foolishness. Of course he was older, how many years since she'd last seen him—three? four? There was more white in his soft unruly hair and his face was savagely scarred about the eyes. Blinded. Because of me. Her breathing turned unsteady, was harsh in her ears.

He heard. "Who is it?" The blind face turned about, searching for the source of the sounds.

"Me," she said, realizing the absurdity even as she said it. "How are you, Vajd?"

"Aleytys."

"I wondered if you'd remember me."

"I've been expecting you."

She dropped onto the bench beside him. "I forgot about your dreaming."

"You forgot a lot of things, your son among them."

She closed her hands hard around the edge of the bench. "Then Stavver did bring him here."

"My son." The coldness in his voice startled her. She stared at him, sensing the suppressed anger in him and an implacable distaste. "You abandoned him."

"You don't understand. . . . didn't Stavver tell you what happened?"

"He came late one night. I couldn't sleep. The waiting was too strong in me. He asked my name and when I told him, he put the boy down beside me and took my hand and placed it on him. The boy flinched and started crying, not the full-throated cry of an angry baby, but the flinching wail of a hurt animal. He said, 'This is your son.' He said that a damn witchwoman called Aleytys had forced him to track down the boy and bring him to me. He said he was done with you and with me and with the whole damn clan. And then he left." Vajd turned his scarred accusing face on her. "He lied?"

"No, but there was. . . . he left out everything. I did not abandon my baby. I couldn't do that. You know . . . you should know that. He was stolen from me by a sick mad woman who sold me to slavers so I couldn't go after her. I made him do it, I had to, I told him to track Sharl to you. What else could I do?" She touched his hand. Quietly he moved it away.

She was cold. She felt like weeping but there were no tears left in her. She wanted to touch the flyaway curls fluttering about his tired, lined face. She wanted to feel his body against her, wanted to know again the warm explosions of those nights in the Vadi Raqsidan. In that moment, she knew that Vajd had been the reason for her return. Her desire for him drowned her desire to find her son. And at the moment she realized this, she knew the futility of that dream. The passion he'd felt for her once had eroded into near hate. The thing in her which reached out and trapped men into her service had betrayed her again. The love she remembered was illusion. She pressed her hands against her eyes, fighting with the cold that threatened to swallow her. "I want to see my son," she said.

"It's your right." He slid his arm through the barbat's strap, reached for the staff leaning against the tree, stood stiffly. He tapped down the path to the back of the Kardi Mari 'fat where he and Zavar lived. He held the door open for her, then brushed past her to tap-tap up the stairs to the second floor. Aleytys shivered. It was like stepping into the past. The night candles cast demon shadows on the walls of the hallway.

He pushed open a childroom door and waited.

Aleytys moved past him. She saw two small forms in the beds but it was too dark to see more. On the ledge of the deep window embrasure she found a stub of candle in a plain pewter candlestick. She lit it at the night candle in the hall, moved softly back inside.

The boy in the bed on her left had Vajd's tumbled dark curls and her cousin Zavar's dreamy vulnerable look. He murmured as she bent over him, but didn't wake. She turned to the other bed. In the candlelight the sleeping boy's hair glowed like fire. "My son," she whispered. Tears blurred her eyes; the candle flame shook. She bent closer. He was frowning in his sleep, a small fist pressed tight against his mouth. She stretched out her hand, but stopped before she touched him. With a hair's width between her palm and him, she ran her hand caressingly over his small body. Swallowing hard, she straightened, blew out the candle, replaced it and stumbled from the room.

Vajd pulled the door shut. "Why did you come back?"

She looked at him, so tired suddenly that it was difficult to keep her thoughts tracking. "I came as soon as I could get transport. It's not so easy moving from world to world if you've got no money and few skills you could use to get money. I wouldn't whore for it." Her voice was dull and slow, one syllable blurring into the next. "I came to get my son. Why else should I be here?"

"My son, Leyta."

She brushed her fingers across her face, did it again. "What?"

"Sharl is my son. I want him." His scarred face was grim in the flickering light. "I won't let you take him."

"You can't stop me."

"What will you do when he wakes screaming for his mother?"

"I'm his mother."

"Zavar is his mother. You're a stranger."

"No. He'll remember. After a while."

"When he first came here, Aleytys, he used to scream at night until he was exhausted then stare at the darkness afraid to go to sleep. It's taken Zavar a full three-year to stop his nightmares. You dragged my son into horror. Don't tell me you didn't know what that woman was. Oh yes, I believe your sad tale. Fooled. Sold. You had no business taking a baby into such danger."

"I had no choice."

He snorted. "There's always a choice. You were set on your road and not about to let anyone or anything divert you. Can you give Sharl a better life than the one he has here?"

"I have a secure position now. I can support him, take care of him."

"If you disrupt his life now, how long will it take to stop the screams this time?"

"You're asking me to abandon him."

"No, Leyta."

"Calling it by another name won't change anything."

His mouth curled into a smile. "Settle here in the Kard." He shook his head. "You didn't even think of that."

I could come back. No! The negative was immediate and unshakable. "No," she said. She closed her eyes a moment. "You've used your knife with skill, Vajd, cut me loose without quite killing me. You've won. I can't take Sharl away from you. And I won't be back to trouble you again." She reached out to touch his face—touched the ragged mane of the sesmat mare. She shifted wearily on the saddle pad, knocking a fretful cry from Sharl as his sling bounced against her hip. (The sleeper shifted restlessly against the solid warm body of the man without waking him or herself, disturbed by the sudden jolting transition from one memory to another). "Hush baby," she whispered, Ahead of her, his outline fuzy in the red-tinted gloom, Stavver rode steadily on without speaking or looking back, getting farther and farther ahead of her, his form elongating into . . . he was painted black lines, swaying, swaying, her hand inside the baby sling was groping, finding only the folds of soft leather, only the folds, she couldn't touch her baby, she couldn't get her fingers through the blocking folds. . . .

She sat cross-legged on the bed looking down at Swardheld as he slept. Quayle now. She made the adjustment hastily in her head, easy enough when she could see his stranger's face—still a stranger's face even after two years. She smiled down at him, wondering how he was dealing with the problem of body image, whether he was still momentarily startled

when he looked into a mirror. This last visit, there were
things she'd seen that hinted he was very much at home in
his new body. His brows rose in the old twisty way; when he
moved and she wasn't looking directly at him, she knew him;
when his mouth flicked up and his eyes narrowed and he
laughed at her, she knew him. She touched her temples
gently, marveling at how easily she wore the diadem now, the
first horror and pain faded like an ancient icon left out in the
sun and rain, only a ghost of what it had been. She put her
hand on his shoulder, careful not to wake him, remembering
when the man inside the warm flesh had been an assemblage
of forces trapped within the diadem—living in her head, in
her flesh. He read her so damn well even now, knew her
from the inside out. She'd come to terms with that at last.
Grey's face rose before her. She winced, took her hand away
from Swardheld, no Quayle, remember it, Quayle. Madar, she
thought, I wonder what he'll do when he hears of this. She
hadn't thought of Grey for days now, not since Swardheld
had come. She ran her fingers through her hair, half-sure
she'd made the final mistake with Grey, the worst of all the
mistakes she'd made before, half-sure she'd planted herself on
the mouth of a geyser that could blow her off Wolff. She was
startled by a new awareness of how strongly she felt about
Wolff, how painful it would be to pull up roots and move
on—and that included Grey. She looked down at Swardheld
and shook her head. She couldn't think of him as Quayle and
she couldn't flush him out of her system. Her feeling for
Grey was different, as strong perhaps, but different. She
watched him sleep a minute more, then lay back down, fold-
ing and tucking the pillow behind her head, lacing her fingers
behind her head. Wolff, she thought. Home? Maybe. Got to
find my mother first. She winced again. Don't know if I'm
ready to face her. Still, better to make a start, don't have to
decide until Swardheld gets back. Wolff. Damris is right. Get
out more, get to know the people here, get into the life.
Mmmmm. Got to get bodies somehow for Harskari and
Shadith. Get rid of the diadem, that peels the RMoahl off my
back. Been drifting too long, putting off too much, drifting. . . . She yawned, slid down farther under the covers,
moved closer to Swardheld and drifted into a sleep where any
dreams she had were too deep to remember or disturb.

THE BOY AND THE THIEF

"A girl? I don't want to be a girl."

The thief grinned at him, lines from nose to mouth cutting deep, lines pressing other lines into the pale flesh of his cheeks. "Think I want to be a wrinkled old richbitch?" He held a veil up to his face, a dainty trifle whose layers of silk tissue were subtly shaded to completely alter the contours it concealed. "I have to be the Vijayne Gracia Belagar of Clovel." The veil altered the quality of his voice, making it higher and lighter. "We value our privacy on Clovel, we do."

The boy giggled, tilted his head and examined the thief with eyes whose color changed with his mood and sometimes with the changing light. "Is that real," he said, "or something you made up?"

The thief dropped the veil back in the box. "Quite real, little brother, and booked on a liner from Clovel. How else could Cazarit Security check on her? They're nervous, little brother, very nervous."

The boy scowled. "I got to wear a veil like that?"

"You're the Vijayne's golden-haired little love."

The boy tugged at a bit of hair, screwed up his face. "Gah."

"Know how you feel, little brother, but your mother's been brought into this and we take no chances, none at all."

"I suppose not."

The thief was a tall thin man with an unruly thatch of fine white hair, translucent white skin, milky blue eyes. He wasn't young, might have been anywhere between forty and sixty standard years old.

The boy might have been nine or ten. He was remarkably beautiful, had a clear fair skin with a rosy bloom on lip and cheek, fine features, and those huge chatoyant eyes. They were somber now, a mixture of green and blue. "I don't like

49

this one, elder brother." He shook his head until his fiery red hair stood out like dandelion fluff.

The thief smoothed the fluff down with a quick pass of his hand. "Maybe so, little brother, but it goes." He frowned. "Is it your mother sticking her nose in that bothers you?"

"No!" The boy jerked away and went to stand in the open door. Over his shoulder he said, "You're slicker than her. I know you can fool her silly, but I got knots in my belly. We've choused more'n enough money out of them, we don't need this snatch."

The thief shrugged, brushed past the boy and strode across the meadow outside the door. With the boy trailing behind him, he followed the river to the fall and stood on the brink of the cliff looking out across the sweep of the valley. The conifers behind them whispered in the off-and-on wind, the water's roar was muted. "This will be the last dip there," the thief said. He smiled at the boy. "We'll ride with a light hand ready to jump."

LILIT

Lilit wrote:

The smuggler. He's been the key to the struggle. And I was the one who called him to us, well, Gyoll and I did it together. There's a cave below the Hold that has been lined, shielded and used to house the conditioners and purifiers that scrub the air and water for the Hold. One of the exits from the passage maze opened into it and there was another well-concealed exit that led eventually to open land beyond the wall. We usually had our meetings in that cave. Gyoll didn't like the shut-in feeling he got from the Hold's massive walls. Acthon and Metis brought him to me for the first time when I was ten. He was home from the mines and not going back again, a sick man but determined to get the rebels in the Wild organized and supplied with weapons and other things they needed to survive out there and more than just survive, medicine and food and tools and clothing, a thousand things. To get them he needed a smuggler who was more than ordinarily daring and trustworthy and he knew just the man.

"You're a clever young one. You've proved that," Gyoll said.

Lilit flushed with pleasure. Metis squeezed her hand and grinned at her, eyes shining.

Gyoll tapped his fingers on his knee, looked from Acthon to Metis, then leaned toward Lilit. "What I'm going to ask of you is dangerous, to us and even to you if we should be caught."

"What is it?" She stiffened, trying to speak calmly but her heart was fluttering with excitement. "I'll do it if I can," she said. She felt Metis's hand tighten on her shoulder, felt her friend's body warm behind her.

Gyoll tapped some more on his knee, his eyes on hers, His face was more mobile than a tiktik's but she found it as unreadable as her father's glacial mask. It was hard to meet his gaze, but she wouldn't look away. He smiled and reached out his hand to her, his fingers dry and chalky but warm as they closed around hers. The touch was a kind of accolade to her, a medal of honor, she thought and smiled blissfully at her parent by adoption though he knew nothing about that. She made the touch of his hand an acknowledgment of that kinship, knowing this was an illusion, a dream she spun for herself, but it was a dream she needed so she took the warmth of his hand for more than it could be. She flushed, felt the heat and tightness in her face. "Metis tells me," Gyoll said, "that you've not breathed a word of us though you've had great provocation from your people. And you've managed to get us everything we asked for without being noticed at it. That's good. Now we need to use the Weksar transmitter. Do you know what that is?"

She glanced at Acthon, nodded. "Yes, but. . . ."

"I don't know the passages like you," Acthon said. "And it's far too dangerous to come out in the halls. Watchdogs. And it's better not to have any record of us up there."

"I see," she said. She put her free hand out and touched the cool concrete to cool her heat. "I've watched Father talking with the tejed. And one night I came through the wall into that place and touched the console. I even started it up, but the noise scared me and I turned it off and went away."

"Can you take us there, is there room in the walls?"

"Oh yes." She got to her feet. "Come."

With Acthon and Metis trailing silent behind them, she took Gyoll through the walls, moving swiftly and surely with no need for light, twisting up and up through the maze, finally around and around the mantower to the room under the roof where the transmitter was installed. She opened the panel but stopped Gyoll before he could step out. "It's warded," she said. "It won't mind me but you'd stir up a mess. I'm not even sure about Acthon, probably he shouldn't come out either."

"Right," Gyoll said. "Listen. . . . ."

He stood in the opening and told me what to do, how to set the dials and what to say into the emptiness of the inter-

split. I did what he said and three nights later came back
with him and Acthon for the answer and that's how we got
our smuggler, a friend of Gyoll's from before, a supplier of
arms while he still ran free on his home world. Again he told
me what to say, words that would identify him to the wary
speaker and they worked out a meeting, all the details, time
and place and what to expect. And he offered Aghir metals
as an inducement for the smuggler to show up.

Nine years ago, that was, nine busy years.

Acthon and Metis and I went over and over the difficulties.
The monorail was automated and shot like a projectile from
the smelter to the warehouses at the landing field. Father
relied on speed and armor and mass to keep the treasure
train from greedy hands. Father knew there were fugitives in
the Wild but he didn't bother himself about them, they had
no way to get the ingots offworld, anyway the Wild itself
would get rid of them for him. He didn't know how many
were there or that their numbers were growing, since they
kept all children born alive and raised them no matter how
deformed and those not sterile had children in their turn; as
the generations gave way they grew closer and closer to the
land. Five hundred years of forced adaptation.

Officially Acthon was assigned to the guards, actually he
was my father's favored aide and spent little time with the
mercenaries that guarded us. He had great freedom whenever
my father dismissed him, he was allowed to move at will between Hold and village, even to be absent for days at a time,
able to do this because of the indulgence of Father and the
unstated relationship between them. Now and then he worked
out with the guards. I sometimes watched. He is a tiger, my
half-brother, faster than most, strong and hard. Father
watched him too, sometimes with one of his rare smiles and
a glint of pride that was quickly gone. Now and then Ekeser
and Selas came to watch also, silent when Father was there,
Selas silent always, Ekeser baiting Acthon when Father
wasn't there, safe in the knowledge that the bastard son
wouldn't dare mishandle the legitimate one. But he knew too
that if he went too far, he'd answer to Father for it and he
was afraid of Father.

Acthon. Yes, well, returning to the tale, where was I? I was
going to tell about how we figured out a way to derail the
monos by mashing up dirty lily pads on the rail so the muck

dried into a hard tough lump glued immovably to the metal, but there's so much more about Acthon and Gyoll—I don't know—

When Gyoll came back from his last shift, Father was offworld buying more laborers, and Acthon was free to go with him into the Wild and help him set up what he called cells of resistance. Gyoll knew his life was measured in months—he lived for several years after that last shift but the last few months were very bad for him yet he never would give in to the pain. He worked on as long as his head was straight. He'd taken Acthon out before, but that was just to talk. Elf went with them, riding on a caticul she'd commandeered from a pride somewhere, a limber predator with warty purple hide, slitted crimson eyes. Acthon told me Elf is eerily lovely with silky white hair and tawny skin, great amber eyes that saw as well by night as by day. She is perfectly formed, a doll-woman—gifted, an empath, a limited sort of telepath, a link, (she can pass images from one mind into another that hasn't the slightest touch of talent) and a more indescribable gift, the art of being loved by man and beast. She came out of the Wild on her own the first time Gyoll decided to visit the dwellers there and led him to their homes and hidden settlements. He returned to these many times, taking her with him as his passport, a tall, lanky man with fire in his eyes, a round amiable face and a flawless memory. He talked and taught, talked and taught—and listened almost as much. For a man with a driving obsession, he listened well.

Late at night, after they got back, Acthon brought Gyoll into that echoing cavern full of humming and sighing machines. I brought a sticktight light down with me and set it on the concrete between us and tried not to stare at Gyoll. I'd seen him walking in the village many times, had stolen an ocular from my father's office (one I knew he didn't use because it was down in a corner with webs spun over it), took it so I could watch him. He'd changed. Large handfuls of his dark brown hair were gone, the tufts remaining were streaked with white. His face was still plump, but the skin was beginning to fold, his gaze was deceptively mild, his blue eyes gleaming in the yellowish light.

The smuggler we called that night ferried Gyoll to each world of the Aghir where he set up communications with the other rebels and runaways. Set up supply lines—arms and medicines, tools, food, transmitters, a thousand other things to make life hard for the tejed and easier for themselves.

Metis, my Metis, you're dead and I don't know how to live with that. Three years almost. Your ghost walks these rooms and I talk to it but I can't touch it, can't touch you anymore.

Little Sister. Her name was Kedarie, but you called her little sister, as you called me little sister, when you told me stories about her. We were born on the same day, almost at the same hour. The two of you have taught me my kinship with all that thinks and breathes. Through you I have made this leap of understanding that none of my blood kin have ever taken. You showed me that I am happy when any man is happy and that I suffer when any man suffers unjustly, that I am a part of all life . . . no need to go on about this, the point is made.

I am a sneak and a spy. Though Metis scolded me and feared for me, I ran the halls even when I was still in the nursery. My brothers left the nursery when they reached five, but I left it long before them, in spirit if not in flesh. I wandered the empty halls at night, poking into rooms, prying into everything my clumsy hands could touch until I stumbled by accident against an ill-shut panel in a long unused storeroom and discovered the passages in the walls. I grew even more insatiable in my spying. I delighted in knowing things my sisters didn't. Of course I never told them anything, I didn't trust them, having watched them tattle on each other to curry favor with Stepmother or even Father, though they were too much in awe of him to speak unless driven to it by unconquerable spite. And oh they did hate me. They played tricks on me to get me in trouble. Lied. I learned early that to protest my innocence was futile. So I trusted only Metis because she loved me and I loved her. She explained many things I found confusing. Explained when she could and told me honestly when she did not. She was seven when she came to care for me, five years older than me, but already older than the earth in the wisdom of the heart.

Her father and teacher, Gyoll, come to Liros II just after Acthon was born, a rebel on his own world, a rebel from birth, I think. His father was a rebel before him, a contract laborer on a world where most people had enough comfort and no freedom at all. The father taught the son well before *he died, taught him how to think and fight, how to organize others in effective action and to use small strength to force large changes. Gyoll the son was condemned as his father had been, sold with others as contract labor (which served two purposes, purging the world of malcontents and bringing in revenue for the treasury, the men in power congratulating themselves on their humanity and providence since they left the rebels alive and wrung a profit from them at the same time).*

As his father taught him, Gyoll taught his children, first to read and write then the lessons from his father, then that they were one with all living things and owed these respect and consideration, that they shouldn't waste time or energy on hate or anger, but should get busy changing things. He wept over the bodies of his dead children and fought passionately for those that lived. And all these things Metis taught me. She was fond of her mother, but adored her father. Through her I learned it was possible for a family to be poor and heavy with sorrow and still be a wonder to see. Sometimes I nearly died with envy. She missed her family intensely those first few years. Each visit home made the return to the Hold that much more painful. She told me some of these things during those first years, spoke more than she should out of that deep loneliness, used to talk endlessly about her family until I knew each of them as well as if I'd grown up beside them. She told me things she should not have, her tongue carrying her into dangerous areas. Young as I was, I knew—instinctively, I suppose—that I should say nothing of what Metis told me. Besides, I didn't want to. I hugged my secrets to me and felt infinitely superior to my sisters whom I disliked as heartily as they disliked me, and I made little secret of my superiority—it was in my eyes, my face, in my stance, even in the way my braids stuck out from my head. This didn't make my life easier. I didn't care. To me, Metis was my family, Metis and her brothers and her sisters, especially Little Sister, my own other self, my age to the day almost to the hour. I loved them with a passion as great as the hate I felt for my blood kin. I had a grudging respect for my stepmother, she got my sisters into order, brought a measure of calm into chaos, and gave me this room where I write. She was not a pretty woman but she had presence. I think even my father was rather in awe of her. She had a strong sense of duty and equally strong ideas about conduct which I came up against repeatedly in those early years. Her punishments were harsh but always fair and if there'd been any love behind them I might have come to love her. But duty is cold and that is all she had for me.

In my wanderings and in my secret thoughts I rejected my blood kin and put more and more distance between myself and them. Without understanding that I was as much a part of the tejed as my father, I began to see the luxury around me with the eyes of an outsider. I grew angry. So angry. I stopped talking to anyone but Metis, even answered Stepmother in monosyllables. I was fierce in my anger, glowering out from the hair I wouldn't leave neat in braids but pulled apart and over my face. Metis talked me out of this, showed me the futility of what I was doing, partly because she was troubled about me, partly because what I was doing endangered not only her but her father.

Lilit laid the pen down, closed the book, and sighed. It was late. Outside, the storm had blown away, the clouds tearing apart until the sky was blazed with stars, painting the shape of the window on the rug in the shadow beyond the cone of light from her writing lamp. She rubbed at her burning eyes and saw with dull surprise that her hands were shaking. The emptiness and silence in the room began to oppress her. Ghost voices and laughter, child's laughter, fragments of memory, came muffled across the spongy rugs, then the heavy bed's grudging protest as two girls rolled and thrashed on it, driven in turn to spasms of helpless giggles as they fought to tickle each other, then other sounds, the sounds lovers make, the sighs and groans, the slide of flesh on flesh.

Lilit bit hard on her lower lip as she fought back the tears her grief squeezed from her. She would not cry, would not let the rage churning in her be lessened by that relief. She needed it, that rage, needed it to feed her resolve, otherwise she feared the years of training in passivity and restraint would make her falter, even fail in her intent.

Beads of sweat clung to her skin, trickled into her hair. She brushed at strands of hair sticking to her damp forehead, wheeled and went swiftly from the room, her feet silent and quick on the carpet, making whispers of sound on the painted tiles of the floor outside, the journal forgotten on the writing

table, the need to move, to be away from her room canceling
all other needs. She moved through dark silent halls, past
doors behind which weary servants slept and dreamed whatever it was they dreamed; sometimes it seemed to her those
dreams rose from their groaning bodies and came to gibber at
her in the night; sometimes she saw laughter made tangible in
children playing, teasing each other, and that was more terrible than the needs clothed in monster's flesh that circled her
bed, howling, whimpering; sometimes there was a sonorous
panting that hung over her for hours, on and on until she
thought the world itself breathed over her, waiting with mon-
strous patience to be relieved of the alien flesh oppressing it.

The watchdogs that drifted in ever-changing patterns
through the halls ignored her. She was family and her father,
ignorant of her habits, hadn't bothered to restrict her range.

For a while she wandered without intent, the automatic
easy movement of her body enough to drain away some of
her tension. She'd never been able to sit for long, not without
something to concentrate on. Her stepmother had tried to im-
pose a polished repose on her but the only time she managed
it was when she was in company, an effort of will that never
reached beyond the surface. Most times, her hands were always in motion, twisting her hair, underlining words, flickering over any surface within reach—flickering because her
need to touch fought always with an equal need to stay remote within herself. Whenever she was tired or under stress,
a muscle twitched by her left eye, a small thing, but she
hated it, it betrayed her, it always betrayed her, she could
never mask herself with anyone who knew her, not completely.

She walked through echoing public rooms, a barefoot,
black-clad ghost, the sounds of her passage swallowed into
the overwhelming silence; even in the twilight of the light-
strips the rooms had an austere grandeur that intimidated
her. For that reason she came here often at night, her
presence a silent defiance of all they stood for.

She drifted into the large dining room her father insisted
on using for the family though their numbers had greatly
diminished with the death of Stepmother and the marriages
of her older sisters. Lilit walked past the heavy wood table,
the heavy wood chairs prodigiously carved and marvelously
uncomfortable, pressed her nose against the glass of the false

vista. Roses and lilacs, ferns and miniature trees, miniature houses, a miniature stream, all shadows now, one blending into the other. Lilit moved her face against the glass, feeling it cool on one cheek then the other, feeling suffocated, wanting to shatter the walls that confined her, the shielding meant to protect her that only succeeded in holding her prisoner. Locking her away from the reality she longed to touch but dared not touch.

With a hiss and an impatient jerk of her head, she turned away from the false vista and went to sit in her father's chair. She looked at her own, far away down the long long expanse of table, and smiled bitterly. Her two half-brothers sat at her father's right and left hand. She was so far from them she could be safely ignored.

Lilit wrote:
Father is a tall lean man with unruly black hair, so black it shines blue when the light hits it right. Pale skin, almost translucent. A wide mouth, sometimes mobile, usually disciplined, its sensuality kept under tight control. Dark blue eyes—most often cool, intelligent, assessing, sometimes narrowed, sometimes blandly unrevealing. He laughs seldom, even less often than he smiles, yet he is not humorless. He appreciates the ridiculous and has a satirical bent of mind which he usually keeps to himself though I've seen him use it with devastating effect when he is scolding the boys or dealing with the stupidity of an overseer. He also has a rigid idea of personal honor. He never breaks a promise, he feels so strongly about it he gives his word seldom, but once given he backs it with his life—or mine. A game player, he is not interested in competition except against himself. He has a strong sense of place and duty and little tolerance for men who fall short of what he thinks they should be or do. He tolerates least well everything he considers self-indulgence. In many ways an admirable man, oh yes, an admirable man in many ways.

From their first day out of the nursery he demanded as much from his sons as he did from himself. He made some allowances for lack of knowledge, none at all for sloppy thinking. After enduring his slashing tongue the boys, especially Ekeser, would be white and shaking, hating him passionately and just as passionately fearing him, in too much inner tur-

moil to acknowledge their very real respect for him and their
need for his approval. The first time I witnessed one of these
sessions, I felt a surge of compassion and tried to comfort my
brother—Ekeser, it was—only to have him turn on me with a
venom greater than Father had ever shown, a cold controlled
rancor that terrified me. He laid on me all the hate, anger
and bitter resentment he felt for Father but could never ad-
mit even to himself. Oddly enough, he did walk away com-
forted, leaving me white and shaking.

He sat with his sons at the head of the table, catechizing
the eldest about security—how he planned to maintain this in
his absence. Ekeser answered calmly enough though there
was sweat beading his upper lip. Watching this, Lilit smiled
to herself. Leave him on his own, she thought, put enough
pressure on him and he'll crack wide. In her night-spying
she'd seen it happen before, seen Ekeser sick, shaking, crying,
cursing. He'd developed over the years a mask effective
enough to pacify their father, but he'd paid a harsh price for
it. Forgotten in her chair at the far end of the table, Lilit
watched the interchange between father and son and knew
she was the son her father wanted and never would have in
either of the boys. She had his strength of will and clarity of
mind. She was his ultimate adversary, his nemesis, but he
would never know it. That was her worst frustration. He
would never know it. She wore her mask better than her
half-brothers, the mask her father had constructed for her
and forced on her. In the end, in the last moments before
that end, even if she told him what she'd done he'd discount
it—a woman's petty resentment, a child manipulated by his
enemies. He'd never acknowledge her as an intelligent, re-
sourceful adversary, never admit to himself that her brain
had directed the most effective attacks of the resistance. Even
if he could somehow know everything the moment before he
died, he would only die baffled at the ill-luck that had over-
taken him.

Lilit wrote:
Father has a stern sense of justice and allows none of the
overseers to abuse the contractees or their dependents. He
makes continual unscheduled inspections and if he finds evi-
dence of such mistreatment he acts. The guilty overseer might

*be fined, stripped of his authority and kicked offworld, or be
forced to labor beside the miners he had mistreated. He
wouldn't last long under the last circumstances as you may
imagine.*

*In winter when there are terrible storms in the mountains,
the mines are closed and the smelter shut down. Then Kalyen-tej would take his sons from world to world in the Aghir
round, visiting the other Lords of the tejed. Father despised
them and got little or no pleasure from the more debased of
their games. As a courtesy of his host, he would join in the
cross-country hunts for malcontents released from the pens to
provide game for the chase, performing his part with calm efficiency, leaving to the attendants the job of collecting the
ears and scalps of his kill. Ekeser enjoyed these hunts far too
much; he tormented me with graphic descriptions of what he
and his companions had done to their prey, boasted how
many he'd killed, how skillful a hunter he was.*

*He rides in comfort on a float, armored, equipped with an
infra-red sniffer and a darter whose missiles have explosive
tips and he boasts about killing some poor, half-starved creature, near naked and unarmed except for whatever he can
pick up in his flight. Now and then a particularly desperate
and ingenious quarry manages to take out one or two of the
hunters. What they'd do to him if they caught him alive. . . .
gah! Ekeser forced me to sit and listen to him tell it. He fidgeted about the sitting room while we were waiting for Father,
sneaking looks at Selas and me, especially me, but I knew
better than to let him see how I feel. I was as unresponsive as
Selas. So he went on talking, starting to sweat as he got into
the parts of his tale he specially liked. He got so involved
with his memories that in his sick excitement he forgot to
watch the door. Father stood there for at least a minute listening to him before he motioned the serving girl in to an-
nounce the meal. Ekeser turned and saw him, went pale, shut
his mouth. He didn't try excusing himself. There was no expression on Father's face, but Ekeser knew well enough the
verbal flaying he'd get later.*

*Funny, it was much the same kind of thing that got me in-
volved with Gyoll; it happened not long after my seventh
birthday. Metis and I were in the garden atop the womantower.*

Lilit lay on her stomach on the grass, her long legs bare to the gentler warmth of the winter sun. She wore only her short lacy chemise; her thigh-slit tunic and long skirt cast aside in a heap some distance from her. She turned sleepily to Metis who sat beside her, dressed in cap, apron, long gown. "What's a warp?"

"Where'd you . . . wait." Metis got quickly to her feet and rushed about the garden, poking behind bushes and into arbors.

"There's no one up here but us." Lilit rolled onto her back, crooked her arm over her eyes.

"Best to be sure." Metis dropped beside her again. "Where'd you hear that?"

"You had your freeday yesterday."

"Well, I know that."

"Well, you know Ael-tej and his heir are here."

"Your sister's wedding."

"Uh-huhhhmmmm." Lilit stretched, yawned, laced her hands behind her head. "Isamu the heir, he was bored. He wanted to hunt. He was complaining to Ael-tej, whining like a baby. I don't think he's very smart. Just as well, Tintu is a real mud-sucker. Anyway he kept at his sire to get Liros, Father he meant, to round up some warps and turn them loose out in the Wild so he could chase them down and cut off their ears. Sounds sick to me, aaaahhh." She stuck her tongue out and mimed gagging. "And he doesn't want to marry Tintu at all, he whined some more about that." She pulled her arm back so she could scratch at her nose. Little trickles of sweat were beginning to creep down into her hair. "So what's a warp? You never told me about those."

"I have," Metis said quietly.

Lilit pushed onto her side, lifted her torso, propping herself on her elbow to stare at her friend. Blood flamed in Metis's face. Her blue eyes glittered with a fury that frightened Lilit. Hesitantly she reached out and touched her arm. "Don't," she said. "Don't, if it makes you feel like that."

"No." Metis scrubbed the back of her hand across her eyes, a quick angry gesture, dropped the hand with the other in her lap. She was pale now, too pale. "Warps," she said. "People, Lili. People born different. Elf. The others. The ones the death squad smothers. People."

With a gasp and a flurry of arms and legs, Lilit came up to

sit cross-legged staring at Metis. "People?" Her voice cracked. "They hunt people? Father wouldn't . . . would he?"

"His tastes don't run that way, but as a favor to his guests?" Metis shrugged. "Lili. . . ." She hesitated, looked away from Lilit. Her fists were clenched in her lap. She began to beat them slowly on her thighs.

"Mimi, don't. . . ."

Metis looked down at her hands, forced them open. "Little sister, I want you to do something for me."

Lilit nodded. "Anything."

"This has to be very secret."

Lilit tried to grin. "Who I got to talk to anyway?"

"I mean really secret. It would be a lot worse than with the tiktik baby if anyone found out."

Lilit laced her fingers together, clutched her hands tight together. "I hear."

"Lili, I've got to go back home fast as I can. You know the passages. Is there any way out, any way I can get beyond the walls?"

"Uh-huh. There's a bit of a tunnel and at the bottom some water from the river. When the river's low like it is now you can see a bit of light on the water at the far end. You'll get wet."

"That doesn't matter." Metis got quickly to her feet. "Come on, show me."

Lilit picked up her skirt and tunic, but she didn't try to put them on, just held them against her chest. "You can't now, Mimi. Someone'd catch you sure. You got to wait till it's after dark. And what can your father do anyway, he can't stop the hunt."

Metis closed her eyes, took a deep breath, pressed her fist against her mouth. After a moment, she sighed. "He can warn the dwellers in the Wild," she burst out, clamped her mouth shut and watched Lilit step into her skirt. She sighed again and began doing up Lilit's laces. "You're right, Lili," she said. "But let's go in soon's you have your clothes back on. I can't sit still when I think of what could happen."

Lilit lifted her arms and let Metis pull the tunic down over them. She tugged her long hair free, lifted it up while Metis did up the back, let it fall. Hand in hand, they left the garden. As they began winding down the spiral staircase, Lilit turned to Metis. "He knows where the dwellers are living?"

"Don't talk about it now. Not till we're in our room."

"But. . . ."

"Don't!"

Lilit wrote:

When Father dies, it will go hard with the people since that will put Ekeser in power here. Yet, it is for this very reason that Father has to die now, before Ekeser is old enough and competent enough to hold on to the rule. Ekeser is jealous of me because I'm going with Father this time and he isn't—isn't that funny? He almost managed to get at my wedding robes the other day, had a vibroknife in his hand. He was going to rip them to shreds and blame me for it, of course. I thought for a minute he was going to use the knife on me but he didn't quite dare. He spat at me, wheeled and ran out. I'm right to do this thing, I know I am. By all the gods that never were, I'm not going to be here when Ekeser takes the rule.

Three days. Three days plus two weeks on the ship. Plus whatever time we are given for settling in. The rest of my life. I am terrified and filled with passion and exaltation and oh—I don't know—there aren't words—he will be dead, dead with me—he will die, like Metis, he will die—

ALEYTYS

The pilot was a slim smiling girl who transferred their luggage and them to the shuttle with a minimum of fuss and an aura of tidy efficiency—impersonally courteous, impenetrably polite and under the mask a bitter anger turned in on herself, a cell-deep wariness that shut her away from any real contact with the other parts of life. Aleytys clamped her teeth together and hardened her shields as she walked ahead of Tamris into the luxurious body of the shuttle. If too many of the Cazarits are like this, she thought, I'd better keep as distant from rank and file as I can, for my sanity's sake. I hate this, Madar, I hate it. She turned to Tamris who was settling herself into one of the comfortable seats. The girl's answering smile—grin really—was an excellent antidote to the depressing effect the pilot had on her. Tamris screwed up her face, started to say something, thought better of it, scratched at her eyebrow, tugged her tunic down, then thumbed on the witness link.

Aleytys lifted a hand to her, settled in her own chair and swung it around so she could see the changing images in the large screen set like a window in the wall. She was annoyed with the necessity that forced the link on them. She liked Tamris's often acerbic wit, and would have enjoyed talking the Hunt over with her. She was glad too that Swardheld had refused her invitation. The overhaul should be finished by now, he would be on his way to Ibex, gone at least six months. There was a small cold knot sitting on her stomach that wouldn't go away, she knew, until he was back. It was hard to realize that the obstacles she'd fought against so long were being swept away with so little fuss. It was quite possible that in a few months she'd be standing face to face with her mother. She shied away from the thought, not ready for it, not yet. With a twitch of her shoulders she remembered the Hunt.

The pilot stood in the open arch between the shuttle body and the steerspace, her green-brown eyes shifting from Aleytys to Tamris and back. She smiled, that professional smile that didn't come near touching her eyes. "This is the Director's private shuttle." She made a brief angular gesture that took in the hand-tied carpet, the grey velour armchairs, the polished wood fittings. "The Director sent it for your convenience, Despin' Aleytys. She wished to save you the bother of clearing through customs and passing through GATE, our entrance satellite. There has been an excess of traffic to Carnival in the past months and the facilities are being strained to tolerance given the current tightening of security. We will land on Center. That is the Island that houses Administration. You will be quartered there but will be provided with a chauffeured arflot when you need to visit any of the other islands. The weather is clear and cold over Center and it will be mid-afternoon there when we touch down. The Director will meet you at the field. There is a small informal reception planned at which you will be introduced to the managers of the various divisions of Cazarit. The trip will take about forty-five minutes. Welcome to Cazarit." She gave them another of her smiles, a small nod, then turned and seated herself at the control console.

In the viewscreen Center expanded from a brown point at the end of a finger jutting out from a much larger island, to an irregular splotch of dull olive against the glittering blue of the sea, to rolling parkland, green and lovely with groves of trees interrupting here and there the meticulously clipped grass and bright flower beds punctuating the grass with rounds of color, every bud open and at the peak of its beauty—nature overlaid with artifice. The landing field was set off at the far end of the island's fat oval, a stark grey interruption of the green, a sweep of metacrete, a tower at one end that looked as if it belonged on a prison wall and in fact did sit on the south side of a fence; woven wire fencing ten meters high surrounded the field, held away from the close-set metal posts by insulators. The woven wire went below the level of the ground, into a narrow metal-lined trench of indeterminate depth. The viewscreen caressed the fence with loving persistence, flowing along it, focussing on details, a

silent lecture on the advisability of minding one's business
and not annoying those in charge.

The touchdown was smooth; the pressure of deceleration,
intensified briefly, was gone, all this in a silence so deep
Aleytys could hear her heart beating. The harsh sounds of the
landing were shut away from them like something vulgar not
allowed to intrude into the elegance of the interior. She shook
her head impatiently and began watching the screen as the
shuttle rolled toward the tower and came to a stop about fifty
meters from it.

"Despini." The pilot was back in the arch, this time ad-
dressing both of them. "Your luggage will be transferred
directly to your quarters here. Unless there is something you
need immediately?" She waited a moment, nodded when neither spoke. "Then if you will remain seated a moment, I'll
have the lock open and the stairs ready for you." She turned
smoothly and bent over the console.

As the lock began to cycle open Aleytys stood, stretched,
smoothed stray wisps of hair off her face, tucking hairpins
more firmly into the braided knot wound around the crown
of her head. "It begins," she said to Tamris. Tamris nodded,
her large blue eyes glowing with excitement, her teeth clamp-
ing down on her lower lip.

Aleytys moved briskly to the lock, raised her brows at the
sight of the carpeted elegant stair now reaching from the lock
to the ground. She went quickly down it, feeling more at ease
when her bootsoles grated on the wind-strewn sand on the
metacrete. She turned to face the tower, the sea breeze tug-
ging at her hair, blowing into her face from the water, carrying the tang of salt, dead fish and desiccated seaweed. Beyond
the fence the tops of trees were swaying and rustling, the
sound pleasant in her ears after being shut in a small ship so
long, as was the distant wash of the surf and the dance of
grit across the field.

A door in the blank face of the tower slid open, a tall lean
door rather like a coin slot. Four people came through, walking two by two, stopped just outside and stood waiting.

TAMRIS

"So it begins," Aleytys whispered. *That's the second time,* Tamris thought. She watched Aleytys straighten her shoulders and smooth her long narrow hands down her sides. *Nervous,* Tamris thought. *Funny to think she's as nervous as me, as if this was her first time out.* Aleytys winked at her, amusement and understanding in her look. Tamris looked away, looked ahead at the four waiting for them. A few steps more and Aleytys stopped walking. Tamris stood a pace behind her and enough to one side so the link on her belt would have full play over the scene.

Two of the four at the coin-slot door hesitated then started toward them.

"Director," Tamris murmured. "ti Ganryn Intaril."

A tall slender woman, long straight black hair loosely wound about a finely shaped head. Tamris had been surprised when she first saw the tapes to find the Director wasn't even pretty, then realized it was the measure of her ability that she'd never chosen or been forced to biosculpt away her individuality, to change a crooked long nose, a mouth too wide, a jaw too pronounced, cheeks hollow until she looked gaunt. Her eyes were long and dark, full of vitality, curiosity, and a driving energy and intelligence she didn't bother to conceal. She had a natural elegance of bone and dressed to it, wearing a starkly simple onepiece, black with a touch of white at neck and wrists. Her face in repose was ugly, though her welcoming smile changed that almost magically. When she came up to Aleytys, she extended a rather bony hand and said, "Welcome to Cazarit, Hunter. Though I could wish this were only a holiday for you, still, it might work out that way, dama fortuna willing." Her flexible voice was full of warmth, a welcome that seemed genuine to Tamris, far more so than the polished plastic welcome of the pilot. It warmed her in spite

68

of her wariness, though she was watching critically both her own reactions and Intaril's actions, measuring her against Head, coming reluctantly to the conclusion that the woman would be formidable either as ally or antagonist. Tamris touched the black box at her belt as a fighter might touch a magic talisman before going into battle, then was furious at herself for the betraying gesture as she saw the black eyes register the movement and file it.

Aleytys touched briefly, formally, the hand extended to her. "My colleague and I thank you for the courtesy of our reception. The trip here was long and boring, as you know all such trips must be in a small ship." Her voice held an impersonal pleasantness that neither accepted nor rejected the Director's welcome. "We will still have to examine GATE as soon as possible. I can't work from reports alone, I'll have to go over your security there myself. We will also need to inspect in some detail the sites of the three snatches, again as soon as possible. You will arrange that?"

Tamris stifled a giggle. Nothing like starting how you mean to go on, she thought. It's like a dance, she thought, the way they're circling round each other.

"Of course." Intaril looked amused. "But not today, I think. You'll be wanting to settle into your quarters first." She made a graceful gesture that was intended to convey rueful apology. "I'm afraid I did assume you'd want to meet the Island Managers and I arranged a small reception. It won't take long, I assure you." She laid her hand on Aleytys's arm and drew her toward the tower. Tamris saw the Hunter stiffen slightly, very slightly, and move imperceptibly away until the Director was forced either to clutch at her or let her go, something she did with a calm assurance, waving that hand at the man waiting for them. "You'll recognize Yagro f'Voine from the tapes. Our chief of Security."

Tamris nodded to herself as she followed silent behind the delicately sparring women. Yagro f'Voine. A smallish man, a head shorter than the Director. A round bland face and round blue eyes, long straight blond hair he wore tied at the nape of his neck with a narrow black ribbon knotted into a small stiff bow. He wore a black velvet jacket with broad loose cuffs, a white shirt with falls of lace at throat and wrists, pale blue velvet trousers tucked into knee-high, close-fitting boots. A sapphire glowed among the froth of lace, an-

other hung from one ear, a long narrow teardrop that flashed
blue fire whenever f'Voine moved his head. A slim rapier
hung from a wide blackleather belt, its hilt of filigreed silver
set with more sapphires. Tamris's eyes widened; she'd seen
the earring on the tapes and the long hair but the whole en-
semble was a bit overwhelming. And a sword, she thought, a
damn silly sword. Playing games. Then she met his empty
blue eyes and no longer felt like grinning. She moved a step
closer to Aleytys, glad suddenly that Aleytys was the one who
was going to have to confront and perhaps coerce this pair.
She tugged absently at her tunic, realized what she was doing
and closed her lips tight. I am not a baby, she thought. I
made the trek into the wildlands and got to the third cairn
and got back out again. She looked at Intaril and f'Voine.
Definitely there are worse things than silvercoats and silence
and cold.

A much taller man stood in the coin-slot doorway, waiting
for them. When they came up to him, he stepped aside and
took his place at f'Voine's elbow, making Tamris wonder if
he'd been chosen more for the contrast he made than for any
abilities he might have—he was, if the elaborate costume was
an accurate indication of f'Voine's tastes. A stone-faced giant
with a shaven head, an attractive head in spite of the shaving
or perhaps because of it, hot yellow eyes, skin like charcoal
spread with thick red-amber syrup. No play sword for him or
fancy dress. He wore a shabby shipsuit whose only concession
to singularity was a multitude of pockets, a number of them
bulging though what he carried in them, she didn't care to
speculate about. The pair of shenli darters strapped on his
lean hips had the same worn but cared for look as the rest of
what he wore. He wasn't introduced, nor was the fourth person, a girl who might have been the shuttle pilot's sister; they
shared an anonymous sort of beauty, the same tidy efficient
air, the same impersonal courtesy, though this version of the
standard model seemed a year or two younger. Tamris was
suddenly glad of her short nose, round face and sprinkling of
freckles; her face was her own, she didn't have to share it
with a thousand or ten thousand others. She gazed thoughtfully at the elegant back of the Director, remembering the
ugly face and the startling charm of the woman. Loki's luck,
she thought, if I don't get ground between them, these wild

women, Intaril, Aleytys and Head. Hah! she thought. No.
Aleytys, Intaril—and *me.*

Tamris opened the small spiral notebook, smoothed the
pages flat, her eyes narrowed, her forehead pinched together
in a frown. She ran her fingers through her short hair, then
took up her stylo and sat tapping the blunt end on the empty
paper, briefly intimidated by the march of the pale blue lines
down the page. She wrinkled her nose, pursed her lips and
started writing.

NOTEBOOK

*Cazarit—Center—assigned quarters (two bedrooms, a
bathroom, a miniature kitchen, all small, a larger room for
pacing, talking, drinking) local time: eighteenth hour (of a
twenty-two hour day) plus thirty-five minutes, about an hour
after sundown—the first day down.*

The ghosthunt—notes, impressions, events.

*Aleytys has asked that I keep this notebook, not for official
showing, but to help me organize my thoughts and arrange
my testimony for the escrow board. Better not leave it lying
around anywhere, she says. She wants me to put down whatever occurs to me without censoring any of it, just let the ink
flow. Hmmm. Never tried anything like this. Should be interesting—*

IMPRESSIONS: *the reception—underground—most everything is underground on this island, for security, I suppose—
not a room, the place Intaril took us to—no—a space—
couldn't see the edges of it—don't even know there are edges
except by faith and common sense—hah!—space filled with
glimmers—deliberate?—light pulled down from the green-
park above, passed down by mirrors, or lenses—amplified
and strangled—eerie, as if light and shadow are painted
in place—rather nice effect—pulling out all the tricks to
impress us—water murmurs coming at us from scattered
fountains—from somewhere comes the susurration of a
stream—air wafted past us, heavy with flowerscents—racemes
of passionflower and suneyes dripping in careful disarray
from hanging pots—note to me: I like our less calculated
world a lot better, got the feeling that everything here was
not here for something as simple as somebody's pleasure in it,*

but intended to undermine and impress the visitor, after a while I started to feel irritated, couldn't even get mad without wondering if that's what they wanted—served us drinks, I waited until Aleytys sipped at hers and smiled at me—good, rather sweet red wine—with everything else there I was starting to get a bit muzzy by the time reception was over—a warning, I think, this reception—opening shot in what is obviously going to be a battle—they want her reputation, that's all—no poking and prying—

THE ISLAND MANAGERS—*what a crew, f'Voine was bad enough, wonder if this is part of the job or something they do to lessen the pressures of the job—or is it maybe the display behavior of competing dominants?*

CARNIVAL—PITAN JEE (manager)
Short and skeletal, stark, oddly hard to see in the patchy black and white of the space, a silver-haired harlequin, a long green drink clutched in one bony claw. A hard-edged smile carved on a face sculpted from flesh like polished whitewood. Androgyne and advertising it.

CARNIVAL—KEMUR YO (subchief of security)
Grey hair like smoke about a grey face, empty eyes, deepset, in the uncertain light, smudges without whites. A long straight robe of matte grey—it looked like leather but I never got close enough to be sure. Long narrow feet in sandals. Hands kept hidden in the wide sleeves of the robe. A cautious type, seems to me, giving away nothing. Should ask Aleytys if she picked up anything interesting from him—not too important, no one was snatched from Carnival. Androgyne, I think—I've never seen a body with such little expression. He's got the most difficult of all security roles on Cazarit—and maybe in a funny way, the easiest, Carnival clients are none of them wealthy or important enough to warrant snatching. Holidaymakers come unscreened to Carnival, having only to have the cost of a two-way passage and something left over to buy bed and board—always rat holes in the walls—those who come and don't leave—those who sell their return tickets for one more turn of the wheel and end in the slum north of the Midway—pickpockets and street gamblers, con men and women, whores of every gender, stranded ar-

tistes and assorted addicts, the thousands of small rats invading inevitably the walls of any place like this no matter how strictly policed.

CHIMAEREE—MALA KOSA (manager and subchief of security)

Long blond hair, seems to be her own, but who can tell anything sure here, braided and coiled atop an elegant head, its massive weight intended to emphasize the delicacy of an over-long neck. Face biosculpted to an icy perfection. Eyes a most improbable violet—she stood under one of the light plays to make sure this was noted—a translucent violet robe over a darker purple halter, low slung tight purple pants— purple! yechh—it was ridiculous, and I never felt so dumpy and grubby in my life and she knew it, damn her—female and flaunting it—first snatch was on Chimaeree—I thought of that and smiled sweetly at her—since hers is a limited operation with a very select clientele and brain-probed staff, she runs security herself—has to be competent or she wouldn't be doing what she is—not at all happy to see us here—instant hate when she saw Aleytys.

BATTUE—DAUN CENZAI (manager and subchief of security)

Of particular interest to us—Battue is to house the Aghir Conference—Hunter's island—a pun, son—hah—inhabited mostly by assorted popular predators not counting man— herds of prey animals—rare species imported to feed the pleasure of those who like to kill things, the rarer and harder to kill the better—Daun's a big man, coarse red-brown hair, sunbleached at the tips, a bristly moustache and short beard, deeply tanned, a reddish cast to the skin of face and arms, deep wrinkles fanning from the corners of pale blue eyes, a small scar above and passing through his left eyebrow, an indentation just above the bridge of his nose—he wore a tan shirt with numerous snapped-down pockets, tan shorts, laced-up boots—in a way he seemed out of place in this space and with the other exotics here—but when I looked at him again, I saw he was as much a construct as this underground garden—just that his construct was a bit closer to the real thing—I have no doubt that he is competent at what he does—but he has shaped himself so carefully to conform to

an ancient stereotype that he is as unreal as the most exotic
of those who waited and hated us.

Tamris stretched, scratched her nose, and grinned at what she'd written. All the description wasn't especially necessary but it was fun to write. No one said this had to be deadly serious, she thought. She chuckled, turned the page and went on with her scribbling.

TRAUMEREE—TANU-ALOM (manager and subchief of security)

A sprite—tiny—glittering with malice—blue hair—blue eyes—even a faint blue tinge to its skin—wore a lot of gauzy stuff that fluttered like a ribbon tree in a high wind whenever he or she—whatever—moved—high musical voice—chattered continually, lots of digs at the others, more digs at us, especially Aleytys—feeling superior, feeling annoyed at having to be here—no snatches from Traumeree—pointed ears that twitched—hands that talked as much as its mouth.

LETHE—MOARTE MATI (manager and subchief of security)

Death Island?—if the name means what I think. Traumeree for drugging yourself silly, Chimaeree for fantasies, Hazardee, gambling—Moarte-Mati—weird—female in form anyway—lush breasts, white heaps of flesh bulging out of a low-cut black velvet dress cinched tight under those breasts with a silver ribbon whose ends fell straight to the floor over a skirt that hung in classic folds—when she moved (her back was to us when we walked up), I had to swallow hard not to giggle—a silver skull mask covered her face—she glided when she moved, only her toes and the tips of silver sandals showed beneath the black velvet—garish ruby and silver jewelry—loaded down with ugly jewelry—no telling what she was thinking—she didn't say a word the whole time.

HAZARDEE—HINTOLLIN (manager)

A smooth bland-faced man—regular features—pleasant, unnoticeable face—brown eyes—thinnish waving brown hair worn short—neat, ordinary tunic and tousers—short plump fingers, broad palms, a plain gold ring on one finger—met us calmly, cordially—me, I think he could be the most danger-

ous of all that bunch—best self image, seems to me, doesn't feel any need for the extravagant costumes of the others— why do they do it—to impress us? No way—Hintollin and Intaril, they're the ones that impress me, they're a pair to watch out for.

HAZARDEE—PROARLUARIM (subchief of security)

Big man—quiet—neat and unobtrusive, dressed like the manager—bald head—pale brown skin, born that color I think—hands soft-skinned except for fingertips, outer edge of palm—knuckles distorted—heaven forbid I ever go unarmed against this one—way he moves, holds himself, better get the hell out if he'd let you—since he is Hintollin's sec-chief, can't be all muscle between his ears—but it's hard to tell about him—besides the obvious, I mean—said nothing the whole time, just stood like an outsize shadow behind Hintollin.

CONCLUSIONS *(Have to be tentative, based on the smell of things and first impressions—a reminder to me not to jump to indefensible or premature conclusions.)*

We can't expect cordiality—except obviously from those so secure in their own positions they're not afraid of us, or from those with the intention of trying to use us for their own ends. Things being what they are, it's understandable. The nature of the beast, Mom said. They walk a tightrope—two different governing bodies involved—Cazar Governors who've got a lot of other divisions under their control (the ones who hired us)—the local execs who have to work with us—if the locals are too free with aid and information about the inner workings of Cazarit, they'll suffer for it after the emergency is over (bad judgment and no leeway given for the difficulty of the situation)—on the other hand, if they're too obstructive and we can prove it—good ol' link, got its monocular on them—that will cost Cazar Company some hefty penalties, especially if Aleytys pulls off the long chance and snags the ghost—and she's already pulled off some damn long chances—and Cazar would be sure to come down hard on anyone who cost them, they bleed when they even think of losing money—Aleytys was right to have me bonded though I think I'm going to get very tired of carrying the damn link with me everywhere—and, sigh, she sure isn't going to be

*talking as free and open as she was on the ship; I'm going to
miss that—*

REMINDERS
*We need detailed physical maps of the islands and the sur-
rounding seabottoms—*

*Ask Aleytys if we should press for blueprints of the struc-
tures on the islands, of GATE, they're going to buck like hell
against giving those away—*

*How hard is it to sneak away from Carnival? seems to me,
right now anyway, Carnival is easiest to get into, might have
been the base of the ghost, the biggest island, pretty damn
rugged in spots, most of the food farms there and contract labor to supplement the automatic machinery, also offenders
against Company law working off sentences—I said something about this, but Aleytys is acting strange, I don't know
what to make of it—is she going to just go through the motions after all?*

THE VICTIMS
*No patterns here, we already checked that out, three
snatches, three different islands.*

OLDREAD CANS—*Hekteer of Kinnarsh, snatched from
Chimaeree*

SAH-KALAH—*y-motz-Yaln Company, a Yaln tie-pair, non-
human oxygen breathers, Rank both untranslatable and
unpronounceable, snatched from Lethe*

SUNG YUL TWI—*world administrator, Weh-Chu-Hsien
Triad, snatched from Hazardee*

MORE NOTES
*Our rooms were most thoroughly bugged, I don't think there
was a centimeter-cubed of space not covered by at least three
sensors—my implants were jumping like I had gnats under my
skin—no way I could fine-tune enough to locate them or
even do anything about them but yell loud and long to the
Director—while this bugging may be standard practice on
Cazarit, it is not something I am accustomed to, not something I intend to become accustomed to—Aleytys was just*

about as mad as I've even seen her but that didn't last long. She winced when we walked into the room, but she said nothing at all, she grinned at me like a hungry silvercoat and went to a couch on the far side of the room, lay down and closed her eyes—watch her work, you snoops—weeeeoooo—watch her work, hah!

Tamris grimaced, started to speak, changed her mind. She yawned, rubbed a hand across her chin, sauntered to the well-equipped bar and began inspecting the bottles racked there. She tugged her tunic down, feeling grubby, tired, irritated with the itch under her skin that was intensifying until it was like the walking of a thousand fleas. She wanted a bath, clean clothes, at least eight hours sleep, she wanted a window open on distance with sky that didn't even have to be blue the only thing but roof over her head.

Equally silent, equally irritated Aleytys crossed the room, scratching at one palm as she walked, rubbing at her nose, at the back of her neck. "Madar," she muttered. "I'd rather a tent in a high blow." She stretched out on a divan after kicking off it several dozen pillows, wriggled around until she was comfortable, tucked a pillow under her head and closed her eyes.

Tamris hefted a long-necked bottle, raised eyebrows at the label—she recognized it from one of the wine parties she'd sneaked into the last year at University; the giver's father owned the vineyard it'd come from and the giver made himself obnoxious by continually boasting about how much any of the others would have to pay for it if they could find it which they couldn't because the whole output of the winery was sold privately and contracted for years in advance. Chuckling at the memory of the end of that party, she started rummaging in drawers for something to draw the cork. A thought struck her and she straightened. "Think this could be drugged?"

Aleytys made a quick face without opening her eyes. She shifted on the divan, her lips twitched. With each movement in her face, Tamris felt a twinge in her implants. For a while she saw and heard nothing, then she began seeing tiny puffs of blue smoke, began hearing tiny pops and skritches. Grinning, she set two glasses on the bar in front of her and began pouring amber wine in them.

A few more minutes passed, Aleytys on the divan, Tamris leaning against the bar watching her.

The lights and the air flow faltered, came on full strength again. More smoke, grey-lavender puffs with an acrid bite to them, wafted from the slots of the airfeed.

And the itch under Tamris's skin vanished completely.

Aleytys sat up, rubbed at the nape of her neck, stretched her arms out in front of her, shook them. Tamris carried the wine to her. "Nice stuff," she said. "Met the winemaker once, a better man than his creepy son. If it's clean, the Director's doing us good."

Aleytys took a sip of the wine and sat cupping the glass between her palms, then she nodded. "No additives." She took another sip, smiled at Tamris. "Feel better?"

"Some. I can talk?"

"If you want. The place is clear for the moment."

"Intaril might be a bit peeved." Tamris settled herself in a drifting armchair, put her feet up on the rest. "Any idea how many eyes you popped?" She sniffed at the wine, sipped at it, sighed as warmth spread through her tired body.

"Too damn many. Intaril won't bring the subject up." She yawned. "Don't forget to make a note of this in your journal." She rubbed at her eyes. "I'm not on local time yet; if I want an early start tomorrow, I better try getting some sleep."

Tamris yawned, catching the infection from Aleytys, yawned again. "Me too. Been a long day. Who gets first crack at the bathroom?"

"Who do you think, lowly apprentice?"

ALEYTYS

She dreamed:

She saw first the shock of white hair, the hair he never managed to keep in order more than a few minutes. His back was what she saw next, he was walking away from her, weaving through a crowd of anonymous backs and banal faces— faces with the forced cheer of those determined to have a good time even if they half-killed themselves, faces with the emptiness of wooden dolls. She hurried after him, knocking the dolls aside, disregarding their reproaches and paincries, hearing them clatter down behind her with half a mind; with no mind at all, she ran after the narrow back and still he kept effortlessly ahead though he never seemed to hurry. As the others cleared away, she saw a second head, red as her own, at his elbow. A child walked beside him, a boy. She cried out, "Sharl, baby, wait for me, wait for me." But the boy didn't turn, wouldn't turn. She ran faster. The street opened into a square, They were in the middle of it, heading for another street on the far side. The square stretched, carrying them away from her, faster and faster as she ran faster after them. When she reached the middle of it, they turned, both of them. Stavver looked at her with cool dismissing eyes, the boy looked at her out of changing eyes filled with anger and resentment. The eyes were a wall of green glass through which she couldn't run. She stood where she was, staring at the man and the boy. The part of her that knew she was dreaming struggled to turn the dream, to turn her away or bring them to her, but she could neither move nor force them to move, though at least they no longer retreated from her. Groaning in her sleep, in her dream she called to them, despair in her voice, stretched her arms to them, in her sleep she cried out angrily, in her dream she cried out pleadingly. The man laughed and turned away, walking away from her, taking the boy's hand; they both walked away from her, hand in hand, laughing and talking; they turned into the street and disappeared, leaving her with her feet sunk into the softening pavement, sinking farther, her body rigid, an unvoiced and unvoiceable pain filling her. . . .

Her cry ringing in her ears, she broke from the dream, jerked upright with such violence the bed rocked under her. There was a film of sweat over her face and body, a brassy taste in her mouth; she opened her fingers slowly, letting go of the blanket. She scrubbed a hand across her face, wiped it on the blanket.

Harskari's eyes and face bloomed in her mind. "Stop whipping yourself, daughter, I begin to think you enjoy it."

"What?" At first Aleytys was angry, then she chuckled. "Is good advice always so astringent?" She lay back, stretched, let her eyes drop shut, her body limp with reaction, deeply calm now. Enjoy it, she thought, smiled into the darkness, after a while she wriggled around until she was comfortable, chuckled aloud, then slipped effortlessly into a deep, deep sleep.

LILIT

She sat at the far end of the table, listening to her father catechize his sons.

"Say the scum hit the smelter train. What do you do?"

"As soon as the alarm comes in, I send Kaston and the search team out in floats. Wait half an hour, send a recovery squad from off-shift miners to collect any ingots left behind and load them on hand trucks so they can take them to the warehouses, send repair bots and supplies to right the mono and repair whatever damage has been done to the rail. Any bodies found, have them brought to the lab so Dr. Akalin can look them over. Live ones, if any, turned over to Kaston for interrogation. Try to track down family affiliation, if any, of such dead as we find. If a family is pinpointed, set sniffers on the individual members so we'll know where every one of them is at every minute." The boy's voice was flat, uninflected. He was reciting a lesson. It was impossible to say how much besides mere words he had absorbed. Kalyen-tej frowned, but after a moment accepted the answer.

"Patrol?"

"Continue as before. Random overland masses—doubled near suspected settlements. Suspicious activity spotted, no overt action taken, infiltration of snoopers and sniffers. If a smuggler is spotted, wait till he grounds before springing the trap."

The catechism went on, the boy given little time to eat, forced to recite, his resentment growing, his face increasingly sullen.

Lilit wrote:

Ekeser will never make the man Father is. I can hate Father because he has killed, one way or another, everything I held dear. But I have only contempt for Ekeser. He is a

*sneak and a sadist and a coward, I've backed him down
many times when he tried tormenting me or Metis. I've
clawed his face, suffered his fists and never surrendered
though I was the one punished for these outbursts. It is not
proper for a girl to fight.*

She suffered the punishment stoically as she'd endured the
pain when he hit her. She was older than he was and could
match his strength closely enough for enough years for him
to learn to let her alone, to avoid her, ignore her, things she
took at first with an irritatingly smug smile though later she
hid her contempt behind her submissive mask, hid her horror
and sick disgust when he switched tactics and described
things he'd done to others, knowing with sly surety that she'd
carry no tales to their father. A year ago he'd thought to try
her again, but she simply lifted cold eyes and stared him
down.

Lilit wrote:
*When the smuggler beams word back that the tejed are
dead, then Acthon will lead the dwellers into the Hold. Ekeser is weak and arrogant. He has already alienated the
guards, most of them anyway, Kaston especially; the man
despises him. Ekeser has learned his lessons by rote but
doesn't understand the principles behind the actions he's been
taught. Father is capable of sudden unexpected strokes, also
unexpected generosities, but my brother has none of this in
him. Sometimes it seems to me he's a changeling. How could
two such strong and intelligent people as Father and
Stepmother produce HIM? If I'd been the boy Father
wanted—no—I refuse to think of that.*

*O Metis, I need you to steady me. I am so wild. Things
fall apart, I am so lonely and so afraid. I don't want to die. I
want to leave this place, to get away somehow, my dearest
one, I did not know how terribly I could miss you.*

*We leave in three days. Three days. All this has been
planned so long. I don't know how I can hold together for
these interminable days. Help me, my Metis, help me not to
be a fool and destroy all of us for nothing. How am I going
to endure those days of confinement on the ship with no one
to talk to?—not even this book. Acthon will be left behind,
he wasn't sure of that at first but is now. Father simply does*

not trust Ekeser. Acthon wants to be with me, but won't try arguing with Father, there's too much at stake to start Father thinking. I suppose Gelana and Ianina will be my attendants. Their men are Father's most ambitious and energetic overseers and he's too canny a man to leave that kind of trouble behind. All the better, less trouble for us, but oh, they are boring.

Canny and uncanny. No, we don't want to start Father's gameplayer mind working. He's eerie sometimes, the way he leaps ahead of other men's thinking. Ahead of us, if we're not careful.

At the same time he is relatively blind where his own blood is concerned. It is as if he puts us all in slots and expects us to fit ourselves to that space. He doesn't understand Acthon at all, though he's right to value him. Acthon's mother, Aiela, was the first of Father's mistresses. He had her before he married my mother. Aiela was young then, fourteen at most. Father was young too, a wild autocratic impatient youth suffering greatly under Grandfather's excesses. He and Grandfather fought over her, just one of the many times he fought with his father, the first time, the first of many times, he backed his father down. I wish I could have talked to her. Metis and Acthon loved her deeply; they and all her children conspired to protect her while she lived and miss her dreadfully since she died. When she was pregnant with Acthon, Father was forced to send her back to the village where he married her to the man he considered the best of the recently arrived contractees, Gyoll of Suyak. Grandfather would have no bastards in the Hold to fight with legitimate sons for the power it represented. Father had to acknowledge the truth of this, that's why he acquiesced in the end. I think, in spite of himself, he has never stopped loving her, or if what he feels can't be called love, he's never been willing to let go of her. That's why Acthon was brought into the Hold when he was fourteen in spite of the danger he represented. Grandfather was dead by then. That's why Metis was the girl chosen to tend me when my mother died. Aiela's daughter. Gyoll's daughter.

Gyoll the rebel, sold into thinly disguised slavery, a man of cold and careful violence, a gentle man, an affectionate man, the father of Metis and Elf and Kedarie and Little Worm who lives in the Wild.

Little Sister. Kedarie. The older she got the more she looked like Aiela, Metis told me. Father had Kedarie brought to him when she reached her fourteenth year. Sometimes I wonder if he was entirely sane about Aiela—if he was trying to find her again in her daughter. He has had two wives, both of whom got little warmth from him, yet I know we are much alike in many ways and I know my own passions and my possessiveness, so I suspect he cared more for Aiela than he was willing to let himself know.

Alike. I hate him with all the passion I can generate, but in all honesty we are much alike. And I'm rather proud of that. Blind man, if only you could see. If only you would look behind my woman's face and see me.

After Acthon told me about Father's selling me, after he came back and got my answer, he brought Gyoll into the cave below the Hold. Gyoll wasn't about to take my commitment on faith. I had to convince him; at least he listens to me, respects me. I think Acthon thought he was going to try to dissuade me, but he just listened.

Around them the machines that purified the air and water hummed their deep rumbling two-note song and the insulated ducts were a cat's cradle woven in and out of the dark. Lilit sat with her back to the wall of dull grainy insulation brick, her legs drawn up, her arms clasped about her knees, her face illuminated by the sticktight light on the floor by her toes. Acthon sat silent and scowling at her left, his narrow high-cheeked face a masculine version of hers.

Gyoll sat at her right. His head was totally bald now, but his eyes glowed with the passion still living in his dying body. He was no longer lanky but a thing of hide and bone, shaky with pain and a growing weakness of body. His skin was loose over his bones, draping in fold over fold and even his dark tan couldn't disguise his chalky pallor. Lilit was appalled at his too-rapid deterioration; Acthon was more familiar with it and perhaps sadder.

Gyoll fixed his eyes on Lilit. "Once this is started, you're committed, girl; you think you can hold the line? More lives than yours will be riding on your will."

"The last wife of Aretas killed herself." Lilit shrugged. "I'm just anticipating an inevitability."

"Stop playing with words, girl, you're talking about lives."

"I've held your lives in my hands for years," she said. "I won't drop them now."

"Words."

"All right, revered leader, look at me. How long would I last in the Wild? And while I did live, how could I stand being an intolerable burden on your people? I'm as arrogant and bad-tempered as my father." She smiled suddenly, the outward sign of the absurd laughter bubbling in her veins, laughter at herself, at Acthon's disappointed glare, at Gyoll's amused complicity. "Ask Acthon," she said. "He knows well enough about my temper." She shook her head. "And I'm used to luxury, good food, hot baths, idleness when I can read and dream. You want honesty? I'd hate living hard. I don't think I could do it."

Gyoll was silent, his eyes hard on her, demanding more from her. Acthon stared at his hands.

"Consider my choices. The Wild? Even to save my life I won't take on a slow dragged-out dying. Aretas? Acthon must have told you about him. Besides . . . well, never mind that. Ask my father not to do this to me? That's a joke. Laugh. He knows well enough what Aretas is like, he didn't want to do this to me; believe me, I know that. He didn't like it but he sold me anyway to get his sacred conference. Run away? Get off-world? I'm useless, I'd starve. I want to mean something." Eyes clamped shut, she beat her fists on her thighs. Gyoll bent forward, cupped his hands over hers, held them still. Lilit pressed her lips together and fought to calm herself. After a minute she said, "I won't trickle my life away. I will not."

Gyoll patted her hands, straightened with a grunt. "Well then, let it be. You say you'll be the trigger. Thought how?"

"I don't know if you know how we dress our women for their weddings. A dozen robes, one on top of the other until the bride is a puffball. At the wedding her attendants peel her layer by layer to present her to the groom, but in the beginning she's a puffball." She reached up her sleeve, pulled out a roll of paper, handed it to Acthon. "That's what the two of you will have to work with. I'll be making my robes myself. I plan to embroider the veil and the outer robe with silver wire and beads, enough, I hope, to mask whatever you want me to carry in." She looked at the roll of paper in Acthon's hand, scowled. "My education is so damn limited, reading just doesn't give me . . . never mind, you figure out how to do it, that's your part." She got to her feet. "All I ask is be sure it will work. I want to go out grandly." There was passion in her whispering voice. "Not with a whimper."

They watched her go, without speaking. She felt their eyes on her, watching her as they'd watch some kind of strange beast. Metis had always told her she was extravagant at times. She felt extravagant, lifted, her feet bounced from the concrete, the black robe's hem-fur swished about her ankles. In the gently humming, warm, oily darkness, she felt Metis beside her, laughing, telling her she was being extravagant. She laughed, paused, startled by the sound, then went silent into the wall.

Lilit wrote:

Acthon and I are too much alike to deal easily with each other. It's a good thing we couldn't meet often or our quarrels would explode the walls of the Hold. Metis, love, since you're gone, we walk like strange cats about each other, sniffing at each other, warily polite and controlled. Otherwise we could not continue to talk and plan. Without your balance, my Metis, we begin to fly apart! When I'm here with your ghost, I see this clean and strong, but when I'm with him, the rage in both of us tries to blank out our reason. I can see him hating me because of the blood in me and I can see him hating himself because it is his blood too. We both reject our father, but we are his children and we know it all too well, especially when we turn on each other. When you died birthing father's child, my Metis, Acthon wept in my arms and I wept into his dark hair and for that short moment we were one. Three years. I see your ghost drifting in the corner of the room, I see you but I can't touch you.

Remember how I used to spy on the people who lived in the Hold, my Metis, how I used to wander through the passages and peer out at people in their private rooms? You scolded me enough times on invading the privacy of people without power to complain. After I started my menses, I spent more time in the maze, watching most of all the guards with the women Father had brought in for them. And I watched Father. You shamed me from the servants' quarters and I plunged deeper into my involvement with Gyoll and your people and their cause; dinners become horrors for me because Stepmother was by then teaching me the arts of the chatelain which seemed at the time my inevitable destiny. Within the next three or four years, if I followed custom, I'd be married to someone, to the son of one of the Aghir lords, possibly to some outlander who father needed to tie more firmly to him. Chatelain. What an elegant word for chattel, a thing to be bartered for gain. At those dinners with Stepmother I was expected to order the servants about, I was supposed to order the meals in the kitchen, I was supposed to watch the servants and read the wishes of Stepmother without her having to say anything. I was supposed to taste the food and praise or reprove the cook, I was supposed to reprove those servants who were dilatory or made mistakes, I was supposed to order the punishment of lazy or thieving servants. Sometimes the words locked in my throat and nearly shut off my breath. Stepmother didn't know what to make of this but she was firm with me—and patient—and got me through this stage. She was pregnant again, eight years atfer the birth of Selas. Why Father made her do that I don't know. Maybe he wanted another chance at producing a legitimate heir the equal of Acthon. Though he always treated Ekeser and Selas well enough—according to his own ideas of that; even his flaying scolds were never without adequate provocation—he simply didn't like either one. Not as he both liked and respected Acthon. And he had reason, if love needs a reason. For all I rail at Acthon and fight with him, he has many of Father's gifts and has honed them with the help of Gyoll. Gyoll recognized and trained his innate capacities and made a leader of men out of him through the power of love and example. Blind man, my Father, if only he could see, he corrupted and ruined his legal sons because he neither loved them nor taught them to value anything beyond their blood; he schooled them hard in duty, but the greatest part of that duty was preserving the Liros system in the hands of the Kalyen line. When this was threatened, all other duties could be disregarded. They were not the kind to stand up to him and demand his respect if not his love; blind man, how could he expect them to give love never having received any. Duty to the blood—and so he sold me to a toad. Duty to the blood!

Father called me to the library six months after I met with Gyoll and Acthon down below and began to plan our course. He sent a servitor with speech functions, not a servant. Obvi-

ously he wanted no gossip about the summons. This time I
agreed with him. I wanted no eyes looking slantwise at me
each dinner, it was hard enough to eat with the excitement
boiling in me. With speculative eyes on me and the
knowledge of how the serving maids would giggle, my throat
would close up completely.

I knew the library as well as I knew my tower room, but
I'd never been in it when my father was there. Sometimes I
wondered if he ever missed the books I'd taken for Metis and
myself. He'd never said anything and I always returned them
(except for this book I'm writing in. Funny, I wonder if
someday this journal will return to sit forgotten on those
shelves?). I thought of all this before I opened the door and
stepped in to face him. It didn't help calm me, only another
burden—look at that, taking myself so damn seriously, poor
baby, bowed down under all her troubles, sorry, whoever
reads this, sorry, my Metis, I'm being extravagant again.

My hand on the latch knob, eyes down, I thought, dull and
submissive, what you've been all these years, eyes on the
floor, hands clasped before me, relax, relax. I regulated my
breath until it was slow and even, then I pushed open the
door. Father was standing by the glass wall looking out into
the same false vista that the dining room windows looked out
on.

"Lilit."

"Father." Her voice was soft and even, she was pleased
with that. She kept her eyes on the floor after her first quick
glance at him.

He didn't speak for a time. She wanted to look at him, to
see what was keeping back the announcement she knew had
to be made. But the situation was too precarious for uncon-
sidered action. Meek and mild, humble and stupid, she reminded herself and kept her gaze fixed firmly on the polished
parquetry in front of her toes.

"How old are you?"

In spite of her resolution, her eyes flew up to meet his. She
quickly lowered them. "Nineteen, Father," she said, fighting
to keep both sharpness and fear out of her voice.

"Nineteen." There was irritation in his voice. She heard the
whisper of his house slippers on the parquetry but forced herself to a measure of calm.

Again there was a lengthy silence. At last he spoke, his words clipped, quick, as if he forced himself to say them and wanted the saying done with. "It's past time you were wed. I have arranged that you be married on Cazarit to Lanten-tej of Aretas. You will have six months to prepare yourself for the wedding. What do you need? Sewing women, materials, jewels?"

It was Lilit's turn to stand silent. She stretched the silence as far as she dared, smiling inside as her usually imperturbable father fidgeted about the room. He knows too much about Lanten, she thought. He doesn't like selling me into that menage. Stew, damn you, Kalyen-tej, my father, stew in your stinking necessities. She bit her lip and forced herself to breathe more slowly. She could feel the twitching of the tic beside her eye but there was nothing she could do about that. She lifted her head when she heard her father swing about, his slippers slapping down hard as he walked toward her. "I will require six meters of heavy white silk, silver couching thread, silver wire and beads, at least a liter of pearls and another of moonstones for the outer robe." She was rather surprised at how softly and smoothly the words dropped from her lips, at the gathering quiet inside her—as if all the knots there had come untied. "No sewing women. I will give you a list of stuffs for the other robes. I have six months, you said. I've nothing else to do."

He stared at her, rather disconcerted. "Do you want to ask about your bridegroom?"

"Could I refuse him if I don't like what I hear?"

"No."

"Then, what's the point? Is that all?"

"Yes." He moved away from her, went back to staring out the window. Over his shoulder he said, "You may go now."

She left, smiling openly now, knowing she'd startled her father, that he didn't like what circumstances and his own plotting had forced him to do. It gave her a deep satisfaction that she refused to question.

My Metis, sometimes writing this is almost like talking to you, it eases the pressures of the passions building in me, eases my grief, my anger, my fear. Talking to you, confessing, asking your pardon for the pain I caused you, the pain of your last months, when I hated you and reviled you and missed you and agonized for you. When I understood nothing and felt everything. Coming to terms with myself—ah, I can hear you, my ghost. I can hear you scolding me for all this me-me-me. I need you to laugh me out of my excesses. Acthon can't do it, or won't.

Little Sister. When we were fourteen Father had her brought to his quarters and installed her there as his mistress. She had even less say in this than I do in my wedding. You, Metis, you were so angry, I've never seen you so angry, yet you spared time to calm Acthon, to help him deal with his fury so he wouldn't ruin himself, you found time to comfort me and help me handle my jealousy and anguish and the rage I thought was going to burn me to ash.

I saw her in the garden outside father's bedroom. She sat on the cool green grass, her delicate head dark against the pale leaves of the willow, her white robe glowing against the red and yellow tulips behind her. Father lay stretched out on the grass, propped on an elbow, smiling up at her, his face relaxed, his hair a little mussed, his tunic falling open about his hard flat chest. He was smiling tenderly at her. I've never seen such openness in his face, I've never seen his eyes alight with contentment like that.

I stood at the peephole, looking through the dusty leaves of the wall plant. I stood there I don't know how long until he moved suddenly, pressed his face against her thighs, his arms circling her hips. I stood there with tears cutting the dust on my face until I knew I'd betray myself if I didn't leave.

You know, my Metis, how I ran unheeding through the secret ways, collecting bruises and cuts I didn't know about until later, not caring what noise I made until I tumbled out into the tower room and ran to you and pulled you down onto the rug, my face pressed against your thighs, my arms tight around your hips. You know how I shuddered and sobbed as you tried to find out what was troubling me. And I know your anger when I told you. Little Sister in my father's arms.

Stepmother died birthing another son. The child was strong and healthy but his hands and feet grew from his torso. He had no arms and legs. They let the mother die and saved the child before they saw he was deformed. When they looked at him, they disposed of him with brisk efficiency. Father went about looking grim, grieving not much for Stepmother, I

*think, but a great deal for his deformed child. Looking grim,
and if you knew him, worried, worried that the world had
gotten to him after all despite his constant and careful pre-
cautions. He went off-world for tests and came back looking
grimmer than before. He said nothing of why he'd gone or
what he'd learned, but I found the doctor's report in his office
and read it. I didn't understand all of it, still, the conclusion
was clear enough—too many abnormal sperm. He had a
good chance for normal children if the mother didn't con-
tribute additional genetic weaknesses. It also recommended a
series of treatments at University, treatments that would have
necessitated his absence from Liros II for several years. I
didn't think he'd do that and I was right. He locked his office
when he left it, but he didn't lock that panel that opened
from the wall, he didn't know about that.*

*I've thought about that ignorance some and come to be-
lieve that the secret of the passages was passed from father to
son and never written down. I never found any references to
it in all my poking and prying through the Hold records.
From the little I heard of him, I know Grandfather was a su-
premely spiteful man. It would be like him not to tell Father
about the passages and go to his grave hugging that secret
gleefully to him. Ekeser has to be a lot like him.*

*Acthon Ekeser Selas. The baby ghost. Sons of Kalyen-tej
Names. Mannen the Kalyen-tej. Tintu Ammayl Claril Yannit
Frens Jantig. And Lilit. Daughters of Kalyen-tej. Metis Elf
Kedarie. Daughters of Aiela and Gyoll. Little Worm. Son of
Aiela and Gyoll. Naoil the Seer, son of Kalyen and Kedarie.
Olyarin, son of Kalyen and Metis. Names. Heartsounds and
Heartwounds.*

*As he'd done with Aiela, he sent Kedarie back to the vil-
lage as soon as she was pregnant. As he had done for Aiela,
he found a husband for her, a younger miner still healthy
and a man more gentle than most. The child was born in
Aiela's house, Kedarie's now. Born without eyes, born not
needing eyes. Acthon hid the baby and brought a borndead
from the Wild to take his place. Father came to the village
and demanded to see the child. Acthon told me later, Metis
my friend, that our father seemed almost afraid. A muscle at
the corner of his mouth jumped and his hands shook a little
before he could still them. He took the tiny deformed corpse
they brought him, looked at it for a moment, then gave it*

back and walked to the Hold, his face stiff, his eyes with a blind look to them.

I almost felt sorry for him, Acthon said. *It's too bad this isn't another place and another time.*

That was a bad time, those years while Father kept Kedarie in his rooms. I went back and back to watch them. Father and Little Sister. I was obsessed by them. Metis made me eat when she could, but sometimes I vomited everything up again and sat clutching myself about the middle, wracked by pains that were easier to face than the agony in my spirit. When I tried to sleep, I sank too often into nightmare and woke you too, my Metis, and you comforted me again and again, loved me, held me, scolded me, and didn't say what I'm sure you knew about me, what I can look at now but only sideways and can't say, can never say even to myself. For those two years I was near destruction but you held me together and you taught me the joy of loving as an antidote to the agony of loving, you got me deeply involved in Gyoll's activities, teased me out of myself, took my eyes off my own wounds and focused them on the needs of the people. I plundered my father's desk, listened to his orders to guards and overseers, listened while he organized ore shipments and flitter patrols, passed this to Acthon. (He avoided prying himself on Gyoll's advice because this would keep dangerous ideas out of Father's head, and, anyway, they got all they needed from me.) Gyoll and Acthon were furiously busy, keeping the threads untangled, soothing the fearful, calming the angry, holding together that precarious patchwork organization scattered over five worlds. You'd think Acthon's involvement with this would show up like black on white, but the guard was long used to his coming in and out whenever he wanted and he was never gone long. Elf and her cadre of wild ones were the messengers on this world, riding the ugly fliers even across the oceans to keep the lines of communication unbroken. They didn't use the local transmitters much, only in emergencies, it was too easy to tap and trace them.

Acthon. We've fought, sometimes we've wept together. We've schemed together, and he's used me. I have Father's gameplayer mind more strongly than Acthon, or maybe because I know few of the people I claim so jealously for my own, I could see more clearly how to use them than he could who loves too many of them. Like Metis, his heart could be-

*tray him. And I can think into Father's mind and find coun-
ters for his plans. I had a good share in planning those first
raids on the treasure trains. They had to change methods
each time they attacked because Father guarded against the
ones they'd used before. The first time they mashed dirt lily
pads and plastered the muck on the rail and let it dry hard.
The mono bucked and screeched and shuddered and nearly
leaped from the rail. The rebels forced the car open, divided
the ingots among them and faded into the bush, no two of
them heading in the same direction. They rode purplecows,
large horned herdbeasts with mottled purple hide and mild
red eyes. They were capable of a surprising turn of speed for
a healthy stretch, cantering smoothly on long thin legs. The
beasts liked to be scratched behind the warty growths that
served as ears, and a mild hopeful attitude toward other life
forms, also something of Elf's talent, a way of binding by affection. How intelligent they were is something Acthon tells
me the dwellers of the Wild often speculate about.*

*I've often wondered what it's like out there in the Wild.
Acthon has told me stories of what he's seen. Their life is
hard but they seem to be thriving, enjoying themselves in
spite of my father's patrols. There are so many ways their
lives will be made better if Father and my half-brothers are
removed. It's as well I won't be here, though, I've got no
place in their lives, not like Acthon, and I'd only remind
them of the hateful tejed.*

I make twenty years the day we leave Liros II.

*I think: we call the smuggler and organize the dwellers in the
      Wild and the miners.
      Our attacks grow quickly more and more annoying.
      Father sees rebellion ahead; he thinks he could handle it
      on Liros II but could be overwhelmed by successful
      rebels from the other worlds of the Aghir.
      He persuades the tejed to hold a conference on Cazarit.
      We plot to wipe out the tejed.
I think: Gyoll is as canny a gameplayer as my father.
      He planned this sequence of events.
      He meant Acthon to take his place; he meant me to come
      to this point, he meant me to see the necessity of my*

passing. He meant Father to gather the tejed in one place, for the tejed must die together or our rebellion is most likely doomed.
I think: This is true and not true.
I think: It doesn't matter.

Metis, you hated Father despised him, feared him a little, and Oh, My Dear One, you did love him. I reached sixteen unwed and unasked, forgotten, content again, busy and loved in my little world.

One day, I didn't know why then, I still don't, Father came up to my tower room instead of summoning me. Maybe he remembered Metis, I don't know. He stood in the doorway that bright afternoon without saying anything. You were on the windowseat, the lowering sun tinting your hair to copper. I was sitting at your feet, my head resting against the padding of the seat. When I saw him, I thought for a minute that he'd sold me at last, wondered what I would do if he had. I got to my feet and stood with my eyes down, waiting—waiting— when he didn't speak I looked up and saw him staring at you, a slight smile on his ice-pale face. I wanted to scream at him, stick knives in him. It wasn't quite like the pain and confusion in me when Little Sister was his mistress. My Metis, when at last you were exasperated at what I was doing to myself, you told me that I was not Little Sister and Little Sister was not me. I shuddered under the words, they were like gusts of wind hammering at me though what could I know about gusts of wind when I've never been out from under the dome? I wouldn't listen, I pressed my hands tight over my ears, I wept until my head throbbed, until my throat was raw and I was so exhausted I felt like jelly.

Father watched you, Metis, when you swung round on the seat, turning your back to the light flooding in the window. He watched as you walked to stand behind me, one hand on my shoulder.

Who are you? he said—but he knew, I'm sure he knew.

Gyoll's daughter, you said.

Aiela's child, he said. He stood there a moment longer, then was gone, saying nothing about the reason he'd come, his feet silent on the silken rug, long strides carrying him quickly down the hall and down the spiral staircase, three

*steps at a time. I heard his bootheels clicking for a long time
until they were only an echo in my ears.*

*I went to dinner already full of fear because Father de-
manded my presence. He didn't speak to me once but he
smiled when he saw me sitting in Stepmother's chair.*

You were gone when I came back.

I knew where you were, I knew.

*For two weeks I stayed in that room. I didn't try going
into the walls, I didn't try finding you or watching you. Not
until Father went to inspect the mines—then I. . . .*

*No. I don't want to remember that. Metis, my love, I
won't—O God, how can I remember what I said to you, how
I screamed and begged you to let Acthon take you into the
Wild. I begged you to leave him. I couldn't endure seeing you
with him, I begged you and cursed you and ended with my
head in your lap, you comforting me and trying to help my
anguish and trying to understand my anguish, not the fact of
it but the extent.*

*I watched you with Father when he came back. I think
you knew that though you never spoke of it to me, never
asked. I sat for hours outside that bedroom watching my father make love to you. Watching as you lay sated beside him,
drowsily stroking fingertips across his shoulders and back,
slow lines that burned into my flesh.*

And then you were pregnant.

And then you were sent home like the others.

*And then you died, but the child lived, like Little Sister's
child, much like Little Sister's child.*

And Father was shown another borndead.

Did he grieve for you, my Metis, or for himself?

*Did he rage against the chance that had warped his seed
and yours into what he saw as horror?*

*This I know, when you died, my Metis, when he saw that
shapeless creature they told him he'd fathered, that was when
he began his shuttling around the Aghir, trying to persuade
the tejed to cooperate against the rebels and their pet smuggler. He wanted, I think, to buy time to visit University and
if not that, to secure the Liros system for his sons, he knew
well enough how ill-equipped they were to handle the rebels.
If he hadn't worshipped at the feet of Order and Blood, he'd
have legitimated Acthon, I'm sure of it, and exiled the others,*

*but he wouldn't do that, couldn't go against his deepest be-
liefs.*

*He took no more mistresses and he grew harder and colder
than stones.*

*Three days. Acthon and I, we've made our plans. Among
my many robes I will carry death.*

She touched the silken green fabric. It had a warm rubbery
feel, a dull sheen. "I can cut this with ordinary scissors?" She
teased open the other two foil packets and touched the
material inside. "These others too?"

"Yes." He handed her a pair of shiny gloves. "Wear these
when you're working. Be best if you work up in the roof
garden where there's some movement in the air. And don't
put any of them directly next to your skin." He looked gravely at her. He was stiff and uncomfortable with her now,
when he touched her it was with a careful delicacy as if she
were some frail ancient creature. He spoke in hushed tones
sometimes, sometimes in a voice so determinedly bright she
wanted to kick him. Rather fervently, she hoped he'd get
used to the idea and relax into the casual give and take they
developed the last three years. "Don't leave any scraps lying
about," he said. "You can give them to me when you're
ready."

"What about when I'm finished?"

"Keep the robes wrapped in the foil and in a place where
they will stay cool." He touched the crumpled metal foil,
smiled suddenly, a wide flashing grin that lit his face. "You
don't need to worry about them wrinkling."

"What about the attendants Father will make me have?
There's nothing I can do about them; it's tradition, they dress
me for the ceremony. Besides, I have to have them, I can't
manage all those damn robes."

Acthon moved restlessly, scowled. "You know more about
that than me. Figure out something. Don't tell me something
as simple as that will stop you."

"Hah! Easy for you to say."

Three days. Two weeks on the ship. And then
O God, I'm terrified of doing this.
*My father will take my hand and lead me into the Hall,
lead me to my toad bridegroom. The doors will shut behind*

us. I know his plans. My father will come to me and take my hand and lead me in and I'll tear away my veil and—I'll tear away the triggering strip and—

Whatever gods there be, help me.

On the night before Embarkation, Lilit wrapped her journal in a square of silk, tied it in a neat bundle and gave it to Acthon to hide away, getting a promise from him not to open it until the signal came from the smuggler.

THE BOY AND THE THIEF

The boy trotted behind the thief as he pushed through the milling crowd at the dome where the incoming pleasure seekers sought the shuttles to take them to their final destinations. He felt a little like a chickling paddlefoot waddling behind its mother, though Stavver even in his present guise didn't make too convincing a mother. Grinning behind the hated veil, the boy kept as close to the tall narrow figure as he could though he took some pains to avoid treading on the trailing robes of the Vijayne. The crowd was noisy and cheerful though here and there the veneer was wearing thin and frazzled tempers broke noisily under the strain of body heat and strange odors, the long waits enforced by the shutting down of all but one bank of four turnstiles. Crowd control bots zipped busily about with stubby metallic calm, restraining with velvet force any altercations that went on too long or threatened to go beyond the heated exchange of insults. Children whined or sobbed or screamed according to their natures or the manner of their cultures if they were old enough. The boy watched them with disgust, feeling infinitely superior to them. And he found time to note and admire the subtle alterations of stance and attitude as Stavver in the robes of the Vijayne brushed past one species, circled carefully about another, stopped to let a third stalk past him. It's like a fancy dance, the boy thought.

As they got nearer the stiles, the crowd shifted and separated into four groups that gradually got organized into lines that the bots shepherded onto the stile-rollways. Stavver stepped onto a rollway and without warning reached down and pulled the boy up beside him, the first notice he'd taken of his companion since they'd stepped from the transfer bubbles into the lock tunnels.

The boy found time now to look around more carefully

not having to keep half an eye on Stavver and another half eye on how he moved his feet.

There was a wizened old sprite in its final female phase behind him, a querulous ancient who had apparently bathed in a powerful, sickly perfume and topped that bath with a liberal dusting of powder whose scent was distinctly incompatible with that of the perfume. The boy edged away from her; a gust of air blew a concentrated cloud of stink over him. He sneezed, sputtered, looked over his shoulder. The old sprite clutched a round silver ball, perforated profusely and putting forth a third strong scent. Lifting the pomander to her beaky nose, she glared at the boy until he twitched and swung back, spent the next few minutes resetting and smoothing down his veil.

By the time they neared the stiles, he was fidgeting again, sneaking looks at the other rollways, putting out tentative feelers for snoops. A cold wave passed over him. He snapped up his shields, edged around until he could see back of him, saw a red head some distance behind him on the next over rollway. His mother. He knew it, though he didn't remember her. The shock of seeing her so suddenly, so close, jolted him. He pressed closer to Stavver, clutched at his arm, fought to clamp his shields even tighter. He sneaked a look at her, glad for the first time for the presence of the muffling veil. She was looking about now, her eyes passing over him without changing; she'd sensed him but he'd snapped shut too quick for her to place him. He relaxed, stared curiously at her as she turned to speak to her companion. She looked younger than he'd expected. And he was oddly pleased with the charm of her mobile expressive face—he hated her for what she'd done to Stavver, done to his father, done to him, but just for a moment he was almost proud she was his mother.

Over the noise of the throng the boy heard a musical note sounded once then several times more. The rollways stopped. He held his breath though he had no sense of danger. On the second rollway over a small red circle of light bloomed on the smooth tan cheek of a baby-faced male who at first glance seemed hardly old enough to be out alone. Two burly guards came quickly along the narrow walkway between the two rollways, stepped up, touched the man on the shoulder. Spoke softly to him. Took him off the rollway and walked quickly with him back toward the dome, his slight figure sandwiched between them. The rollways started up again.

Computer spotted him, the boy thought. He looked up, starting to feel a bit nervous, wondering if the inner robe was as good as Stavver thought. It was supposed not only to fool the eye but the probes of the stiles. He forced himself to remember the other times they passed without incident, though they were not pretending to be female at those times. Preparation, he thought. We did a lot of work to get here. Stavver knows, we'll pass easy, he knows.

On Messab where GATE was designed they'd got at the man who held the computer keys to that section of memory that held the plans of GATE, they'd got into the computer and plundered it of those plans. Before the first snatch they sneaked onto Cazarit in Stavver's shield ship, the one he'd killed Maissa to get. The boy didn't remember the woman who'd stolen him so long ago, all he knew about her Stavver told him to explain a nightmare once. They'd crept about the world taking photos until they knew the sea and the land as well as they could without actually traveling it. Then they came in through GATE as innocent holiday makers, pulled the snatches off with an ease that made the boy smile and hop from foot to foot in a tiny dance of triumph every time he thought of them. And each time they left again through GATE, calling the ship after them to the pre-set rendezvous—that was another thing Stavver explained—Maissa's connection with a Vryhh engineer who'd made *Butterball* into something almost alive. There was nothing to connect them ever with the snatch victims, nothing the boy could think of that might endanger them, still he was nervous as they rolled past the scanners and the stile probes.

The rollway they stood on ended in a long narrow platform that led into a second domed hall thronged with tired, restless people moving into the lines that led to the shuttles that would take them to their various destinations. High overhead, signs in interlingue and a dozen different scripts blazoned the way to the various terminals. CARNIVAL. CHIMAEREE. HAZARDEE. LETHE. TRAUMEREE. The Battue board was dark, no one around it. The boy smiled, feeling a thrill as he saw this first sign of their prey. He laughed silently behind his veil. Only one group would be going to

Battue for the next several months, the Aghir tejed. And us, he thought. The milling crowd surged and split unevenly, was pushed from behind by newcomers, began oozing out the various exits, most of the beings heading for those under the Carnival sign.

As the pseudo-Vijayne began edging toward the Hazardee exit, the crowd began to thin before "her." Intent on their own goals, none of the visitors paid any attention to them beyond a few impatient mutters as they crossed in front of some hurrying being.

At the entrance to the shuttle lock, a smiling young woman waited for them. She murmured apologies for the discomfort they'd suffered, assured them there would be no more of this, the only problem was that GATE's facilities were a trifle strained at the moment. Directly ahead of the pseudo-Vijayne and her companion was a pungent Cavaltis triad, their red fur ruffled, their scent glands aggressively active, ears alternately laid back against round little heads sitting almost neckless on narrow shoulder, or pricking forward, tufted points quivering. Their short black boots—polite in company to confine the tearing claws, necessary here where all three looked ready to tear themselves bloodily from all this irritation—were stamping in arrhythmic annoyance on the yielding floor surface while they hissed complaints—but let the hostess soothe them with spitting compliments in their own language.

The boy felt a series of touches across his back and buttocks, twisted his head around to glare at the Lazone behind her. He (or she, Lazonen didn't go in for sexual dimorphism) blinked slowly at the boy from round golden eyes—rather his (or her) nictitating membranes flowed over them and retreated repeatedly, keeping them moist in spite of the dryness of the air in here. He (or she) stared with bland innocence at the boy until, fuming, he turned his back on the creature and moved up until he was closer to the thief.

Stavver looked down. Eyes now a washy brown twinkled at the boy. "She wasn't groping you, loveling." His voice was lighter, higher, quavering. "Just practicing her trade to pass the time."

"Trade?"

"Dip."

"Oh." The boy thought a minute. "She?"

"Odor," the thief murmured. "Going into heat, she is."
"Oh."

They were herded into the shuttle two by two and settled
in the comfortable seats. The triad objected loudly to being
separated and no one wanted to sit beside an irritated and
odorous Cavaltish, so one set of chairs was turned about to
face the ones behind and the purring triad settled in to enjoy
the ride.

The air was filled with a spicy melange of body odors and
perfumes, with an oddly rhythmic mixture of languages as
the travelers chatted cooly or fervently in their home languages or practiced their interlingue. A double dozen besides
the Vijayne Gracia and her companion. The boy glanced
swiftly secretly about, his eyes slitted over the top of the veil,
his head swinging in small dips, the despised golden curls
tumbling prodigally from under his headcloth. He was not
very interested in any of the other passengers except perhaps
for the Lazonen pair, but the Lazonen were near the back,
too far away to watch or listen to without being too obvious
about it. He slanted a glance up at the thief, smiled as he saw
how the veils and robes altered the apparent shape of the
body beneath. He sighed. They'd passed the next-to-worst
part, the entry through GATE—still, there was that persistent
cold knot below his ribs.

He thought about seeing his mother, but this made his in-
sides churn. He didn't want to think about her but he
couldn't stop thinking about her and that made him remember things he thought he'd put behind him except for nightmares. His gloved hands clenched and the knot moved up
into his throat. Damn her for leaving me, damn her for
somehow sending that man. . . .

He was lying on a flat rock staring down at the rushing
water of the Kard when he heard his name called. He
jumped to his feet, stared at the man standing on the white
sand of the road.

A tall man, with hair redder than the boy's, a pale man
with skin like alabaster, a smiling man who looked at him
from eyes brighter green than the horan leaves dipping low
over his head. He held a shining crystal egg in the palm of
one hand. "A present from your mother," he said.

He laughed, tossed the glowing crystal egg into the air, caught it, said something else the boy didn't understand, tossed the thing into the river beside the rock.

The boy followed the glittering arc with his eyes, started at the splash. Questions quivering on his lips, he turned back to the road, but the man was gone.

The boy plunged into the water and searched among the water weeds and gravel until he found the crystal. He took it to the bench where his father liked to spend his mornings and evenings and sat with it, turning it over and over until it warmed with the heat in his hands and a few sparks of shimmering color licked through it. It spun glowing veils of color about him, showing him moving dreams in its heart. It began whispering to him, telling him to come into it, come, come, come, telling him it was the gateway to a thousand worlds and all of them were his. Then the bell rang for the evening Madar chant. The whispering grew more intense, he was falling into it—but he shook himself free, hid the crystal in the roots of the tree and went inside.

The next day he quarreled bitterly with his brother and when he went to their room he set the crystal beside his brother's bed, went to bed himself, pleased with himself, thinking his brother would oversleep and be punished for it. But in the morning the crystal had sucked the soul out of his brother leaving him hardly alive, a hollow thing. Unable to face what he'd done, the boy fled the vadi Kard, wandered about, starving, begging, thieving until he ran into another stranger, a tall thin man with wild white hair, an angry driven man drawn back to Jaydugar by memories he couldn't escape, seeking out the woman he'd run from. He found the boy instead and took him away when he left, taught him the finer points of thieving, used him in his own jobs when he discovered the boy's special talents.

And the man who tossed the crystal into the river was somehow related to his mother, or so the thief had told him.

And his mother was responsible for his father's blinding.

And his mother was a witch who should have been drowned at birth, or so the thief told him, a user of men, throwing them away when she was done with them.

And his mother had run off and left him.

They landed, accepted the chains with the marker medallions, and pleasant courteous young men and women came to lead the guests to their quarters and show them the many pleasures waiting for them.

TAMRIS

Tamris wrote in her journal:

The day started smooth as cream. The shuttle took us up to the GATE. Out of the kindness of their hearts, they let us wander through the place as we wanted, not encumbering us with guides. We saw the scanners spot one professional, a thief with a tendency to turn violent—or so we were informed when we inquired. There was one odd moment. Aleytys jumped and squeaked like something bit her, then turned to look around as if she'd spotted something, but when I asked, she shrugged it off. Damn this link, I wish I could talk to her. Anyway, it was obvious that Security would catch known thieves easily enough, lesser ones who'd been careless enough to get body-prints and faces in the files of Company worlds elsewhere. Troublemakers and criminals on Company worlds have their records transferred to the files of Cazarit, nice little bit of this for that, sensible too. Our ghost obviously isn't one of these.

It took a bit of doing to pry even that small bit of information out of Security. Funny, though, even then I got the feeling that she had a notion who's doing this, though I didn't say that to her, not with the link recording everything we say. Nice to know I'm not wholly stupid; tonight when we got back to our quarters she admitted she had a suspicion that was wholly without evidence to support it. More about that later.

The people taking the shuttles down to Carnival haven't been checked out before they arrive. Security depends almost entirely on the computers and the scanners to weed out the bad ones. All one has to do to get to Carnival is buy a ticket to Cazarit, some with hotel accommodations included in the price. You can do that on a hundred worlds through a hun-

*dred different passenger lines. Cazarit. The longer I'm here the
more I see why Mom didn't want Aleytys anywhere near it. I
watched her today; if she were a cat her back would be
arched, her fur on end, her tail high. She fought it some, but
most of the time she was pulled in on herself, listening, I
think, to what f'Voine was saying. putting in a question or
two in a cool remote sort of voice. Oh yes, we were honored,
the Security chief of the world, the top man, he took us
round.*

They didn't give us maps.

They didn't let us land—except on Chimaeree and Battue.

THE OVERFLIGHTS
CHIMAEREE.

*Shaped rather like a bodylouse. A few deep inlets, a long
sweeping curve around the hind end. Mostly rolling grassy
plain. Some low mountains marching across the eastern end,
rather like a collar on the louse's neck. Shuttle field is about
where the eye would be. The guests are ferried to the "estates" in arflots. Watchtowers around the coast in visual
touch with each other. The estates were rich green velvet
patches against the paler green, brown and yellow of the
grasslands, small round patches of new cloth on an old
jacket. On the north and west the water was very deep close
in to the coast. Along the southeast edge the shallows extend
out over a kilometer. There was a line of small islands in the
distance, rugged, like the tops of mountains poking out of the
sea. In the clear shallow water large black shadows swam lazily along, working their way slowly along the bottom past
the south side of the island.*

Aleytys touched the screen, her fingernail clicking over the
shadows. "What are those?"

"Merkrav." F'Voine didn't bother looking where she was
pointing. His voice had a weary superiority that Tamris
found more than irritating. "The watchtowers check out every school or individual passing the islands."

"But they do swim close to shore?"

"One man might get to shore that way, but he couldn't
carry weapons or tools with him. A naked man isn't going to
get through the estate defenses."

"One did. So one could." She looked at him, coolly amused. "I could."

F'Voine said nothing.

HAZARDEE

Rugged island shaped vaguely like a flying lizard with its two mountain ranges the spines of the wings. There is an elaborate racetrack winding through them. As we flew over this, a half dozen small bright wheeled vehicles were racing along the track at a speed that looked lethal even from our height. They were fighting for the front with a ferocity that reminded me of half-starved snagtooths fighting for places at a kill. Their vehicles seemed to be equipped with assorted attack weapons, blades projecting from the axles, spouts in the rear that shot clouds of smoke or gushes of some turgid slippery liquid. Our guide would not let the pilot dip lower, and after a moment Aleytys acquiesced, not wanting to be a distraction to men or women who were battling for their lives. At least, that's what I think. One car was knocked off the track as we watched and went tumbling over and over in a hell of flame. The others kept up their high-speed battle. We didn't see the outcome, f'Voine told the pilot to take us over the Casino.

"Why do the drivers struggle so viciously? That's no sport." Tamris winced as she heard the frazzled note in the contralto voice. She put her hand lightly on Aleytys's arm. Aleytys glanced at her, nodded, a quick sharp jerk of her head.

"It's not meant to be. The winner has ten days off the track and anything that Cazarit can offer him or her."

"Then he races again?"

"Then he races again."

"The towers along the track—eyes?"

"Yes. Clients are watching the race. A webbing of wagers is involved."

"Whether or not someone dies, how soon, how it happens?"

"Whatever pleases them."

"What happens if a driver loses his nerve?"

"He's encouraged to recover it." A shrug. Empty blue eyes stared past them out the transparent bubble over their heads.

"If he doesn't, he's transferred to another division until his contract runs out."

"And?"

"He either finds other work or is transported offworld."

"Lovely. Use him up and throw him away."

As Aleytys shifted restlessly in her seat, Tamris once again touched her arm. Conscience on her shoulder, she thought. The muscle under her fingers was knotted hard. Anger flowed like electricity under the pale golden skin. Alarmed, Tamris chewed on her lip wondering if she should say something or if that would be all Aleytys needed to set her off. "They choose to do it," she said mildly and waited.

Some of the tightness went out of the arm beneath her hand. Aleytys sighed. "So they do."

The silence that followed was uncomfortable and didn't get easier as the arflot approached the coast. On the screen they could see a complex of domes, arcades, towers, cubes, a lacy intricate structure beside a wide white-sand beach.

"Casino," f'Voine said. "No eyes and ears in the suites, clients won't have it. However, the casino itself and all public places are fitted with viewers. Computer scan plus a bank of watchers behind one-way glass. Psi-alarms set in the walls. You'd be surprised what the clients get up to trying to manipulate the games." He glanced at her but her stony face gave him nothing. "Guards patrol the perimeter with pairs of hunting cats, they clock in at measured intervals; there's not much wild life and the fence is electrified to keep them off—sensor webbing's strung round the perimeter to back up the patrols."

Aleytys smiled tightly. "Sung Yul Twi," she whispered.

F'Voine ignored that. "Battue," he told the pilot.

BATTUE

A plump island with a ridge of mountains cutting it almost in half. On the east side, plains and desert, the marginland between them a shifting vagueness. Here are the greatest herds of grazers, the packs of hunting tagreda, the night prowling tartals, their front paws like clawed hands, their muzzles blunt. There's a move to outlaw hunting them since folk on University suspect that they're something more than animals. Well, that wouldn't make any difference here. I sort of got the feeling there isn't much illegal here, not if someone can pay for it. In fact, such a ruling by University would

*make the tartals even more valuable for Cazarit, forbidden
fruit being sweeter. It's not quite the same thing as hunting
down people, but verges on that. And they are quite deadly
game; there's supposed to be an appreciable chance that the
hunter will turn out to be the victim according to the brochures. The clients of Battue must sign waivers before their
reservations are confirmed and provide proof of their skill
with weapons. I suspect all this is just hype, part of the service to the clients, letting them boast of their toughness on the
hunt. Other rare beasts, in pairs or alone, here and there in
the grass. F'Voine pointed them out as we went over.*

*On the west side of the mountains there's a patch of
swamp in the north near the equator. This fades into rolling
tree-clad hills that descend in great waves to the sea. The
mountains have snow on their peaks but most of it is gone
from the slopes. Much of Battue is south of the equator and
enjoying the first warmth of spring.*

*We landed beside one of the lodges. Each of these has had
to be specially built to the specifications of the Aghir tejed.
They are massive structures with a front like half a hexagon
and the back with twin towers whose walls must have been
six feet thick. On the top of each tower, there were guns capable of shooting down anything less than an armored
destroyer. More guns along the tops of the high wall that
ringed the place. F'Voine led us around the outside first,
showing us the wall with its metal mesh capable of carrying a
current strong enough to fry a man stupid enough to touch it.
Inside the wall were generators for a force dome. The Aghir
wouldn't feel at home without a bubble over them, f'Voine
said. Inside the circle of the bubble, there were elaborate
formal gardens, the flowers in bud, timed to bloom at the arrival of the Aghir. He took us inside. The water supply was
completely self-contained, wells within the hold and a shielded cistern in case the particular tej housed here wanted to
bring his own water supply, a water evaporator in case he
wanted to purify water from the wells. Womantower, Mantower. Dining hall, servants' quarter, guards' barracks,
kitchen, closets for serviteurs. No eyes inside, no screens
except in the top room of the Mantower—had to be guaranteed—f'Voine looked peeved—stupid, he said—wouldn't consider being tagged—won't allow a single Cazarit on the soil
of Battue once the Aghir have landed at the shuttle field—*

won't allow any checks on personnel or let them be tagged—Aghir paranoia was making the job unnecessarily difficult —Aleytys was more tactful this time, didn't remind him again that all the security he wanted was in place when the Ghost walked through it without wiggling a needle, slick and neat as if he reached through some warp in space and sucked up the victims one by one, schlluppp—

LETHE

North of Battue, on its way into Fall. Mostly desert. Mountains in the north, rugged and barren, white as old bones. Below the mountains, the desert stretches south to a narrow fringe of salt marsh. Sand dunes dotted with scattered and very lush oases. We were not permitted to land, even at the shuttle field and administrative offices. F'Voine argued with Moarte-Mati for several minutes but she wouldn't budge. She said there were no empty slots and the clients of Lethe were adamant about maintaining their privacy, that even she was not allowed inside one of the slots when a client was there. F'Voine told us it didn't really matter, other than the added deterrent of the arid land surrounding the oases, the security arrangements were much the same as those on Chimaeree. It's getting late, he said, there'll be just time for a preliminary walkthrough of the estate where Oldread Cans was snatched. It happened that it was empty at the moment.

CHIMAEREE (again)

We landed near an estate built close to the sea—as f'Voine said, it had gotten to be very late afternoon. I was tired and hungry, getting to be irritable, my knees aching from all that sitting, my back worse. We landed on an open bit of lawn next to the house—the house was a surprise, it looked half dismantled, floors and roofs solid enough, walls like metal lace, wiring and lenses, solid state lattices, the whole thing preserved in a force field like some bit of leftover wrapped in clear plastic wrap. I was glad enough to be out of the arflot for a while but didn't expect to learn much, going by the rest of the day. Mala Kosa came round the side of the house and stood waiting as we climbed out—wasn't wearing her purple flash outfit today, was wearing a blue onepiece that looked like a coat of paint, her eyes tinted blue to match. I could really develop a dislike for that woman. She was smiling pleasantly enough, but it hurt. Hah!

"I need to walk through the house. As it is now and as it was when Cans was here."

She's about had it with them, Tamris thought, all this so-called cooperation which is grudged every second of it. She watched Aleytys stop in front of the gap-mouth hole which served as a door, finger the force shield and swing around.

"You want to turn this off or shall I?" There was a snap in her voice, an acid reminder in the words of the thorough cleansing she'd given their living quarters. Tamris didn't try to hide her grin. Rub their faces in it, she thought.

"That would involve subverting the entire energy system of the house." Mala Kosa watched her, curiosity in the newly blue eyes, maybe a touch of apprehension.

"If I need to make the point?" Aleytys brushed tendrils of hair off her forehead with a quick impatient gesture. "I would prefer not to brangle any more and get this business over with. Push me and I'll do it the hard way. Might I remind you that time is getting a bit short?"

Mala Kosa smiled graciously. "All this heat about nothing." She glanced at Tamris, frowned at the witness link, peeled back the padded satin cuff of her glove, tapped a quick sequence on the wristcon.

The doorway cleared. Aleytys stood to one side and waited. With another glance at Tamris and the link, Mala Kosa walked briskly past her. Blank-faced but watching both of them, Aleytys and Mala Kosa, f'Voine followed Mala Kosa into the house. Poor femme, Tamris thought, damned if she do, damned if she don't. Still grinning, she joined Aleytys and together they walked inside.

ALEYTYS

As Aleytys followed f'Voine and Mala Kosa deeper into the house, twisting up and around the half-formed walls, Shadith's purple eyes opened, her pointed elfin face materialized about them. The Singer was frowning, her eyes flicking from side to side as she examined in a way that wasn't seeing those walls that they were passing. Aleytys could feel the tickle of her activity, something like the ghost feet of many moths. "Something funny, Lee," she murmured after several minutes of this.

Aleytys slowed and turned inward. "Yes?"

"Got a lot of holo projectors everywhere."

Aleytys frowned, subvocalized, "Two-thirds of the completed structure would be holo. Plan your own decorative touches, that's in the brochures, they'll be programmed by the computer. You read that with me."

"As advertised, uh-huh, that's all right, but the Cazarits are pulling a sneak on the clients. At least, I think so. Needs a bit more checking before I'm sure. Be a help to get the house turned on so I could check them when they're working, wouldn't take long for that. The point—it seems to me some of the instrumentation in the walls isn't there for making pretty pictures but for taking them. Privacy in a gnat's fat eye. The Cazarits want their security and they mean to have it. Bet you there're tapes of all three snatches. If so, the ghost's damn good."

"Spy eyes." Aleytys pinched her lips together, beginning to feel a rising excitement. All day she'd been left with guesses, dreams, a lot of sterile fact and observations that were more irritating than helpful, but this was something that promised to provide material that she could chew on and digest. "Maybe I'm a detective after all," she subvocalized, almost singing the soundless words.

Shadith chuckled, went back to her probing of the walls.

In the same silence the four of them moved through the skeletal structure, seeing the nothing much there was to see. Tamris looked tired and irritated, Aleytys knew she saw no purpose in all this traipsing about and wanted to get back to a bath and a hot meal, but she wasn't about to explain what she was doing, not with the two Cazarits keeping carefully in hearing. All through the "house," up the graceful curving stair, through the many levelled, many shaped rooms, looking blankly at the webbing of wire and crystal, of chip and bubble, a flittery glittery parody of walls. Lice in the walls, little spy eyes everywhere, not functioning now, still itching under her skin.

"That's the house," Mala Kosa said.

"Not quite." Aleytys flicked a hand at the walls. "Where's the computer that turns this on?"

Mala Kosa stroked a long thin finger wrapped in blue silk along her jaw. "Computer's below, you need to see that?"

"Since the ghost obviously got to it, don't you think I'd better?"

Mala Kosa shrugged a blue shoulder. "Come then."

The computer was behind a metal door with a code lock that Mala Kosa tapped open with a few quick touches of ungloved fingertips that her body hid from them. The door slid open. Pulling the glove back on, she stepped into a short brightly lit hall. Over her shoulder she said, "Anyone coming in without the code would trip a gastrap here." She waved a hand at the door, the far end of the hall. "Plates slam down there as the gas is released." She stamped a dainty heel on the floor. "The floor tilts as soon as the plates come down, dumps the intruder into a holding pen." She walked on.

The computer room was cool, white and still. "The set-key is voice-cued. My voice." She stripped off her glove again and danced her fingers across the sensor plate, talking as she worked. "No one came down here. We've been over this until we broke it down to bubble fractions. No one got in here, no time, no way. Yet computer went down, locked the house in the shield, that's automatic, stayed down for about twenty minutes, came on again with everything perfectly the same except that all breathing personnel are gassed, out. And Oldread Cans is gone. There. Except for the personnel we provided, the house is what it was then. Satisfied?"

"For now. We have time to walk the perimeter?"

"If you want." She looked down, grimaced at her elegant spike-heeled boots.

"No need for you to come." Aleytys nodded at the screens just visible in an alcove off the main room, alive now, showing sections of the surrounding estate. "You can watch from here." She swung around, took a step toward the hallway. "Any problems about going out?"

"Go." She waved a gloved hand at the doorway. "The gate will be open by the time you reach it. You'll find a double barrier, the outer part a woven wire fence with a pulsing charge in it, enough to fry a man." She smiled and smoothed one glove over the other. "Not on right now. I saw to that."

The house was on. The walls were translucent alabaster draped with silk, a delicate floral scent played through the halls, from somewhere in the distance came bursts of joyous laughter, an infant fawn toddled on his soft new hooves about a fountain playing musically in the center of the largest room. Beyond the windows in the suddenly solid walls, several tall, scantily clad blond girls were playing a complicated and noisy game with a bright blue bubble that kept popping as they touched it and reappearing in another place. Somewhere unseen, flute song was joined after a few bars by a lute and finally a liquidly rippling woman's voice. The gaping hole was now a great bronze door that swung open as they neared it. It swung out to a fanfare of trumpets.

Tamris laughed. "Do you believe that?"

"Some of us got it." Aleytys stretched, rubbed at the back of her neck. "All that sitting. I'm beat."

"Nothing like a nice long stroll to rest the weary body."

"You want to wait here?"

"No. Wouldn't miss this for worlds. Of course, I could work up a bit more enthusiasm if I knew what the hell I was looking for."

"Just look." Aleytys grinned at the face she made; together they strolled down the white sand path that curved around behind a house now sporting vines heavy with bunches of grapes, or trumpet-shaped purple flowers that dropped down a delicate sweet scent, singing birds nested in the vines, giant butterflies, flecks of brilliant color, floating about overhead, weaving through complex patterns in an aerial ballet. "Rather

nice, this." Aleytys sniffed at the perfumes on the gentle
breeze. "A dream but not such a bad one."

Tamris moved a shoulder. "Makes me itch."

Aleytys chuckled. "Gate ahead, should be better outside
the walls." She looked up. "Gilt onion domes. Not cheap in
his dreams, Oldread Cans."

Aleytys knelt beside the woven wire fence, looking at the
two-meter stretch of bare beaten earth between it and the
even higher wall of fieldstone crowned with elaborate and ra-
zor-edged steel spikes. At some time in the recent past it had
rained in this area, leaving behind a mud puddle, softening
the hard earth into a sloppy goo. It had hardened rapidly as
the puddle dried but while it was still plastic, several beasts
had splashed through the shrinking puddle and left behind
some deep clear paw prints.

"Found something?" Tamris had been looking idly about,
but now she came and leaned against the wire, touching it
rather warily since she had little trust in f'Voine, less in Mala
Kosa. She raised her brows at the prints. "Big suckers."

Aleytys asked, "Recognize them?"

Tamris frowned. "Should I? Is it important?"

"Not really. More of the same. Thought you might have
picked up something about them at University."

"Jumping again. Hop, hop." She drew her brows together
and examined the prints more closely. "Four lobes, non-re-
tractable claws, pads a long oval, running stride, mmmm,
looks like almost two meters and what else would these lovely
people have prowling the perimeter? Hidunga hounds." She
shivered. "I'd rather face a silvercoat pack any day. I'm
working up a real respect for our ghost. Hidungas. Brrr."

"Huh. Mala Kosa didn't mention them."

"Didn't, did she."

Aleytys straightened, strolled on, glancing about with interest, looking for what she expected to find, a clump of larg-
ish trees outside the walls, a similar clump inside. She could
hear the muted roaring of the sea, the cliff edge was curving
in toward the fence. "Coming up on something, I think," she
said. Tamris glanced at her, wrinkled her nose and looked
away, muttered, "Hop, hop." Aleytys laughed, ran her hands
through her hair. "We're close to the water here." She
scraped her hair off her face, knotted it on top her head and

held the knot there with one hand to let the freshening breeze cool the nape of her neck. "He came by sea. I can think of a dozen ways to beat those detectors without even trying hard." She left the fence and strolled to the cliffedge. Hands on her hips she looked down at the seething swirling water rising about the formidable rocks. "Cliff's not that steep. Weathered. Easy climbing."

Tamris leaned over and looked down, her hands clasped behind her. "Fifteen minutes at most, even loaded."

"Oldread Cans is a wisp. About this big." Aleytys patted the air a handspan below her breasts. "Hang him over the shoulder and go bounding from rock to rock, tuck him in your pseudo-merkrav and there you are."

"How come you're so sure?"

"Simple and quick; our ghost won't unnecessarily complicate his life." She looked along the cliff. A watchtower was distantly visible on each side of her. "Even with those on the watch. Pick the right section of cliff where a fold of the earth hides you, wear neutral colors nicely mottled, or drag around a crawl sheet." She stopped talking, narrowed her eyes at a clump of brush and a few sturdy trees halfway between her and the northern tower, close to a section of cliff that dipped precipitously inward, precipitously out again. She laughed, flicked a finger at the trees. "Almost like they planned to make it easy for the ghost." She started walking fast, almost running, for the trees.

Tamris ran after her. When she caught up, she said, "Those trees are over three meters from the fence. You think he climbed a tree and flew over?"

Aleytys laughed. "Not flew, walked." She slowed as she drew near the outer circle of brush. "Leave me my mystery, humble apprentice, respect for your elders, please, didn't your ma teach you?"

"Ma taught me to ask questions when I don't know something." She slanted a glance at Aleytys. "You're all of a sudden riding high."

"Riding an idea, hoping it won't throw me before I get a chance to tame it." Aleytys pushed through the prickly brush into the more open spaces under the trees. The rising wind sent the stiff-edged leaves scraping against each other and the long whippy branches they grew on, made the main limbs groan just a little as they shifted under its pressure. The twilight under the trees was filled with this rustling, whispery creaking, with shifting shadows flicking about, a pungent spicy odor; ghosts of the same odor rose from under their feet as they kicked through desiccated leaves and bits of bark. Aleytys moved from tree to tree, examining the trunks with care, running her hands along them, sniffing at them. Tamris watched a moment, shook her head and joined the hunt.

"This what you're looking for?" Tamris rubbed her thumb across a smallish abrasion in the papery grey-green skin on the trunk of the largest tree, slid her hand up the trunk, locating several other scrapes. "Heavy-footed for a ghost."

Aleytys grinned. "Useful apprentice." She patted Tamris's shoulder, then walked about the tree, stepping carefully over the coiled and knotted roots lying like tangled string above the ground. "He always did like the biggest and best of everything." She jumped, caught a large limb and swung herself into the crotch where the trunk split in half and continued upward a short distance in the two parts. The inland half split again at a point just above her head when she stood upright in the crotch. She pulled herself into the second crotch and straddled it, looking at the bruised ring she'd expected to find. The skin was stripped away from the yellow-white wood and the wood itself though hard and tight-grained was crushed inward with a fringe of broken fibers. She rubbed a finger along the scoring. "You shouldn't boast about your skills when you're drunk, my friend," she whispered, but said no more because she was sure f'Voine and Mala Kosa were hunched over the screens in the basement watching avidly. No need to gift them with her guesses. She sighted past the limb, saw where several of the branches had been cut away to leave a long narrow opening in the foliage. Through it as she looked across the wall, she could see another clump of trees, something else she'd expected, one of the trees appreciably taller than the others and partially denuded of foliage as if it had some kind of vegetative mange. Her cheek pressed against the pungent tree-skin, she stared at that tree, at a long bare section of thick limb with a small dark blotch marring the pale grey-green of its skin. Eyebolt with a ceramic point, she thought. Line should stream a manheight above the stone wall. I can see you, my ghost, or rather I can't, running along that line, a puff of air in your fancy suit, half a minute, that's all and there you are. How do you get my son in, thief? No web for him. I wonder where you got yours, you never told me that. What is he? Your watchdog? Or does he handle computers for you?

Below her, Tamris kicked at old leaves, cleared her throat loudly. "Found his nest?" she called.

"Found something." Aleytys swung down, landed lightly beside Tamris. "Let's head back, no use going farther, this is where he got in."

"Hunh, I suppose I keep guessing."

Aleytys chuckled. "Mindsets, they wreck us all. All this, it's set to catch an intruder who attacks it on its own terms. You have to remember, humble apprentice, I grew up in a place where most things were powered by human or animal muscle except for some mills that used water power, a low-tech culture with a different sort of mindset." Aleytys stretched, kicked at a clump of grass, grinned at the flash in the blue eyes watching her. "This has a point. I'll get there sometime." She looked toward the house. It was dark again, dismantled. "They've turned the house off. Ever seen a wirewalker?"

"What's that?"

"Where I grew up . . . hah! I see from your face there she goes again. Patience, apprentice, cultivate humility, even these maunderings do have a point. Wirewalker's a sort of acrobat. Stretches wire or rope between two points and does tricks on it, you didn't see one even on University? I'm surprised. Now I know you must've come across a crossbow."

"Metal."

"Doesn't have to be, there's a kind of horn that's almost as strong and resilient as steel, organic material, wouldn't register. He gets here, leave how for the moment, climbs that tree, shoots a bolt with line attached across to the tree inside the wall, ties it taut, gets himself on it, runs across and lo, there he is, neatly and undetectably inside, not at all bothered by current, spikes or even hungry Hidungas." She laughed. "Simple, uncomplicated, effective."

"What about the roving eyes, why didn't they see him?"

"Because they couldn't. Any practicing ghosts need to disappear now and then. Seriously, ever heard of a chameleon web?"

"They're myth."

"Not quite. I've seen one."

"They really as good as the stories say?"

"Close enough. The web's a sort of parasite, powered by the wearer's body, can't wear the thing too long, but there are no heat radiations to register on a seeker. You look hard where you know he is and there's nothing, it's eerie, I tell you; there's a slight blur when he's moving but you have to know where to look to see it."

They walked in silence for several minutes, Tamris mulling over what she'd heard. As they came around the last bend and headed for the gate, she said, "It all seems so—well—obvious when you explain it. How come Security didn't find those traces and figure out what happened?"

"Who says they didn't? F'Voine hasn't been very forthcoming about what he does or doesn't know. Vague generalities that's all and bragging about the security systems."

"There's that." Tamris tugged at her tunic. "Mmm. You went for those trees like you expected what you found."

"Later."

They went through the gate and followed the path around the house. It was back in its skeletal state and the garden was diminished to late autumnal barrenness, melancholy in the developing darkness.

F'Voine was waiting alone by the arflot, stroking gently the back of one gloved hand with the fingers of the other. Behind his apparent calm, however, his mind and body were in turmoil. Aleytys felt it suddenly, stumbled, caught herself and moved past him without a word, settled herself in the airflot, bemused by the possibilities the turmoil suggested—that f'Voine and Mala Kosa both had missed the marks on the trees—or their search squad had, which was the same thing—had circled the fence looking for signs the wire had been tampered with, had searched the tree clumps cursorily if at all. Mindset, she thought. She leaned back and closed her eyes. I wonder if he got *Butterball* away from Maissa. Must have, that has to be how he sneaks the victims offworld. How old is the boy now—nine, ten? Hard to keep track of time, so many different worlds, so many different time systems. Nine or ten. If it's him, nothing yet but guesses. Maybe tomorrow we can get us some proof.

Aleytys sipped at the wine. "Ahh," she said. The chair adjusting smoothly to the new angle of her body, she leaned

back, lifted her feet onto a floating footrest. After a moment
she opened one eye and smiled at Tamris. "Ran right at that
bunch of trees. So I did. I was looking for them. Thing is,
looks like an old . . . um . . . acquaintance has dropped
back into my life. No direct evidence yet, but it gets so easy
when I plug him and what I know about him into the situation. Without him, I don't see how the snatches could be
worked. And look what happened. I think what he would do
and go there, and lo, I find his traces. To me, that's a good
indication that my hunch has hair on it." She sipped at the
wine, sighed. Tamris made an impatient gesture, leaned forward, started to speak, pressed her full lips into a tight line.
Aleytys smiled. "Here's something to stir your blood. For all
their boasts of perfect privacy, that house was swarming with
eyes. All nicely camouflaged from detection by the projectors
and receptors of the holo equipment."

Tamris jerked upright, grinned, grabbed one of the pillows
and spun it across the room. "Whoops," she said. Then she
sobered. "You sure? Not just along the fence?"

"Remember the eyes here? How do you think I spotted
them? Which reminds me. I think I know how the computer
was taken out. Visualizing telekineticist. Mouthful isn't it.
Describes me, describes the person with the thief, ah, your
eyes light up, I see. I don't want to talk about that person,
not yet. Not till I see the tapes on Oldread Cans, if I can pry
them out of Intaril."

"Ah." Tamris punched up a pillow and shoved it behind
her back. "Then you think there are tapes around somewhere
of all the snatches."

"That I do. They probably wipe the tapes after each visitor
leaves, there's that much truth in them, self-interest really,
don't want that kind of thing lying around as a temptation to
blackmail. But when the visitor is snatched? Not a chance
they wiped those." She chuckled, sipped at the wine again,
held up the glass and looked through the drop of amber wine
in the bottom. "Can't you see the poor souls bent over their
screens, hour after hour, day after day, slaving away, looking
for some clue to what happened? You know, Mari, for all
their boasts, Security here hasn't been really tested for a long
time. They're good enough catching the little fleas and slapping difficult employees back in line, but a real predator?"
She lowered the wine glass until the base was sitting on her

stomach. "F'Voine was eating worms on the way back. I'm sure now his men didn't think of looking at the trees, they weren't looking for something as simple as a wirewalker with a crossbow, not when the ghost managed to take the computer down. Enough. Tomorrow I want you to visit Security offices and pry the entry records out of them, those from the stile scanners at GATE, the five days before each snatch, two days after. I want to see if I can spot a familiar face or two. Me, I'll be facing the Director in her nest. This is one time when I think I'll do better keeping the argument off record. If she doesn't have to face reporting on just what is said, she can be more flexible—if she wants to be."

"Rather watch her than chew on Security." Tamris scowled, looked up. "Eh-Lee, you going to keep me from seeing the tapes because of the link?"

Aleytys thrust out her glass. "Fill this, you. What are apprentices for if not to humbly and assiduously cater to the whims of their teachers?"

Tamris bounced up and took the glass. "If you didn't scare me almost as much as Intaril does, I'd empty this bottle over your head."

"Waste of a truly fine wine."

"Hah." She filled both glasses and brought them back, settled herself on the footrest by Aleytys's feet. "You didn't answer my question." She looked down into the clear topaz liquid, tilted the glass, watched the wine shift about, catching the light in gleams from bright lemon to deep ocher. "You think the ghost's your friend?"

"Not friend." Her voice was too sharp. She grimaced. "He's got good reason to be annoyed at me."

"Some day, if we're both drunk enough I'd really like to hear the story of your life. My question?"

"Do my best if you're sure you want in on that boredom. I need your help." Aleytys sipped at the wine, smiled, feeling a gentle fondness for the girl, feeling also slightly drunk and very tired, so tired she was already half asleep. "He used to boast he was the greatest thief in the universe. You'll have to meet his ship one day. I traveled in it a long time ago, seems like a long time, before he acquired it actually. Whistle and she'll follow like a pet puppy." Lazily she lifted a brow at Tamris's skeptical snort. "I'll expect an abject apology for that once this is over."

"You're getting fuddled."

"More exhaustion than wine." She yawned, watched the rise and fall of the wine glass sitting again on her diaphragm. "If," she said drowsily.

"If?"

"Tomorrow tells the tale." She yawned again. "Maybe."

TAMRIS

The young man was a bland and impersonally beautiful as the two girl pilots, with the same characterless beauty biosculptured out of his flesh. He smiled at her, at least his lips curled upward in a parody of a smile. "Yes?" he said.

He knew who she was, she was sure of that, but he wasn't going to volunteer anything. Young, she thought, but he already knows how to cover ass. "I want copies of stile data from the GATE," she said.

"You have authorization?" He made no attempt to move a hand to start the process of getting the tapes.

"We were promised cooperation."

"I can't do anything for you without authorization."

"Then who do I see to get it?"

"There's no one here who can authorize non-sec personnel to have access to restricted information." Smiling, pleasant, giving away nothing, giving no offense—but she had a strong feeling that he was enjoying himself. Not only did the secs resent the Hunters being called in—a constant reminder of their own failures—but Aleytys had piled nettles on their heads by pointing out their shortcomings as security. Something had leaked down into the organization about Aleytys's discoveries on Chimaeree, not the details perhaps, but f'Voine's rage on returning was there; everyone in this upsidedown building would be feeling the effects of it and like any other highly motivated group would be adopting the attitudes of their leader.

She narrowed her eyes at him, nodded. "I want to talk to f'Voine."

"Do you have an appointment?"

"No, my sweet thing, however if you continue being obstructive you might find your precious little self shoveling shit on a farm instead of where you are now." She stepped back a long pace so he could see the witness link, tapped the top of it very gently in case he didn't take her point. "I want to see f'Voine in the next ten minutes." She smiled. "Hunter Aleytys asked me to get those tapes and I intend to do so."

ALEYTYS

Aleytys settled herself comfortably in the floating armchair, smiled as she sensed the tiny prickle of sensors probing into her. Working with some care so she wouldn't disrupt the field that kept the chair afloat, she popped the tickles as she'd have popped small intrusive bloodsuckers.

Intaril sighed as the concealed readouts on the desk went dead. "You're getting expensive."

"It would be easier on both of us if you just shut them off when I'm around." Aleytys tilted back in the chair, smiled at the ceiling. "That too."

"I'd prefer to have a record of this conversation."

"No, you wouldn't."

Intaril eyed her thoughtfully. "That's interesting." Hand poised over a sensor plate, she said, "Where's your young friend?" She played her fingers over the plate, looked up again, frowning at Aleytys.

"Picking up some tapes for me from Security. Finish what you're doing."

"Or you will." Intaril laughed, giving no outward sign of what the laugh cost her. After working a minute more, she sat back and said lightly, "Satisfied?"

Aleytys closed her eyes. "Satisfied?" she subvocalized. Shadith's face formed around twinkling eyes and a broad grin. "She's not stupid, Lee. You made your point. Better stop enjoying this so much or you might start missing things." Aleytys swallowed a laugh. "Yes, little mama," she subvocalized. She opened her eyes. "Satisfied," she said.

"Why the visit?" Intaril looked calm enough, but there was a rigidity in the line of her long neck, in the way she was sitting. "If you don't mind getting to the point, I've got a lot of work on hold while we talk."

Aleytys tapped gently on the arms of the chair, imitating Head though she wasn't aware of what she was doing. "I want the pretty pictures. The unreleased tapes."

"You didn't need all this fuss, why not just ask f'Voine? He has general charge of the investigation."

"I'm not talking about the exterior scenes or after-the-fact scans. I want the tapes recording the activities of your clients before and during the snatches, the record of every moment of their occupation of that particular facility, whatever it happens to be."

"There are no such tapes. We guarantee privacy." Intaril's voice was icy, she was no longer relaxed, she was leaning forward, poised on the edge of her chair. "If that's all you have to say, I'm very busy."

"You have also guaranteed security." Aleytys didn't move. She sat relaxed, her eyes closed, following the flurry in Intaril as she considered what to do—a quick spurt of excitement and anger, a surge of cooler caution, the brisk snap of a decision. Aleytys opened her eyes. "I accept there are no suite tapes from Hazardee. Since you don't use holos in the suites there's nothing to camouflage such spies from your clients' own electronic sweeps. However, you will have tapes of the activities inside the casino. I'd like to see these from about five days before the snatch till one day after. Chimaeree, the same time span. I saw the eyes in the walls so don't bother protesting that. Lethe—from your own brochures I know there's holo equipment in the walls and that means you've sneaked in some eyes and that means tapes. Eyes. In every room, swarming like fleas over a carcass. End of speech. Your turn."

Intaril tapped her forefinger against her lips, dropped her hand flat on the desk. "Good of you to stage this in private."

"Was, wasn't it." Aleytys laughed. "Make up your own account later. Not to labor the point—even without your authorization, I do intend to go looking and without really meaning to I could probably make hash of your records."

"Threat?"

"Certainly not, merely a warning of intent."

"Accepted." Intaril tapped lightly on the desk. "Continue your courtesy. I don't want the contents of those tapes recorded in the witness link."

"And I need my associate with me, Director. That poses a slight problem, doesn't it."

"Your associate could remove the link and leave it outside the viewing room."

"Could, but that would seriously compromise the integrity of the link, unless. . . ."

"Unless?"

"Unless you authorized under your own seal, registered in the link, your approval of the removal of the link and testify that we both went nowhere other than the viewing room during the interval. One of your employees who is also bonded will take over the bearing of the link and spend whatever time necessary outside the room. And when we come out, you will again swear into the link that you have witnessed the resuming of the link by my associate. All this repeated each time the link is removed since we're probably going to be a number of days at the viewing. With that set in the link there should be no difficulty, eh?"

"You don't ask much." Intaril settled back in her chair, smiling absently, rubbing a long forefinger beside a long nose. "I would prefer the girl be left outside."

"I have already said I need her with me."

"And I heard you. Still, that's not urgent, is it?"

"Yes. Time—remember?"

"The tapes are that important?"

"Could be, could be not. Depends."

"Very forthcoming."

"More than your pretty shadow, wouldn't you say?"

"Here—now—yes." Intaril stretched, smiled. "Feels good for a change." Her smile widened to a grin, her dark eyes twinkled. "Only for a change. F'Voine gave me some interesting information last night. Was your young friend right? Did you expect what you found?"

"Oh, I don't think I'm ready to talk about that yet."

"Mmm. You know, I didn't believe half the things I heard about you."

"Don't." Aleytys grimaced. "Big mouths, bigger boasts. Look what we owned once sort of thing."

"Useful though. For you, anyway."

"Not really." She smiled gently at Intaril. "We look at things from the opposite sides of an insurmountable fence. I

don't like being constrained by you or by anyone even those I
consider my own. I don't like this job or this world. If I
could, I'd blow you all to hell this next minute. When I was a
little younger, I might have tried it, but not now. Too many
debts I owe to people I respect and have a fondness for. I
will do the job I've been hired to do, all of it, I'll catch the
ghost for you if that's at all possible, do my best to keep him
from zipping off with your Aghir clients, I'll explain how he
does his dance with you so you can counter it. You needn't
worry about the secret tapes, I keep my word and I keep my
mouth shut about the business of Hunters clients. I recognize
the pressures you are working under, I have my own pushing
me. You're intelligent enough to recognize my need to get the
hell away from this world before my gorge rises to the point
I do damage both to my people and to you." Aleytys
shivered. "All right, end of speech. You wanted this over
with. Do I get the tapes?"

"Yes."

"Good. In one hour then. I'll be in my quarters, send
someone to fetch my associate and me." She rose, laughed. "I
know, I wrecked hell out of the phones."

"I could fix them for you while you work."

"No, I think not. We'll have to put up with a little inconvenience. I might not be able to locate passive ears." She
chuckled, "Then again, maybe I could. Irritating, isn't it?"

Tamris stretched, laughed, said, "Oh, I do feel free."

"Good." Aleytys was in no mood to echo her lightness. She
settled in a chair she suspected was deliberately chosen to be
uncomfortable, touched on the screen in front of her, drew a
deep breath as she fed in the record of events in Oldread
Can's fantasy.

"Want me to start the GATE tapes?"

"No point yet. Slide that chair over here and watch this
with me. Look for anything even a hair out of place. Don't
say anything until the tape is finished, then we'll compare
notes."

"Right. Want me to pick off the fleas, oh revered elder?"

"What?"

"The ones biting you."

"What!" Aleytys swung around, saw Tamris's broad grin,

shook her head, sighing. "No respect any more." She tapped Tamris's arm lightly. "Thanks, Conscience."

CHIMAEREE
OLDREAD CANS

The little man's fantasy began playing on the screen. According to the notes provided there were half a dozen days of it before the record went black then came on again with Cans gone.

Oldread Cans was a god king of infinite power, instant anger at times, but not too often, just enough to impress his might on his subjects. As subjects he seemed to prefer statuesque blondes a good foot and a half taller than him, and slight boys as the male figures, none of these taller or more robust than him. From the beginning he was thoroughly enjoying himself, bathing almost in the fulsome speeches about his power and his sexual prowess (which rather amazed the two watchers since the women didn't need to exaggerate much when they praised him; he was a considerate lover with a remarkable capacity for recovery). He flew about the house, created jewel-like beasts out of thin air, played in the water with his blondes, watched the boys wrestle or race or play endless games with balls and cesta-gloves. The first hour was relaxing and rather touching, but the watchers found themselves growing rapidly bored watching Cans being noble and generous and exaltedly romantic for what seemed the thousandth time, listening to the chants of praise to him for the thousandth time.

"Wonder how many times Security went through these?" Tamris kept her voice even but her impatience was evident.

"Doesn't matter." Aleytys rubbed at her neck, wriggled in the chair. "So. Look for a tall fair man and a nine or ten year old red-haired boy."

"Boy? What. . . ?"

"Not here, not now."

"Damn."

"Watch."

The day passed with agonizing slowness. The tapes were realtime, one hour of tape representing one hour of Oldread Cans's experience. Aleytys would not skip anything, or skip ahead to the snatch, afraid she would miss something important. Yet by the end of that first day, her eyes were burning, her head aching, and she had nothing at all to show for it.

On the second day:

Aleytys settled rather grimly into her chair, Tamris silent and grumpy beside her. She started the flow of images and began watching the second day of Oldread Cans gamboling through his dreamworld. The third time she sat through a fervid and all too lengthy song of praise to the godking, she sat back in the chair with some violence and shoved at the hair falling onto her sweaty forehead. "Enough," she said.

"More." Tamris wrinkled her nose. "One more speech and I'll be sick all over me."

Aleytys stopped the flow, called up the last day. "It's half a day only," she said. "But it'll be more of the same, I'm afraid."

"You'd think he'd get bored."

"Well, we're not there enjoying it, only watching."

The images began to flow again, the same as before, fawns gamboling in the shrubbery, tall blondes dancing in veils of gauze, wretched prisoners dragged in so Cans could pardon them and listen to their paens to his generosity. The day dragged slowly on, wholly predictable. Cans had little real imagination, enough for a day's elaboration perhaps, but after that he only repeated himself, not that he knew it, of course, he was still blissfully involved in his dream.

Aleytys was starting to drowse when a flash of red caught her eye. Cans was watching the boys and the fawns play with a ball of blue light. Suddenly in among the boys was one who had not been there before, the real boys paid no attention to him, perhaps thinking he was an invention of Cans like the fawns or the winged girls circling overhead.

Cans tired of the game and went inside, the boys trouping after him. The red-haired boy was always in motion, circling behind another when passing the eyes as if he read them as easily as she had. There was only the occasional flash of red to mark him as his head shifted before or behind that of another boy. She leaned forward, watching intently for that moment when he finally moved just a bit wrong and exposed himself more than usual, enough to get an image of his face or a piece of it.

It happened. She stopped the flow with a soft satisfied

sound, ran it back. Fingers flying over the sensor plate, she enlarged the bit of face, enhanced it, took a print, fiddled with it milking the machine of all it was capable of giving her until she had to be satisfied she could get it no clearer, then she returned to the flow of action, looking for another chance. She didn't get it. The boy guarded himself with a skill even she'd have problems matching; except for his hair he seemed to be remarkably unnoticeable. He glided like a ghost half-seen, face hidden, gracefully quick, sure of himself, through the playing boys and out of the room. A moment later the scene went dark.

Aleytys sat back, her head bowed, the heels of her hands pressed hard against her eyes. She dropped her hands into her lap. "I got my proof. Wish I hadn't."

"Why?"

"Later." Aleytys picked up the best of the prints, handed it to Tamris. "Look for this face on the first set of GATE tapes." She sat with her hands limp in her lap, suddenly so weary and dispirited she didn't want to move, couldn't move. She stretched out across her chair, the nape of her neck on the hard plastic back, her legs pushed out stiff and straight before her, her buttocks barely on the edge of the seat. After a long moment of this she exploded out a breath, collapsed and sat up. "Call me when you see him."

"Mmm."

She swung around. Tamris was hunched over the screen, working busily, using a light stylus, entering points on the print into the computer. She looked up as Aleytys came to stand beside her. "Thought I'd try this first." She touched on the flow and leaned back watching the shifting blotched blurs slip across the screen. "If it doesn't work, we can go back to the eye work. Could save some time through."

"If the boy hasn't come in disguised some way."

"If. You said there were a lot of ifs. Hah, look." The swimming blurs halted abruptly. "After what we saw at GATE I thought the computers would have this capacity." The boy's face swelled until it filled the screen, unmistakably the same boy, then slid off as the flow continued at normal speed. Hastily Tamris backed up the flow, shrunk the image until they could see the man with the boy, a tall fair man with a worn clever face and a shock of white hair. "That's him?"

"Uh-huh."

"You were right, look at them, walking in innocent as . . . as . . . well."

"Pick up the day after the snatch. Look for them leaving."

"You think . . . but . . . what about Cans? What did they do with him? You can't tell me they're smuggling him out in a trunk."

Aleytys whistled a few notes, said, "Here pup, here pup."

"You're joking."

"Nope. Look."

A flow of blurs, a short interval of dark, another flow, stopped to focus on the boy's face again, reduced, showed him and his older companion leaving again, as empty-handed and innocent as they'd come. Tamris scratched at her nose. "I begin to think I'd better work on that apology."

"Clear those tapes. That's enough for now." Aleytys yawned, stretched. "I'm hungry." She watched as Tamris shut down the systems and gathered up the scattered prints of the boy and the thief. She stood, stretched again, moved to the door and waited.

"How did you know how to look for the boy?" Tamris rubbed at her back. "Is he the thief's son?"

"Mine." Aleytys pushed the door open.

"What?"

"Later." She stepped through the door and waited, her mouth twisted in a half smile, as Tamris took the link from the silent boy who'd spent a dull day watching a shut door. As they waited a bit more for Intaril to arrive and confirm the transfer, Aleytys said, "Part of that life history you want to hear, matter for the trip back to Wolff, not here."

Intaril arrived frowning, obviously in a high hurry. "Anything?" she snapped. Without waiting for an answer, she took the link from Tamris, gabbled her certification and handed it back.

"Ask f'Voine," Aleytys said.

Intaril scowled. "What?"

"He's tapped into our lines, you know that. Let him tell you." She strolled off down the hall toward the lift tube that would carry them up to the transport chutes. In silence they drifted up the considerable distance to the small floats that they could ride to the other buried building where they had their quarters.

In the float, Tamris shifted uneasily. "I don't like this being underground all the time, makes me itchy."

"Over and above the probes?"

"Oh, I'm getting used to those. No, I'd just like to see a bit of sky now and then, breathe some unprocessed air."

"With today's break, we could possibly finish this tomorrow or possibly the day after that. Depends. I want to check the other tapes, see if I can find that pair again. I want to know as much about his operations as I can. Enough so I can fill in the blanks myself."

"You think he's really coming back." Tamris groaned and sat up as the float came to a stop at their building. She stepped out, extended her hand to Aleytys. "Respect to the old folks, ma'am."

"Imp. I think. . . ." She ignored the hand and stepped out beside the girl. "I think Cazar made sure he'd come when they brought me here. He's a gambler, Mari, he couldn't resist this challenge if he was dying; he'd love making a fool out of me."

"And the boy?"

"Don't ask me about him."

"I can't help being curious."

"Forget it, I shouldn't have said what I did."

Tamris pushed the door open, stepped inside, held it open until Aleytys was in, then slammed it shut with a sigh of relief. "Ah, I hate the eyes on me." She flattened her back against the thin veneer of wood covering the metal of the door. "Think f'Voine got that?"

Aleytys threw herself down on the couch, laced her fingers behind her head. "No, not then, not after you shut down the viewers. Intaril and I, we made a bargain. She shuts off the eyes around me and I don't pop them."

"You trust her to keep it?"

"Of course not, she knows that, so she shuts them off. I check, just to keep her honest." She pulled a hand loose and patted a yawn. "I'm hungry enough to gnaw on raw silvercoat and too tired to eat. Disgusting."

Tamris pushed away from the door and crossed to the bar. "I could get used to the wine they keep here."

"Be a nice little Hunter and one day maybe you can afford it. Speaking of Hunter, you tell me. What are we going to do tomorrow?"

Tamris poured the golden wine into two glasses. "I suspect another miserable day looking at tapes. Seeing in what guise the boy and the thief appear, locate where they spent the time they weren't working the snatch. See if there's any pattern in this, how many days they spent here before acting, how many after the fact, more like that. And Intaril knows exactly what we discover."

"Right."

"And f'Voine will have half a hundred secs checking out the tapes, probably got them started already."

"No doubt."

"What chance they'll spot the boy? Or the man?"

"Some, depends how flexible the watchers are, or how desperate."

"If I had f'Voine standing over me mad, I'd be pretty damn desperate."

"Mmm. We'll see in the morning. If Intaril shows to authorize the shift of the link and isn't bouncing, then the thief still has them fooled." Aleytys sat up, took the glass, sipped at the wine and sighed. "She might decide to get tricky, but I think I can read her." She threaded fingers through sweaty hair. "Bath. I need a bath. Damn them for having only showers. I want to soak and soak until I'm wrinkled as a raisin. You dial supper or me?"

On the third day:
HAZARDEE
SUNG YUL TWI (the second victim)

The flow of the casino, a flickering of faces around and around the machines, the games, the tables, the pits, the screens where fighters fought and the racers raced on realtime transmission, silent intense faces, distorted faces, silently shouting, blank faces refusing entry, but most of all the eyes traversed hands and bodies, this wasn't for the security of the clients but the security of the casino, they were watching for gimmicks and sleight of hand tricks. As with the first tape, the fourth day proved the key, this time the stab came early in the evening rather than in the afternoon. Only a flash, a second's image, immediately gone, but her hand stabbed the flow frozen, backed it up and there he was, again altered, expertly turned into a young-adult sprite, drifting with grace and sly impishness through the crowd of larger persons.

Tamris was skeptical until Aleytys brought the face up and matched it to the first.

LETHE
SAH-KALAH the tie (the third victim)

Lethe was difficult to watch, dedicated to death in all its forms, no holos these, the dying screamed real screams, bled real blood, suffered real death and pain. The clients sometimes watched, sometimes entered into action, up to their elbows in blood and entrails, delicately touched rheostats that increased in slow stages the pain of the victims, drinking in the pain they saw before them.

"That's not real, it can't be real," Tamris whispered. She pressed her hand against her mouth and her throat worked.

"It's real enough. Phah! no wonder they're hardheaded about their privacy, this would sicken a. . . ." She stopped talking and brought up the last day. This was no better. Tamris gasped with relief when Aleytys picked out the boy now fitted with wings like a small demon.

Grim and silent, Aleytys took the print, switched to the viewer with the GATE tapes.

In the float on the way back to their quarters, Tamris clutched the folder with the pictures and data in it, held it on her lap and tried to relax. Aleytys watched her, knowing she was still a bit sick with what she'd seen in the last tapes. "Tomorrow we'll start looking for the latest incarnation of our ghost," she said.

"The Aghir are due in tomorrow," Tamris said. She leaned back against the cushions, a little more relaxed.

"I know."

"How long you think it'll take to run him down?"

"If the computer can pick them out, thirty minutes. If not, depending on our luck, one day or five. This one won't be easy. Saving his best for last." She settled back, sighed. "It's going to be a tight race, Mari, but we're getting close."

THE BOY AND THE THIEF

The Casino

Late in the afternoon, a beautiful senset going unnoticed.

The boy, swathed in layered robes of multicolored gauze and the long veil, stood at the elbow of an adult in the same dress, wearing in addition shimmering film gloves. The boy watched the thief, worried and uncertain. For the past few days he had spent more and more time in the casino, gambling with a growing intensity. The boy was near sick with worry that for once he would forget what he was here for, lose himself in the gambling fever that was the worst part of the times between jobs. Watching the faded brown eyes above the veil, the boy fought for control. He was tempted to intervene, one way or another, but the thief had told him over and over and he knew from his own observations that anyone who tried mental manipulations in this place rung alarms all over.

To his relief, the thief kept to the plan, though he had to fight with himself to pull out of the game. He stood, swayed a little for effect and tottered from the room, leaning heavily on his companion's shoulder. Or rather the Vijayne Gracia did, muttering incoherently to herself as she walked out. She'd been exhibiting a progressive weakness, something that was planned to peak with the arrival of the Aghir, a weakness that would keep her secluded but not sick enough to require the services of a doctor.

A storm was ghosting in from the west, its edges obscuring the thin spray of stars overhead, the spray of surf at their feet. In slick black bodysuits the thief and the boy slid into the water and started across the narrow channel between Hazardee and the little unnamed jag of rock that held the *Butterball,* one of many other jags in a sweep of small rocky

136

islands trailing south into the open sea. The current was fierce, the waves were whipped up by the rising wind, but they were both expert swimmers and made the island with a minimum of difficulty.

Butterball sat invisible, tucked under its peculiar shield, on the far side of the island on a crescent-shaped bit of beach facing Battue distantly visible to the east.

Shield clamped tight, flying almost blind by gyro and by nanosecond licks at the air around them, silent, shut in the claustrophobic egg-shaped shield, they crept across the tumultuous channel, felt their way over the land to the mountains that bisected Battue, landed a comfortable distance from the Aghir conference hall.

The boy crouched on frosty grass as the thief got the dirigible ready. Protected by the shield from the buffeting of the winds, he couldn't see the storm gathering overhead, but he could hear a little of it and accepted this promise of shelter with a slight lessening of the ice in his belly.

Tucked up close beneath the small black gasbag, two black figures dangled side by side, passing in and out of the clouds, bumped about by erratic winds, tossed up, forced down, the twin airscrews whup-whupping with sturdy determination, the chemical motors driving them against the wind with slight but sufficient force, creeping north along the mountain range, weaving in and out of the peaks, in and out of the clouds.

With nothing to do but dangle beneath that black sliver, the boy began to tense again in spite of the exhilaration engendered by the storm—ordinarily he gloried in storms—began to let his mind ramble over the things that bothered him, to contemplate the image his continual anxiety had suggested to him, a black mouth opening before them, waiting for them, a terrible sucking mouth. He stared down, saw only soft rolls of nothing beneath him.

The meeting hall on the mountaintop was finally before them, copiously floodlit, a squat heavy structure, five-sided, with five tall bronze double doors, five landing stages, one by each door, a pointed five-sided pyramid for a roof. One of Cazarit's ubiquitous electric fences circled it, random rolling robots crossed the open space between the hall and the fence, rolled in and out of the structure, the bronze doors opening and closing before and behind them with a quiet elegant precision. Hovering outside the fence, the boy and the thief watched the activity for some minutes then began to circle the mountain top, high above the fence, watching the changing patterns of the robot patrol.

As one of the robots entered the structure, the thief smiled. "As if they want to make it easy for us." The clouds moved around them, flicking cold tails at them, the air was chill and fresh, clean except when wisps of lubrication stink and exhaust gas from the robots swirled up past them. The thief turned a little in the harness so he could look at the boy, pointed at one of the doors. "That's the next one to open."

The boy nodded.

"Think you can make it?"

The boy was taut with a shivery excitement, part fear, part anticipation. "We should circle up a bit more, I'd like the angle steeper."

The thief slipped some ballast and the dirigible swept around and up until the air was thin and sharp and they were on the verge of needing breathing equipment. The boy eased himself free of the harness, held himself in a hover for a moment as he checked to make sure the four bladders of compressed sleepgas were strapped firmly to his legs, then he reached within, steadied himself and began angling downward, falling fast, lifting only enough to keep the angle of fall he wanted. Once he reached the hall, he hovered in the shadow of an overhanging lintel until the door slid open to emit a robot. He popped inside before it could shut again.

It was dark and quiet inside, with the smell of newness still clinging though the building had been finished for several weeks. Straining, growing more tired than he liked, tired enough to frighten him, the fear weakening him further, he felt his way to the angle where roof and wall met. To his intense satisfaction, there was a narrow ledge there, sufficient to hold a smallish boy. His control slipping rapidly from him, the boy unsnapped the bladders, shoved them onto the ledge, pulled himself up beside them and stretched out along the ledge between two of the broad beams that supported the roof. His legs were trembling, he could hear the soft scrape of his darksuit against the stone, he was weak in the middle, muscles twitched in his back. He'd never tried so long a drop or so long a hovering before and he was frightened now, wondering if he could possibly manage to get out of here.

He had hardly managed to steady his breathing a little and stop the betraying trembling when the dark was suddenly gone as doors across the hall slid open and a robot rolled inside. As soon as the doors closed a searchlight on the robot's head flashed on. The finger of light probed about the huge room and the boy heard the soft pings of a sonar system. He squeezed himself into the small opening as far as he could, stopped breathing as the robot came swooping around the walls toward him, kept holding his breath as it rolled past, its soft rollers near noiseless on the polished stone floor. He closed his eyes to get his dark adaptation back and waited for the robot to finish its inspection and leave.

When it was dark again, he stayed where he was for some minutes, resting and gathering himself for the job he had to do. Very carefully he freed one of the bladders, tucked it as far back in the angle as he could, its matte neutral skin making it close to invisible. When he was satisfied with that one's placement, he started crawling very carefully along the ledge, scattering the other three bladders at fairly equal intervals about the hall. After he wedged the last one in place, he stretched out flat again along the ledge, its sharp edge cutting into his side a little but not enough to bother him. He closed his eyes, laughter bubbling up in him, the ice in his belly melting for the moment, this moment of aching weary triumph. He lay on the ledge and giggled, softly, a whuffling intake and outgo of air, then he did his breathing exercises, slow the breath, in-out, in-in-in until his body ached, out-out-out until he was empty, again and again, until he was wholly relaxed, limp, almost asleep, breathing the cool odorous smell of the stone, the sealants that made the room potentially airtight, fugitive traces of robot stink and other traces it was not possible to identify.

He was nearly asleep when the next robot came in. He crouched on the ledge, waited until it moved past him, then he floated off, easing closer and closer to it until that moment just before the robot reached the door and the light on its head blinked out. In the sudden darkness, the boy surged forward, bouyed as much by excitement as by his talent—or so it seemed to him—pulled himself through the door, angled his body and began to climb. He shut his eyes, tensed and rose, faltered, tensed, rose, edged outward, afraid to look down, afraid to see how far he had to go. Ice again. Fear. He fought to ignore it because it drained his concentration, could kill him. Rise and halt, falter, dip toward the ground, rise, halt, gather himself, rise again, desperately tired, suddenly sure he would never finish, never reach the fence, it was too far . . . too far. . . .

Strong arms caught hold of him, a wiry nervous body was hard against him. He gasped and collapsed, too weary to think or worry any more. Distantly he heard the whup-whup of the airscrews, dimly he felt the flow of damp cold air around him. The thief shifted his hold and began fitting the harness about him, he could feel the wide straps slipped over his arms and shoulders, around his chest and waist, could hear the harsh breathing of the man, feel the nervous intensity in him. The boy sucked in a breath, suddenly stronger as if he sucked some of the energy out of the man.

When the snaps were shut, the thief let go of him. "You all right?"

The boy nodded, decided that wasn't enough. "Tired," he said.

"Where'd you put them?"

The boy explained, cold now, once again aching with the need to sleep.

"Good," the thief said.

The boy looked at him, saw his gleaming grin, grinned back.

"Set," the thief said. "We're set to go."

They floated back toward *Butterball*, the return to Hazardee before them, some need to hurry so they could slip back into their suite before the rising of the sun.

The Aghir were due into Battue late the next day.
The first meeting was set for the day after that.
Two days to wait, two days.

LILIT

THE EMBARKATION FROM LIROS II

They all marched across the stained and gritty metacrete to the squat powerful ship—

Mercenary guards in utilitarian grey shipsuits, guns and leather gleaming.

Ianina and Gelana, bustling across, bundled in bulky robes they clutched at whenever the strong wind tugged them up and away. (I hope they are annoyed, Lilit thought, look at them pick up their feet, their slippers are getting muddy, dirty, scuffed, look at the wind blowing them about; envy me my prison, you stupid old bores, envy me.)

A cadre of silent nervous servants.

A collection of stolid serviteurs and watchdogs.

Lilit smothered in a veil, angry, sealed into a sedan chair, shut away from the wind and the smells and the possible taint riding the wind. She looked out through a round window in the front of the chair, its glass obscured by elaborate scrolls etched into it. She sat with her hands clenched, her arms aching with the strain, furious at being shut into the stuffy prison, at being denied even now a free breath of free air, not even now, not even when she was leaving forever.

Kalyen-tej. (She knew he was there though she couldn't see him, as she knew Acthon was watching at the edge of the field; they'd said their private farewells last night knowing they could not speak together at the field. Ekeser and Selas were there also; briefly she wondered what Ekeser was thinking, then let the thought go. It didn't matter, nothing mattered but finishing what she'd started.)

Ameersin and Heydall, the two overseers, husbands of Ianina and Gelana.

Another squad of mercenaries.

When the loading was complete the ship was filled near to its capacity, with little room for privacy and almost no place for exercise.

THE PASSAGE TO CAZARIT

Boredom and irritation, endless games of cards, petty quarrels between serving maids, petty sniping between Ianina and Gelana, her women, hers in name only—they were carefully polite to her and otherwise ignored her. She didn't protest, she was back to being meek and mild. For the sake of her adopted people, she swallowed the fury that threatened to choke her at times, the exasperation at actions of truly formidable stupidity. She had a small cubicle that was hers and hers alone; on that she made her stand—they were never to enter there unless she invited them.

She spent long hours in that room that was more like a coffin than a place to live in; that thought pleased her—a coffin for the not-quite-dead, sometimes she laughed at the thought until the shrillness of her laughter frightened her. She needed some one she could talk to, but there was no one. More and more she retreated to her bed, lying there in a state between waking and sleeping, reliving her joys and the reasons for her rage. She felt pressure building and building in her, tried to run from this into the past, the only freedom open to her though even that was not enough, never enough, she wanted to scream and pound the walls, but she couldn't do that and didn't do that, and it cost her. The pressure built and built until she dreamed of and yearned for an end, for the explosion that would crash the walls of her prison, freedom at last.

THE HOLD ON BATTUE, CAZARIT

"It's a nice room." Ianina looked around with a trace of envy at the luxurious fittings of the room, the jewel-bright, hand-tied rug, the glowing wood panelling, the heavy silken drapes, the rich furnishings, the drift-art on one wall, its pigments shifting in slow dreamy flows along randomly determined free forms. "A nice room."

Lilit ignored her, ordered the serviteurs to set her dress box on the floor near the window.

Gelana bustled over, stopped with her hand on the lid of

the box. "You want us to help you unpack, dear child?" Curiosity and a touch of malice gleamed in her black eyes.

"No," Lilit said, a sharpness in her voice she couldn't help. "No," she repeated more quietly. "I'll do that."

Gelana's thin face sank into familiar sour lines. "If you say so." She'd never seen the wedding robes and didn't like having her curiosity thwarted.

"The wedding will be tomorrow afternoon. Would you like us to stay with you this night? It's customary, you know, the bride should have her women with her the night before the wedding." Ianina was merely foolish, she had no malice in her, she'd be a little hurt when her offer was refused, but Lilit had no choice, there was no way she'd spend the last night of her life in the company of these two.

"No," she said. "I'd like to be alone. If you don't mind. . . ." She walked quickly to the door and held it open, her mouth curved in the semblance of a polite smile though she could feel the stiffness of her face and knew it was not convincing. She wouldn't look at them, kept her eyes meekly on the floor and waited for them to leave.

Even Gelana didn't quite dare challenge her. She was very much in awe of Kalyen-tej and some of this awe was involuntarily transferred to the daughter of Kalyen-tej however much she might despise her. She swept past Lilit, muttering something about seeing the tej, but Lilit knew she'd do nothing of the sort, anyway it wasn't important, let her complain. Ianina wavered past, fussing and uncertain whether this was right. But she went. They both went and Lilit was left alone except for the serviteur.

The silence closed in around her, frightening her a little at first, then comforting her, it was so filled with memory and ghosts that there was scarce room to breathe. Metis laughing at her. Old Gyoll, a real skeleton now with no flesh left on his bones, his dead eyes shimmers in his fleshless skull, glowing at her, filling her with his energy, his purpose. The dead babies. Even her mother was there, watching her with bewilderment, wondering what she was doing in this gallery. She walked to the window, plucked at the green silk drapes, put her back against them. "Come," she said to the serviteur, smiled as it rolled smoothly to her. She took the key from around her neck, unlocked the clothes box and turned back the lid. "Hang the robes in here in the closet across there."

She went quickly across the room, slid back the door to the large walk-in closet. "Here," she said. She spoke slowly and carefully even though she knew its capacity to understand speech was considerable. "Each robe hangs alone on one of the wooden hangers you'll find in the lid of the box. Leave a handwidth's space between each robe. Do you comprehend?" When she had the affirmation, she went back to the window.

This time she pulled the drape aside and looked out. Beyond the wall the green hills rolled away to blue mountains with pure white caps. Pale blue mountains against a pale blue sky, cool, soothing, restful. She pressed her face against the glass and began to cry, a quiet gentle crying like the gentle welcoming world beyond the wall.

Still weeping, unable to stop, she turned from the window, stretched out on the bed, her forehead pressed on crossed arms, weeping until she cried herself into a sodden sleep.

She woke with a throbbing head, burning eyes, a foul taste in her mouth, a knot in her stomach—and the serviteur standing with metal patience against the wall; she'd forgotten to dismiss it once its task was finished. She dragged herself up; the thought of food revolted her but the shake in her back, arms and legs meant she needed to eat. She sent the serviteur to fetch some food and tottered into the bathroom feeling a thousand years old. After bathing her face in cold water, she went back to the window.

It was dark out now, the sky curiously empty of stars. The mountains were dark, almost invisible, the snow pale and eerie against the velvet sky. Ghostly snow, she thought. You're ghosts, all of you. You don't mean anything, Acthon, Gyoll, my people. "My people," she whispered but the words had an empty hollow sound. Tomorrow, she thought, and felt nothing, no exaltation, no fear, just nothing.

The door chimed. She left the window and went to admit the serviteur with the food.

"Mid-morning," the serviteur said when she asked the time. "The fourth hour since dawn local time." It waited a moment to see if she had more questions, settled the tray neatly on the table and left.

Lilit lifted a cover, saw the row of fingerling fish and felt a revulsion in her stomach. She touched a warm crusty little fish but couldn't make herself eat it. She went back to the window and stood gazing out at the green hills.

Lilit smoothed the shift down over her body, her hands trembling as they passed over the corset with the triggering mechanism wired into it, the detonating charge pressed between the inner and outer layers of silk. She took the shimmery green robe from the closet, handling it with a shrinking eagerness, pulled it over her head. "One," she breathed. She fished the tearstrip attached to the corset from under the robe, pulled it with great care over her shoulder and up under her long loose hair, pinned it in place. The second robe was a paler shade of green, had a hint of blue in it. She thought of Acthon and felt a hot ache behind her eyes but didn't weep, there were no tears left in her. She thrust her arms through the sleeve holes and smoothed the front closure shut. The third robe was the key. She took it from the closet. It was the heaviest and palest of the three. She held her breath as she lifted its heavy slippery folds over her head and let them fall around her, slide with a deadly inevitability down her body. She didn't smooth this one into place but shook herself instead until it was settled. She walked to the mirror and looked at herself, trying to see if anything suspicious showed about the robes, but they hung still, fell in smooth folds, bulking out her slim body. She sighed, went back to the closet and took out the gauzy fourth robe. She slipped her arms into the sleeves, tugged the insewn waist cincher together in front and threaded the lace through the grommets. She pulled the cord tight, tied it into a knot, tied a small neat bow over the knot. She hesitated a moment, but she knew only too well what she had to do; she squared her shoulders, closed her eyes tight, didn't breathe for several heartbeats, then she marched to the door, pulled it open and sent the serviteur waiting outside to bring Ianina and Gelana to help her with the last two robes, her head covering and veil.

She rode in the second flitter, rode alone because of the bulk of her robes. There was no room for her attendants and she was glad of that; the pilot was there but he ignored her and she found it easy enough to forget about him. Ahead of her Kalyen-tej rode a float, other floats swarmed around and over hers, guards, her attendants, guards, the serviteur musicians, the overseers, guards.

The land rolled away under them, below her—to the side where she could see them—herds of hooved beasts exploded into flight as the fleet of flyers whined over them. Not too far away she could see several birds about the size of her fist with bright red feathers. She watched them with a touch of wistfulness then jerked her eyes away and fixed them on the mountains ahead.

The flitter began to slant upward, pressing her lightly toward the back of the seat. In another few minutes she could see the squat brutal bulk of the conference hall. Her heart beat erratically, there was a strange almost pleasurable shiver running through her body.

At the landing stage outside the door marked Liros her father waited and watched, stone faced, as Gelana and Ianina helped her from the flitter, straightened her skirts carefully, fluffing out the outer robe with its thick crusting of silver wire until it stood wide from her body, spreading out and smoothing the veil and headcloth. The outer robe was lovely, she was proud of that, she'd put her heart into it, heavy white satin, couched silver wires in elaborate curls and spirals, in leaf shapes and vine shapes repeated over and over, pearls catching the light and glowing, moonstones catching the light and glowing. The headcloth and veil were a fine white gauze embroidered in arabesques of silver thread with tiny pearls nesting among the curves. Her father examined her and let a touch of surprise show in his face. "The dress is beautiful," he said. "You have a gift."

She bowed her head. She wanted to speak and she didn't, she couldn't explain the confusion even to herself. She extended her hand. Her father took it, accepting for the first time she could remember his responsibility for her. For a moment he continued to stare down at her, then he straightened, led her through the great door, the musician serviteurs following, taking her in on a swell of sound. He led her across the glowing stone floor toward the inlaid multipointed silver star set in the center of the empty space, his boot heels ringing on the stone, her feet whispering silken beside him, the slight sound lost in the march played behind them. Walking. Walking. Toward the sloppy, bloated figure oozing over the edges of the chair. The doors clicked shut, that sound lost also in the music.

She swallowed, her mouth was dry, there was an odd sweetness suddenly in the air, she could smell it, almost taste it. She thought about Acthon. She thought of Metis and Little Sister and Elf. She thought of the faceless people of the villages, she thought of the dwellers in the Wild that she knew better than the villagers from Acthon's tales. She looked at the man her father had sold her to, looked up at her father. She raised her free hand, worked it up under her veil until she could touch the tearstrip pinned to her hair. She felt as if she were floating, it was hard somehow to concentrate, that didn't really matter, except things were starting to be fuzzy in her head and it was hard to control the movements of her fingers. She swallowed. The sweetness was thicker. She began to wonder about it, began to feel alarmed. She tried to close her fingers about the tearstrip, nerved herself to rip it loose—

TAMRIS

Tamris wrote:

We viewed one day's arrivals today. The computer search didn't work, came up with several almosts, but Aleytys says she doesn't think any of them is the boy. There were no matches at all for the man. Twenty-four hours. We could squeeze it a little. There was congestion when the liners arrived and some long dull stretches between we could skip. All I can say is after the first few minutes it was boring as hell. And Aleytys paid almost no attention to the screen. She was looking at it all right, but I don't think she saw a thing, sort of sat there turned inside, her lips moving now and then as if she were talking to herself. She does that sometimes and it's driving me crazy trying to figure out what's happening. I suspect Mom could tell me, but trying to pry information out of her about her Hunters is about as easy as taking a ved haunch from a hungry silvercoat. Ah well, all this is off the point.

When we came out of the viewing room, Intaril was waiting as usual. She was looking a bit grim but whether that was real or put on would be hard to say. I was a bit surprised to see her since I hadn't transferred the link today, it wasn't necessary because we were finished with the sensitive tapes.

"The Aghir are settled in," she said. "The conference starts tomorrow afternoon."

Well, we didn't need reminding—maybe I should qualify that—I didn't need reminding but Aleytys was in a funny mood, she doesn't really want to catch this ghost, track down her own son, what a thing to have to do.

Aleytys laughed, a soft little sound that seemed to scratch at Intaril like nettles. "I know that well enough," she said. "And you know equally well how much progress we've made in there." She waved a hand at the door, started strolling

148

toward the lift shaft. "You've had f'Voine watching us since
we started playing with the tapes." She smiled then, not much
of a smile. "I've got no doubt at all," she said, "that you've
got a herd of sec-serfs working on the tapes, slipping that
boy's face over every child or midget passing through. I
imagine—" she laughed again, enjoying the look on Intaril's
face—"you've had about the same luck we had today. That's
why you're so antsy."

Intaril didn't say anything. She couldn't. She wasn't about
to admit the truth of what Aleytys said and wasn't about to
get an outright lie into the link, not one it would be easy
enough to prove a lie by putting f'Voine or one of his secs
under the verifier.

In the float Aleytys did her trick again with the eyes and
the lips. She was looking worried and a bit cranky. I think
maybe she was just a bit afraid that the secs would stumble
over something and get to the ghost first. After all the trouble
she put Mom to to get that agreement—I think maybe she
was stalling today, trying to make up her mind what to do,
maybe that explains all the talking to herself. God forbid that
I ever have to make a choice like this.

When we reached our quarters, she dumped herself in the
chair and plonked her feet on the rest. Me, I went straight to
the bar. I'd been thinking about a glass of wine, food and a
hot bath for what seemed centuries. I may come out of this a
confirmed misanthrope. Go spend a year looking at trees and
rocks and no faces. Anyway, I poured the wine, took Aleytys
her glass and headed for the couch with mine.

Tamris settled on the couch, tucked a pillow behind her
back, the glass tilting precariously as she wriggled about getting comfortable. As she started to lift the glass, Aleytys said
sharply, "Don't!"

"Huh?" Tamris stared at Aleytys, then at the gently slosh-
ing liquid.

"Hunch," Aleytys said. "Don't drink till I test this." She
sipped at the wine, frowned, emptied the glass in three gulps.
Great beads of sweat popped out all over her face, she
shivered, shivered again, flushed bright red. She reached over
the arm of the chair, making it rock a little, set the glass
down with exaggerated care that told more eloquently than

her clipped words how angry she was. "I'm tired," she said. "I'm hungry. I hate this."

Tamris stared at the wine, set the glass gently down beside the couch. "Drugged?"

"Yes." The word was snapped out. Aleytys leaned back in the chair until she was stretched out almost flat. She closed her eyes and her face went blank. Tamris felt her skin start to itch but couldn't tell if it was just nervousness or a bug activating her implants. Before she could say anything, Aleytys opened her eyes. "Despin' Intaril," she said. For a moment Tamris thought Aleytys was talking to her. "I want to see you here in fifteen minutes or you might have to redefine the word expensive. My companion and I are seriously annoyed." She slid her fingertips slowly up and down the chair arm. "Whoever you are monitoring this, I suggest you get that message to the Director two minutes ago or sooner. If you take it into your pointy little head to ignore me, your ass will be kicked from here to the slave pens of Lethe." She closed her eyes again. Briefly her face and body went taut. Tamris rubbed at her shoulder as the itch intensified suddenly then went away.

"That too?"

"That too." Aleytys flexed her knees, shifted about a bit, sat up. She smiled drowsily at Tamris, all her anger apparently dissipated.

"Clean?" Tamris got to her feet and took the glass to the bar, set it there beside the bottle.

"Now."

"Why today?" She lifted the bottle, put it down again, swung around to lean against the bar, her arms crossed over her stomach, hands cupped over her elbows.

"They want to get a jump on us. Time's getting tight."

"The fee."

"In part. Honor-points if they can get it cut in half."

"Our data."

"Prove they didn't stumble on him by accident."

"Accumulated data. Too many coincidences. Your testimony and mine."

"Might do it. Chancy. And there's always the claim of tacit agreement."

"But. . . ."

"You knew what was happening."

"Suspicion, not knowing, not me."

"Say anything?"

"What good would that do?" Tamris pulled herself up on one of the two stools, sat with her legs dangling. "They'd just deny it."

"Tacit agreement."

"No fair."

Aleytys chuckled.

"That's funny?"

"Not that. Intaril's going to be mad enough to spit. I wouldn't want to be the genius who overstepped his or her instructions and drugged the wine."

"So?"

"Today was a bust as far as information is concerned."

"Hop-hop, you're skipping connections again."

"Patience, flea. The tape we'll see tomorrow covers our visit to GATE."

"So?"

"Remember the twinge I got?"

"I remember you jumping and squeaking like something bit you."

"Squeaking? Felt more like a sneeze that won't fruit. Faded to nothing as soon as I felt it. The boy, I think—with his heritage he has to be talented one way or another."

"What are you going to do about him—the boy?"

"I don't know." She drew her hand across her face. "Don't ask."

"Why hasn't f'Voine or one of his serfs spotted them? And if you do better, how can we trace them without alerting f'Voine?"

Aleytys grinned. "Go down on our knees and pay homage to the great little jerk who decided to bug and drug us. One. The ghost is a damn good ghost. Looks like he's putting on a special effort just for me. Two. Joke's on Intaril. I was mad enough to start ripping the place apart till I stopped reacting and started thinking. You look confused. Think. Want to try getting that bottle away from me?"

Tamris shook her head. "Not me. I'm not stupid."

"What would happen if I took that bottle to Helvetia where the escrow board could test it?"

"Hah! Not stupid but sadly slow. We got ourselves a hostage."

"Caught up?"

"For now."

A quick rat-tat on the door.

"What timing. Be a nice little apprentice and open it for me, I don't feel like moving. And ditch that grin, we don't want to terrify the woman."

Aleytys swung the chair around to face Intaril who sat at apparent ease on the couch.

"You chose an odd way to summon me," Intaril murmured.

"Should I offer you a glass of wine?"

Intaril's mouth thinned momentarily. "Not at the moment, thank you."

"Just as well. One of your lesser rats has been into it. It's drugged."

"You have proof of this?"

"Sufficient to convince me. Sufficient to be quite sure a competent analysis would prove the presence and disclose the nature of the adulterant." She laced her fingers together over her stomach. "Our rat didn't do its homework. I'm a healer. You can kill me, but you can't drug me." Her smile broadened to a grin. "When I say you, I speak generically not personally."

"Thanks for that at least." Intaril gazed down at her knees, her face gravely thoughtful, giving nothing away. "I can't accept your guesses, Hunter. You have no evidence." She lifted one hand in a quick graceful gesture of negation, dropped it into her lap. "Even if you happen to be correct, you might have some difficulty proving that you had no opportunity to drug the wine yourself."

"And I might not." Aleytys smiled at Intaril then sat watching her thumbs circle each other, a look of intense interest on her face. Tamris sat very still on her stool, afraid even the slightest movement or sound would disrupt the tension Aleytys was building into the silence. Her nose started to burn, she thought she was going to sneeze, she gritted her teeth and hoped fervently that Intaril was half as uncomfortable but doubted it, the Director was relaxed and cool, perhaps a little wary but only a little. Aleytys lifted her hand up and let it fall in a parody of Intaril's gesture. "A nuisance, whatever the circumstances," she said.

After a nearly imperceptible hesitation, Intaril said, "That is possible."

"Trade," Aleytys said. "Nuisance for nuisance."

"You'll have to be more specific."

"Really?"

"Really."

"Then let me lay it out. I've got a fee to earn. I want your Security force to climb off my back. You've had a full year to catch the ghost and he's laughed at you. Me, I've worked hard the past few days and got a lot farther than any of you. Your little rat must be pretty damn sure I'm getting close. I'm willing to accept the rat's evaluation. Flattering in a way." She smiled. "I presume your personal access to the computers is shielded."

"Yes. Of course."

She didn't hesitate this time, Tamris thought, she saw this coming.

"Have the rest of the GATE tapes transferred to your office and expect us early tomorrow."

"My office? Certainly not."

"As an alternative to that, certify that any discovery your Security force makes from now on is due to leads I developed and provided to them—without my permission, of course, this provision."

"Do you seriously expect me to certify that nonsense?"

"What I seriously expect is the use of your shielded access."

"For how long?"

"How long is a piece of string?"

"Your idea of brilliant repartee?"

"Your answer?"

"Your original description was accurate. Nuisance." Intaril stood. "The tapes will be transferred. Anything else?"

"Well. . . ." Aleytys swung her feet off the rest and sat up. "A small thing. I'm hungry enough to eat the rug and I suspect my associate is fading to a thread too, though she's too polite to mention it. We'd like a fresh supply of untainted food and wine. You can collect your embarrassment—" she flicked a finger at the wine bottle and glass beside it—"when the food arrives."

Intaril's smile was small and pained. "Thoughtful of you. Good night." She nodded to Tamris and walked out with unhurried dignity and apparently undisturbed imperturbability.

Tamris pushed the bottle a few inches farther from her. "You just going to give her this?"

"The threat's more apparent than real. I don't want to have to spend the rest of our time here hovering over that blasted bottle. Besides, sooner or later we're going to have to move fast and hard. No time to be cuddling that thing."

"You trust her."

"Her, yes. In this. The weight is on our side. She'll be waiting to see if she can find an opening that gives her a bigger edge. The other rats—well, watch your back." She groaned and turned herself stiffly out of the chair. "Madar, I wish this was over." She stretched and yawned. "Time, I think, for a shower before the food arrives."

Tamris wrote:

> *So Aleytys pulled it off. I think, really, she worked that hard so she can keep her promise to herself not to turn the ghost over to the Cazarits. I got a twinge myself tonight, wondering if she really needed to check the records of the snatches. She could have started with that day we were up at* GATE, *but if she did, the sec-serfs would have scooped him up before she could get near him. Still, maybe she did need to be sure it was him before she started looking. Damn this link. We've needed it and will again, but I don't like this floundering. Guess and guess and not even able to ask because the answer might say too much in front of the link.*

Tamris looked at what she'd written, flicked the page over, pressed it down and began to write again.

> *When Aleytys told me to keep this notebook, I thought I'd just note down a few facts and dates—didn't stick with that not even the first day, these damn empty pages, they're seductive—like having a discreet friend to talk to—helps me get my head in order—but definitely not for outside consumption—is a good idea—think I'll keep it up other Hunts—*
>
> *The end's close—I know it—I can feel it—almost smell it—God, don't let me mess up—*

ALEYTYS

She dreamed:

She was running toward the boy who stood looking at her out of a face filled with hate. At his feet lay the bloody body of the thief, stretched in boneless death. She ran toward the boy but before she could reach him, Intaril and f'Voine were there, clutching his arms and gibbering at her. Oldread Cans giggled and pranced on crooked legs about them, pricking pointed hairy ears; the tie Sah-Kalah whirled about them, screaming, swinging bloody entrails, throwing gobbets of twitching flesh at her. She slipped in the blood and screamed

and woke shaking. "Harskari." Her throat hurt, her voice was a husky whisper.

"Daughter?"

"I dreamed."

Shadith was suddenly there. "Anxiety dream," she said.

"I don't know. We're both getting close, Intaril and me. I'll tear this place apart before I leave him in their hands."

"Your son?"

"Them both. Sharl or Stavver."

"You've bought your leadtime." Harskari shook her white head and laughed. When she sobered, she said, "Watch it, Aleytys, don't trample too glibly over others simply because you can."

"That's one cool femme," Shadith said. "Anything we can do to help?"

"Don't know. Keep an eye on things." She smiled into the darkness. "Laugh at me now and then. Good for my sense of proportion."

"Even if you've acquired another conscience? I think I'm jealous." Harskari was in a playful mood, something rare enough to startle the others and tease their spirits high.

"Oh, never like you, my mother, she only pinches me on the outside." She yawned. "Damn, I'm tired. Sing me to sleep, Shadithi, mmmh?"

Shadith's laughter tickled through her head. "Yes, little sister, a lullaby for a sad lady, but you'll have to tuck yourself in."

IN THE ALCOVE WHERE INTARIL HOUSED HER ACCESS AND OTHER INSTRUMENTS

eighth hour plus twenty minutes CENTER
eleventh hour plus twenty minutes BATTUE

The flow drifted past, faces and faces until they blurred into a visual rhythm, widening, narrowing longer, shorter, round eyes, slitted eyes, bulges and pits, faceted and simple, hats and no hats, head cloths and helmets, fur and hair, robes and armor, harness and naked skin. Aleytys caught a glimpse of red, checked the flickering time in the upper right corner and knew she saw the top of her own head. She leaned closer, eyes devouring the four images on the screen, one for each of the four turnstiles, reached out, touched Tamris's arm. "Slow it."

She watched the faces crawl past, saw herself look around then turn to speak to Tamris. "Stop it there. Good. Back it up, about three minutes. Good. Now—very slow forward."

Her hands closed tight about the chair arm as if by squeezing the plastic she could squeeze the face she wanted out of the screen. The faces crawled past. Nothing. She watched herself pass through the stile, watched the rollways, all of them, watched most intently the several families that came into view. She flattened her hand across her mouth, drew it across her face, pinched her nose. There were a few children the right age and general conformation. She stopped the flow at each, stared without blinking at them, ignoring the apparent sex of the youngster—but she felt nothing for any of them, not even for a small brown-pelted youngling perfect in size and almost matching in certain points, the differences nothing beyond what could be taken care of with inserts and fills. Three times she had Tamris send the flow back past him. She watched him move, had Tamris play over and over the other bits of tape with the boy on them, watched him move. Finally she shook her head, leaned back, closed her eyes.

"That's the best match," Tamris said after a moment's taut silence.

"I know. It's not him."

"Maybe the twinge wasn't what you thought it was."

"Could be." She sighed, clasped her hands behind her head, eyes still closed. "I was being so sly and sharp," she murmured. "Maybe we started too late. Cycle it back a couple of minutes before I show up on the tape. The boy was looking at me, I'm almost sure that's what I felt. But whether he was in front of me or behind. . . ." She opened her eyes, sat up. "It was just a flicker, I couldn't catch the direction." She sighed. "Try again. I said a couple minutes, better make it more like five. If I don't get a touch this run-through, we go back to the tedium."

"Then I hope this is the one that makes it." Tamris busied herself at the sensor plate.

The flow went dizzily backward, stopped on a four-fold blur. One part cleared into the form of a tall man with blue-black skin and a bramble of dark red hair. She didn't remember seeing him at GATE, but there'd been so many faces, so many different types there. His body was too thick and he was at least a foot taller than Stavver, so she wouldn't have noticed him because he was so obviously not what she was looking for. The second gelled into a small slim female who wore a few bits of metal and leather. The third was a Cavaltis triad. The fourth was a very young couple clinging to each other, interested in nothing else.

Faces again, bodies. Change the fourfold image. Freeze. Change and freeze, a dozen new faces and forms—among these the gauze-wrapped Vijayne and her companion. Four at a time the faces flicked on and off the screen, on and off, her own face appeared and vanished. She held up her hand. Tamris stopped the flow. "Nothing?"

"I don't know."

"You want me to take it back to the beginning?"

"Yesss . . . no! Run it through once more from the point you started last time. There was something about the way one of them moved his head . . . her head . . . oh hell . . . start it again, I'll stop you."

She stopped the flow at the Vijayne. "The taller one. Enlarge the area about the eyes."

"The shape of the face is all wrong, besides, the stile probes say that's a female."

"I know. Do it anyway."

Washed-out brown eyes filled the screen. "Wrong color," Aleytys muttered. She scowled at white brows plucked to a thin line arching high over the eyes, making them look rounder than they actually were. If the flesh was puffed and pinned to enhance that roundness, it was a clever job, difficult to see even under magnification. She was sure it was him, not that she recognized those eyes, there was no real basis for her sudden conviction, but something intangible, the very perfection of the disguise, if it was a disguise, whispered to her of the thief who'd once boasted he was the best in the universe, the thief who'd stolen the diadem out of the RMoahl treasurehouse and was indirectly responsible for setting that soultrap on her head. Old woman. The veil shadows shaped his face into that of an old woman. She laughed. Clever thief, clever, clever man, but I know you, yes I do. "The companion," she said, "enlarge her eyes."

There was a shifting blur then large round violet eyes looked at her from under a froth of blond curls. She stared into those eyes. The shadow of the lower face was different, radically different from that of the other images she knew so well, so she ignored it, stared into the imaged eyes as if she could force them to answer her. "The other images, match them. Upper face only."

Silently Tamris complied, half-believing because of what had gone before, skeptical when she looked at the frozen faces. She brought the faces up, restructured them to fit the tilt and angle of the companion's face. At first she had considerable trouble matching any points at all.

Watching her, a small smile on her face, Aleytys read the growing skepticism behind the bland outer expression. *She thinks I've blown it this time, let my impatience push me off balance.*

Tamris reangled the image slightly and tried again. The line of the nose above the veil fell into place. The inside corners of the eyes matched microscopically, the points of the bony structures fit over one another exactly though the curve of the skull was wrong, the line of jaw and the shadow of the mouth through the veil matched nowhere.

Aleytys let out the breath she'd been holding. "Let me see the companion move, give me all you can of her." She watched intently as Tamris called up every scrap of image she could from the computer's records and sent them moving across the screen. "Enough. Try matching the man's face now." She watched in silence for several minutes more, then she leaned back and closed her eyes. "Trace them. Identity and destination."

"The mushti boy was a closer match."

"Moved wrong. Felt wrong. The companion's eyes, I know them. The eyes of his father before they were burnt out. Because of me." Eyes still closed, she said, "The companion has a trick of moving his head—I can't say her—one eye narrows a little when he's startled or amused, there's the way he jerks his chin up, a lot of other tiny things. Enough." She lay back silent as Tamris worked, opened her eyes finally. "Well, who's the ghost being this time?"

"Mmm, right, got it. The most honorable the Vijayne Gracia Belagar of Clovel, registered in the Southhive at Casino on Hazardee."

"Get a print and shut down. One minute." She blinked at the ceiling. "Give me the time. Here and Battue." She closed her eyes again.

"Mmm. Here, tenth hour plus thirty-five. Want more accuracy?"

"Not running a race."

"Oh? Looks like it to me." Tamris grinned. "I'm grinning," she said. "It's a joke, revered elder. Thirteenth hour and thirty-five at Battue."

"The conference is started then."

"Uh-huh. You think the ghost is moving on them?"

"Don't know. Got the print?"

"If you opened your eyes you could see it. Want me to wave it so you can feel the air?"

"Don't be snippy, apprentice. Be quiet, I have to think."

"But . . ." Tamris stopped talking, she shifted position.

Aleytys smiled. Tamris had realized only a little late what a dilemma she was in. No need to prejudice the record before they had to. The smile went away. What am I going to do? she thought. I haven't much time, five minutes at most. The

Lethe tape flashed through her mind as she sat frozen in her chair, eyes clamped shut, struggling to weigh her loyalties. Harskari and Shadith bloomed out of the darkness in her mind, but they said nothing, were there to comfort and strengthen her whatever she decided. She asked them nothing, this was a decision she had to make for herself, one she'd have to live with whatever the outcome. Tears burned in her eyes, trickled from under her closed lids. Both sides called to her with equal force and in the end, it was the hope that the ghost was already gone that dropped the weight on Head's side.

Aleytys dabbed at her face with the backs of her hands, asked the time.

"Tenth hour, forty-four." Tamris dug out some crumpled squares of tissue and handed them to Aleytys.

She wiped her face with quick nervous swipes, blew her nose. "Call the Director," she said. "I came here to do a job."

tenth hour fifty minutes CENTER
thirteenth hour fifty minutes BATTUE

Aleytys handed the printout to Intaril. "I can't guarantee the Vijayne is the ghost but I'm convinced of it."

Intaril read the few lines of printing, dropped the sheet on the desktop, began tapping a code into the comweb. "How'd you pick this one?" she said absently as she worked. Hintollin's face bloomed on the screen. Intaril didn't waste time with greetings. "The Vijayne Gracia Belagar and companion," she said. "Suite 17GB, South hive. Get them. Report when you have them." The screen went dull and Intaril settled back in her chair, her eyes fixed on Aleytys. "How?"

"When your hordes couldn't after working on the tapes for days?" Aleytys smiled wryly, a knot in her stomach, an ache behind her eyes. "As you know quite well, I've met your ghost before, lived with him awhile, got familiar with small habits of the body, the way he moves his head, the way he holds his hands, the kind of thing that lets you recognize at a distance someone you know before you can possibly make out any specific features. Is that sufficient?"

Before Intaril could answer the comweb chimed. Aleytys sucked in a breath, leaned forward, hands clasped to stop their shaking.

Hintollin again, tight-lipped and scowling. He held up a square hand. Two chains with guest medallions dangled from it. "Computer located them in their suite. No answer when the house manager called. Had to break in, the locks were jammed. The place was cleaned out except for these."

Intaril didn't wait for more. She tapped in another code. Daun Cenzai of Battue answered. "Get a man to that Hall soonest," Intaril snapped. "If the Aghir are there and get nasty, refer them to me." She didn't wait for an answer. Cursing under her breath, she danced her fingers across the plate in a complex sequence, lifted them, thought, coded the comweb again. F'Voine. "No one going in or out of GATE. Stop all shuttles. I've got the guard nexus activated and the patrol on battle status, the arflots grounded except those on the Security feed. I want you and a squad of your best on the way to Battue in a minute or less. The ghost is loose somewhere on Cazarit. If he's on Battue at all, get him. Was the Vijayne Gracia of Clovel, God knows what now. You've got the prints, get more from Hintollin as you go. Questions?"

"On my way." The screen went dull.

Intaril swung around to face Aleytys. "You heard. Any suggestions?"

Aleytys shook herself out of her relieved collapse. Now that Stavver was moving he'd be much harder to catch, though there was still some danger that they'd get him on the ground on Battue. She couldn't do anything about that. The problem now was to catch him before he left the system. Obviously he wasn't going to leave by liner this time and whistle the ship after him. She rubbed her hands on her thighs. "Yes. This. Get my associate and me up to my ship as quickly as possible. If you don't catch him on the ground, he'll slide through your defenses as if they didn't exist."

eleventh hour plus ten minutes CENTER
fourteenth hour plus ten minutes BATTUE

A man's voice on the speaker, relayed up from the ground.

"The force dome is down. Doors all open." A pause. The sound of feet, a few distant curses. "Bodies all over the place." Pause. A shouted question. "Not dead. Gassed. Medic hasn't placed the gas, but says it looks like they'll be out another hour at least." Another pause. More shouts—questions and answers. "The Aghir are gone. We got one of the outside guards stimmed enough he could answer questions. Said something he couldn't see or hear came out of nowhere and zapped him. Said that wasn't so long ago, far as he could tell about thirteenth hour plus twenty, no sooner than that. Said the flitter his tej came in was gone. Ghost probably used it, had five men to carry. Cenzai got his perimeter guards here ten minutes ago; they've started a gridded search pattern centered on the hall. Hope to find the flitter. Nothing yet. It's rugged country. Lots of trees, enough metallic ores about to screw the magnetics. That's about it for now." The speaker went dead except for a soft hiss.

Intaril frowned. "Missed him by a half hour. Maybe less."

Aleytys shrugged. "I gave the data to you within five minutes after we had the printout. What's left is hope. Hope I can locate and catch him before he hits Teegah's limit and skips into the intersplit. Hope he doesn't get excited and try to blow me away so I have to retaliate. If he gets into the intersplit, good-bye." She shrugged again. "You pay and get the Aghir back, Wolff loses the greater part of the fee."

"You wouldn't know where to look for him, you seem to know him well enough?"

"No, I wouldn't know where to look for him."

"You'd swear to that under verification?"

Aleytys shook her head, laughed. She felt more like laughing now with the greater part of her anxiety gone. It was working out—she could be loyal, to a degree at least, to both her ties—if she worked it right, if she could catch him in space. Intaril began to tap irritably at her knee. Aleytys quieted. "Despin' Intaril, you're a lot more persuasive than I if you can get the board on Helvetia to let me anywhere near their verifier. The one time they tried it, it had fits and no, I wasn't fooling with it, I was really trying to cooperate." She rubbed her thumb across her chin. "Point is to catch him here. My ship's no match for his, but he's handicapped by having to move under full shielding, slows him, and he knows what I can do if I get in range."

"The tikh'asfour."

"As you say."

"May I remind you there are five of our clients aboard?"

"I'm aware of that. Given a chance to talk, I'll probably have to offer safe conduct out of the system in exchange for the return of the Aghir." She eyed the silent Director. "You agree to that?"

Intaril was silent a long moment, then she nodded. "We must get the Aghir back."

The pilot appeared in the archway. "The transfer tube is locked in place. If the Hunter will cycle open her lock, we can complete the transfer."

Intaril stood. "I'm coming with you."

Aleytys stood. "Up to you. Don't interfere, that's all."

"I'm not a fool, Hunter."

"We'll see." Aleytys started for the lock, Tamris behind her, Intaril following them.

THE BOY AND THE THIEF

third hour plus five minutes HAZARDEE
fourth hour plus five minutes BATTUE
first hour plus five minutes CENTER

Black and cold. Overcast. Late. Water heaving up and
down with a heavy sullen rhythm as if oppressed by the sluggish air. An unpleasant night, sultry but not threatening rain,
not yet. With bouyant swimpacks the thief and the boy
slipped into the water, they wouldn't be coming back this
time, so the Vijayne's money and jewels and anything else of
value were coming with them. They swam the channel between Hazardee and the nameless island with rather more
ease than before, climbed the ridge and slid under Butterball's shield.

Again they crept across the water toward the tight-drawn
ring of warning stations now surrounding Battue. Thanks to
Maissa's Vryhh and the work he'd done on the ship in pay-
ment of his debt, they slipped past the guard ring without
wiggling a needle and felt their way over the land to the
mountains.

eighth hour plus thirty BATTUE
fifth hour plus thirty CENTER

The dew had burned off the rock. The snow caps and gla-
ciers were dripping in the warm brilliant sunlight even this
early in the morning. The day promised hot and bright. No
clouds now, not a sign of any to come. The thief eased back
on the shield, opened a window in it so he could see where
he was going, flew slow and low among the mountain peaks,
winding in and out of them in leisurely curves, in no hurry
now.

164

He put the ship down on a small flat not far from the peak that held the hall, clamped the shield down tight again and sat back, a grin on his face. "Almost home," he said to the boy.

The boy wrinkled his nose and rubbed at his stomach, the cold knot back again. He didn't say anything but started collecting the gear they'd need, the thief's tools and the chameleon web.

It took them a little more than two hours to climb close to the truncated peak that held the hall. They stopped in the shelter of some prickly spindly brush and a few stunted trees not far from the chewed-up ring of naked earth outside the fence. The boy narrowed his eyes at the stretch of red earth. "It's mined," he said.

"Nasty minds they got." The thief snapped a blanket open and spread it on the grass and leaves beneath the trees. He dropped onto it and sat with his back against the trunk so he could see the hall through a thin screen of brush. He reached into the pack and pulled out a thermos, unscrewed the mugs, handed one to the boy, filled them both with hot sweet cha from the thermos. The two of them settled down to wait.

Silence. The song of birds. The crackle of small beasts in the grass and brush. A series of barks suddenly cut off. A shattering bray of some larger animal, annoyed, a good distance off. The robot guards were gone. The hall was squat, powerful, and serene, deserted. The sun was very warm on them, coming strong through the spotty new spring foliage. After a while the boy went to sleep.

twelfth hour plus three minutes BATTUE
ninth hour plus three minutes CENTER

The pulsing whine of several floats woke the boy. The thief was on his knees, watching, as five floats came from five directions converging on the hall, timing their arrivals so they set down on the five landing stages separately but simultaneously. The boy and the thief watched as five men came walking around inside the fence. Sounds carried well in the calm crisp air. Voices came, words indistinct, as they attached small generators to every tenth fencepost. Still working they disappeared around behind the hall. A moment later a force dome clicked into being, clicked off again. Shortly af-

ter that two men came walking around the hall and climbed
up onto the two landing stages visible to the boy and the
thief; each stood guard with his back to the great bronze double doors marked with his master's sigil, waiting the arrival of
the tejed. It would take five keys applied together to open the
hall—the Aghir trusted each other even less than they trusted
the Cazarits.

Out in the brush, time passed slowly now. The boy was beginning to grow tense with excitement and a generalized foreboding. The excitement was familiar and welcome, the foreboding was not.

thirteenth hour plus two minutes BATTUE
tenth hour plus two minutes CENTER

Small flotillas of flitters and floats came from five points
and converged on the hall. The tejed applied the keys and
stepped back. The boy watched the doors clash open then
slide closed once the tej and his entourage had marched inside leaving a single guard standing on the stage. The dome
went up as soon as the doors were shut. Behind the boy the
thief was climbing into the chameleon web. Leaving the cowl
hanging and his hands free, he came up beside the boy.
"Force dome bother you?"

"No, you know that."

The thief ruffled the boy's hair, still a bright blond since
they hadn't taken time to strip off the dye. "Huffy, aren't you.
They've had time to settle. Pop 'em."

The boy *reached* into the building, felt about for the gas
bladders. One by one, he twitched away the patches and let
the gas out. Near odorless, colorless, slightly heavier than air,
it wouldn't take long to fill the room. They waited, boy and
thief, for what seemed an endless interval but was only a few
minutes, then the thief stood. "My turn," he said. He pulled
his hands into the web, smoothed the wrist slits shut, pulled
up the cowl and clamped the mask in place.

The boy could sense him and hear the soft brush of his
feet but he saw nothing—as the two guards facing this way
saw nothing. On the edge of the bare strip the boy saw a
circle of light bloom on the grass then begin rising, almost invisible in the brilliant sunlight. It tilted a trifle and drifted inward over the strip of ground, over the fence. It hovered for

some minutes before the forcedome. The boy heard a faint whine and a few snappings, then the light merged easily with the dome, oozed through it; once inside, the circle sank quickly, vanished as it touched the ground.

The boy watched, grinned as the guard jerked then collapsed. A moment later the same thing happened to the second guard he could see. He sat on his heels and waited, the birds singing in the distance, the wind rustling through the soft new leaves overhead. Then he laughed and got to his feet. The forcedome was down.

He ran quickly up the hill, stopped at the edge of the cleared ground, strained, lifted himself in a slanting rise over the fence, curled into a ball and let himself fall inside. He came up onto his feet with a bounce and another laugh, ran to the tall bronze doors. A head appeared, resting on nothing. The thief peeled out of the web, rolled it into a small compact bundle, tucked it into its pouch. "Ready?" he said.

The boy nodded. He flattened his hands on the door about the lock; he studied it a minute, then tripped it. All around the hall the doors slipped open. A sudden whoosh of gas-tainted air blasted past him along with strains of music, swirling, skirling, incongruously lively music. The boy snorted out the gas that crept into his nose, tucked filters into his nostrils, and followed the thief inside, swaggering to the beat of the music.

"The Aghir tejed." The thief spoke with intense satisfaction, the gambling fever glistening in his eyes again. "We beat her, little brother."

The boy nodded again, stopped beside a girl lying among a puff of crumpled robes. She'd been wearing a veil, but her hand had caught in it and dragged one side loose when she went down. She wasn't exactly pretty but if she had some life in her face, she might come close to being beautiful. As she lay unconscious on the stone floor she was scowling and her face was haggard as if she hadn't been sleeping much lately. "What about the girl? She looks important."

"Leave her. We have enough work with the five. Get this one's heels. He's Liros, the only one from what I hear worth what we're going to ask for him. I got the flitter open back there. We'll use it to take the men to the ship."

The boy caught hold of the gleaming black boots, lifted them as the thief lifted the man's shoulders. They carried him

out, stuffed him in the back of the flitter, went back inside
for the next one.

The *Butterball*'s shield was on flicker when the first Cazarits arrived. The boy was on watch in the control room, getting a series of quick looks at the surrounding countryside
while the thief was in the hold adjusting the sleep machines
on their captives' heads. The arflot whipped in from the east,
circled the hall, hovered a moment, then landed on the stage
where the flitter now outside their ship had been. In one of
the flicks the boy saw a vague undetailed figure jump out and
run into the hall.

The thief came in, saw what was happening, swore. "Your
mother's doing, little brother. This place will be swarming."
He settled himself at the console. "Strap in, we're moving."

Shieldflicker at a minimum, the ship crept across the rolling hills, enough eyes out to protect against running into a
flitter or float rushing inland to the search. Twice the boy
caught a glimpse of a large flier of some sort, but these were
too distant to be a worry. What did worry him was the drain
on the fuel cells; all this hovering was expensive in fuel. The
thief watched the quiver of the needles, shook his head. "The
first jump will have to be a short one. We'll have to stop at
Hadelvor to refuel."

The boy looked at him thoughtfully, watched him smile
with a flutter behind his diaphragm, but he said nothing.
Hadelvor was a wide-open world, a crossroads tavern of sorts
for small traders, smugglers, mercenaries, assassins, thieves on
the run, most anyone not affiliated with a Company. There
were games there of all sorts for those who liked to gamble.
The only hope he could dig out of the situation lay in the five
sleeping bodies in the hold. The thief usually managed to dis-
regard his weakness when they had a bit of business going,
but after that. . . . The boy bit back a protest that would be
worse than useless, would probably goad the thief into doing
exactly what he wanted to stop him doing. Lately it seemed
to him the fever in the man was burning hotter, maybe the
time would come when it burned out of control. He looked
down at fisted hands, slanted a glance at the thief's intent
face. Keep him busy, he thought. Working. He thought, if my
mother catches up with us and takes the Aghir back, then

he'll have to fix up another job that much sooner—and felt
like a traitor for thinking it.

"Water ahead," the thief said. "A few more minutes and
up we go."

They edged away from Cazarit, the shield hardened to
near complete impermeability. The ship's nose poked delicately at the web of detector fields between the guard satel-
lites, teased open a hole large enough for the ship to squirt
through. Without troubling a single alarm it passed the guard
ring and began spiralling outward. The heat inside grew near
unbearable since the shield would not allow it to radiate away
and the thief couldn't spare the power to operate the coolers.

At the end of the first hour the thief dropped the ship a so-
lar radius below the plane of the ecliptic and started the
flicker going. Slowly, very slowly, the heat began to dissipate.
While that made them more comfortable, it was also dangerous since it made them vulnerable to heatseekers should a
ship pass close enough—something not too likely where they
were traveling now.

Another hour passed. Nothing much seemed to be happening. The thief didn't talk, just watched the screen with a
small tight smile. The boy grew tired of sitting and seeing
nothing, left his chair and wandered away. He went down to
the hold to look at the snoring bodies. He moved from one to
the other, gazing gravely at the slack faces. He didn't know
them or what they were like, though most seemed people to
avoid. The man who'd sprawled beside the girl had a cold
look the boy didn't care for. Cold look, cold belly. His stomach was turning to a single block of ice. He stared at the five
men, hating them for tempting the thief with their fabulous
wealth, hating them because the man who was now father
and elder brother was destroying himself and there was nothing the boy could do about it. One day—not now, not a good
while yet, the boy hoped—the thief in his need would take an
extra risk and lose it, lose everything. He scowled at the men,
hating his mother. It's her brought us here, he thought, we
don't need this snatch, we got plenty money, she's why he
went after this game. We beat her, the boy told himself, but
he couldn't make himself believe it. He wouldn't believe it
until they were safe in the intersplit.

The boy wandered about the small ship a bit more, made some cha, went back to the bridge with a cup for the man.

The thief was hunched over the console, tense, shoulders stiff, hands clutching the chair arms. Stiffly the boy crossed the room, the steaming mug cradled between his two hands. He stopped by the thief's arm, saw the small dim blip in the screen. It moved off the screen, the ship it marked forging ahead of them. Ahead and above, the boy thought. He started to speak, stopped. The blip came back, began to grow larger as the ship came toward them.

LILIT

She stirred. A sweet smell lingered in her nostrils a moment, then was swept away by gusts of very cold, greenly pungent air. She moved her hands. One hand was caught in her veil. She was lying down, her robes bunched uncomfortably beneath and around her. Head throbbing, mind sodden, she fumbled her hands to the stone and pushed at it. Her hands slipped, the bulky robes bound her, making movement awkward, the satin and wire and beads slid noisily across the polished stone. She struggled upright after minutes of floundering. Around her she heard groans, other noises, voices. She blinked repeatedly, trying to clear the persistent mist from her eyes, the fog from her brain. Absently she snapped the veil back in place. Her face and hands were cold, but her body was very hot. She blurred, felt herself falling over, came out of it still sitting in the pouf of her robes. She took a deep breath, looked around.

Several strange men stood in the center of the hall, not far from her; near them was a pile of something, she couldn't see, her eyes were blurring again, yes, sidearms, yes, a careless heap of darters, stunners, an energy pistol or two, knives and other deadly looking things, chains and sticks. When she found herself beginning to count them, she wrenched her eyes away. She wiped at her forehead, stared at the film of dust and sweat on her hand. She swallowed, turned her head slowly, inspected the hall, realizing suddenly that there was no music. They stopped playing, she thought, and wondered why that felt odd to her. Gas, she thought suddenly, we were gassed. How long ago? She looked about for her father, expecting to see him bustling about, taking charge—and noticed for the first time that the thrones were empty. The tejed were gone.

Gone.

No.

Heat flashed through her. Her head felt as if it were about to explode. No, she thought. No. No.

Around the conference hall guards and overseers were getting to their feet and staring about, dazed, feeling at their heads. Confusion. An overseer shouted close behind her, a roar of anger that bit into her head. She gasped, started to raise her hands to her temples but her arms were too heavy. The overseer came lumbering past her. She saw it was Ameersin, Ianina's husband. She forced her arms up, pressed the heels of her hands against her temples. What's wrong with me? So slow. So heavy. Can't think. . . .

A smallish blond man in blue velvet pants and a ruffled shirt stopped Ameersin; their voices burred in her ears like insect noises, were lost in the growing clamor as other overseers and guard captains found their tej vanished. Someone behind her flung an accusation at another unseen someone, got an angry obscene reply. There was the sound of scuffling, the meaty smack of flesh on flesh, the hall filled with echoing noise. She couldn't think, could scarcely remember to breathe. . . .

A sizzle-crack, a flash of intense, blue-white light, the smell of hot metal, melted plastic, charred stone. The man in the blue velvet pants tossed the energy gun atop the pile of smoking ruined weapons. In the sudden silence his rather high voice was like the cracking of ice. "Return to your places," he said. He didn't have to say that the next target could be one of them. He waited.

The guards shuffled sullenly back to the empty thrones. The overseers followed more reluctantly. Ameersin stayed where he was.

"I am Yastro f'Voine, chief of security on Cazarit," the blond man said. "Your tejed has been snatched—shut your mouths!" he roared. "Snatched because they were fools. We have a Wolff Hunter on the snatcher's tail. Within the next hour we should have the tejed back here. You can wait or return to the lodges. You'd be more comfortable there."

How long were we out? Lilit thought urgently. She moistened her lips but couldn't make herself speak. Her voice would shake, she knew, and she didn't want to draw attention to herself. She trembled with relief when Ameersin said, "How long were we out? What time is it now?"

"Four hours," f'Voine said. He was smooth again, spreading soothing oil on the outburst that followed. Lilit closed her eyes and shut out also the indignant questions, the silky answers. No, she thought, it can't all be a waste. Four hours. She thought about the three robes rubbing against each other, reacting on each other. We can't just go home and come back tomorrow, we can't, it can't be dribbled away.

"We'll stay here," Ameersin said finally; he moved his massive head around, saw the nods of the other overseers. "About an hour, you said." He scowled at f'Voine.

F'Voine bowed, a slight inclination of his sleek blond head.

After a quick look at Lilit, Ameersin snapped a series of commands at Ianina and Genlana.

Play the game, Lilit thought and was glad of the veil that hid her face. Play the game for me, you greedy muddog. You hope Father is killed because you think if he is, Liros is yours. Keep them here, dust me off, don't take chances, play the game.

Flustered, the two women bustled to the center of the hall, lifted Lilit to her feet, fussed about her, straightening the crumpled outer robe, fluffing it out. Lilit stood docilely enough, swallowing her unease and annoyance. It seemed to her she could smell an acrid tang coming from her underrobes, but they made no mention of it, attributing it, she thought, if they noticed anything, to fear's effect on her. Each one holding an arm, they led her across the room to the Liros Throne. As she moved, she felt more strongly the heat in her body, a burning sensation on her skin whenever the thin shift brushed against her legs. Ianina and Gelana lowered her on the steps leading up to the throne. They seemed to find her lack of response rather daunting, even the more acerbic Gelana. Leaving her to her silence, they retreated to the wall and stood whispering together, watching the others in the hall.

Lilit sat and waited.

TAMRIS

She watched them face each other on the bridge, two dominants walking carefully around each other, sniffing at each other. Intaril looked about with casual curiosity that was hardly as casual as it seemed, moved with the wariness of someone penetrating for the first time into alien territory. And Aleytys had insensibly relaxed as soon as she stepped from the transfer tube. Homespace, Tamris thought with a surreptitious smile.

Aleytys flicked fingers at the control console. "You can make yourself useful," she told Intaril. "Get this ship cleared for free access to all space within Teegah's limit. I don't want to have to argue and I don't want to be blown out of space before I have time to defend myself."

Intaril eyed her a minute then smiled. She settled herself at the console and began working, no need for argument or explanation, never was with her, if she pushed, she did it for what advantage it would give her. Once again Tamris smiled, looked around, saw Aleytys watching her.

"You, my grinning young friend, you'll be doing the driving. I'll be in the pilgrim seat searching my own way. Be careful you don't run us into anything."

Tamris snorted.

Aleytys frowned. "Dip in close to the sun, spiral out, push the heatseekers to their limit, switch axes now and then. He probably went up or down to avoid difficulties with incoming ships or the patrol ships of the Cazarits. Stick to the plane of the ecliptic the first time out. Maybe he's close enough to give us a hint."

Tamris tugged at her tunic, sniffed irritably.

Aleytys laughed. "All right, lowly apprentice. All right, so

I'm telling you things you know perfectly well. It's the role of the dutiful apprentice to put up politely with the maunderings of her master." She shook her hands vigorously, moved her shoulders. "Right, let's get started."

ALEYTYS

The ship began the turns of the spiral, those turns quickly widening, the three women silent, watching, each in her own way, what was passing outside, Tamris and Intaril watching screen and readouts with quiet intensity, Aleytys stretched out in the pilgrim seat where privileged passengers rode, her eyes closed, reaching out and out—

Disturbing the silence of the bridge—

Three breathings—

Aleytys: soft, slow, long long breaths

Intaril: light, shallow, rapid, the panting of a hound on trace, not forced, a little excited, steady and confident

Tamris: steady rhythmic breathing, deep and slow, an artisan lost in her craft

Sub-audible vibration of the sub-light drive

steady tik-tak of heatseekers

challenge—now and then—from patrolships quickly silenced by code squirted at them by the computer

Slide of cloth across leather—Intaril or Tamris shifting position

She was only tenuously in her body. Buoyed up by Harskari and Shadith, she expanded out and out, reached for the remembered feel of the man, the flicker of fire and bright pain that was the boy.

The ship turned in the bends of the spiral neither slow nor fast, a smooth swing, Tamris doing her job with quiet efficiency, a good girl she was, a splendid young apprentice, a good hunter one day, Aleytys thought, smiled with affection.

An hour passed. Another.

Aleytys felt a tickle in the ghost body that was turning and elongating with the movement outward of the ship, feet in the sun, head—somewhere—she felt the teasing touch—she

176

turned and flowed, seeing herself as a huge amoeba flowing to engulf its prey, was gently amused by this—briefly—then was flowing around the little ship, the painfully familiar little ship, her amoeboid self quivering with the memories it woke, knowing it by touch, nearly every inch of it.

She flowed into it, feeling her way along. She hovered about two sparks, separated, one sitting still, the other moving about, knowing both of them, coiling about them. Her son was in the hold with much dimmer sparks, five of them, the Aghir, she winced away from them, not liking the way they tasted, like touching her tongue to nettles. She swirled about her son, wondering if he would sense her presence, but she was too tenuously there. He didn't feel her, but he was uneasy and growing more so. His foreboding shivered through her. She turned to the other spark. He was humming with contentment, perhaps not audibly, she couldn't tell about that, but she could feel his triumph and it made her sad.

She focused on her son again and was sad again, wanting to take his troubles on her shoulders and give him ease, knowing there was no way she could.

She brooded. It would be easy enough to let them slip away with their prey, she could lie and say she couldn't find him, go through the motions of searching while making sure they got nowhere near him. The link would show she'd done her best, done it only a few minutes too late. No one, not even Head would question this. She felt a kind of curdling in her ghostbody. No. She couldn't do it. Pride, self-respect, or something as simple as not wanting to look like a loser—good or bad reasons, she simply couldn't do it. She argued more with herself as she felt the boyfire huddle against the manfire, felt the shock as her ship must have appeared on their screens. I want my son, she thought and that woke in her an anger and a longing so intense it shook her from her outreach, snapping her painfully back within her body. She felt a tightness in her skin, a stickiness rolling across her face into her hair and knew she was weeping, silently steadily weeping.

She opened her eyes. They burned and blurred. She pressed the backs of her hands against her eyes until the burning went away. When she took her hands down she saw Intaril watching her; beside her Tamris was still intent on the console. This is why she came, Aleytys thought, to watch me.

With a sense that she was losing something inexpressible but intimately, necessarily a part of her, feeling old, weary, grimy, she said, "Down. Back toward the sun. You should get a reading in the heat seekers within the next few minutes."

She dropped her head back, closed her eyes. It wasn't over yet, Stavver had to be convinced, Intaril persuaded, the Aghir carted back to the hall. I wish this was over, she thought. Let it be over soon.

THE BOY AND THE THIEF

The communicator chimed. Stavver listened to the repetition of the musical sounds, fingers tapping on the chair arm. "I could wish that stomach of yours was a poorer prophet, little brother."

"We got to be faster," the boy said. "Dump the shield and run."

"Not enough faster, little brother, not with your mother that close." He tapped on the communicator but left the imager shut down. "Well, well," he said. "Bad luck herself."

"Cautious, aren't you, my ghostly friend."

"I'm choosy about who gets pictures of me."

"Too bad, there're quite a lot of them in Cazarit computers."

"Thanks to you."

"You provided the source, not I."

"Name, history?"

"Not yet."

"Ah. Incentive?"

"I want the tejed, my friend."

"Ready to do a deal?"

"Depends. If I have to."

"If I have to, I can blow the ship. That you can't stop. No company slavepens for me."

"You know me, my friend. What I promise, I perform."

"If you can."

"Yes."

"No ransom, I suppose."

"No."

"Escort to Teegah's Limit?"

"In exchange for what?"

"Five peacefully sleeping bodies."

"Delivered here and now."

"Delivered at the Limit."

"No. Here and now. I'll escort you to the Limit, turn you loose."

"And Cazarit will let you do that?"

"Let me?" She chuckled.

"Stop bragging and answer me."

"Cazar Company has a registered agreement with Hunters. If I get the Aghir back, I can do what I want with you."

"Registered. Some consolation if I'm a gaggle of isolated atoms. I'll deliver them at the Limit."

"No. You're a touch too slippery, my friend. I want them now. If Cazarits try to interfere, I'll take them out. And it'll cost them heavy. Double my fee. You ought to see my fee."

"Looks like I'm in the wrong business." He was relaxed now, playing word games with the woman. The boy rubbed at his stomach; the foreboding ache was gone, but he still hurt. There was a shine in the thief's milky blue eyes not unlike the fever shine they got when he was deep in a game. The boy stared at his mother's smiling face, sick with hurting and hating. He wanted to get out of the room. He couldn't move. He wanted to scream at her that he hated her, he wanted to ask her why she went away and left him.

"Looks like. Well?"

"Been a long time."

"You seem to've kept busy."

"You too or so the rumors say." He pulled at his nose. "Too bad. Anyone else, I'd have beat it."

"Kind of you. You never could resist a challenge. A weakness, my friend, you ought to fight it. And all those pictures in a company computer, careless of you." She smiled suddenly, her blue-green eyes glistening with laughter. "But you know how to handle that, I'm sure. Stop stalling. Lay to, or. . . ." She raised a brow.

"Or you'll do it for me. Well, can't say I didn't try." He shut off the drive, left the ship drifting outward; the boy smiled then. They weren't that far from the Limit, if the thief could just stall a bit more. . . .

"Drop the shields too, you forget I know that ship." The pleasant contralto voice was still quavering with laughter. "And I know your tricks, you're not going to slide away on me."

"I get the message. You got a lifeboat in that fancy piece of junk?"

"Yes. Big enough to haul five sleepers."

"Bring it over. I'll have the slip open."

"You never give up, do you. Wish I could bring it myself, but I don't think that's a good idea. My associate will bring it across. I'm getting a bit impatient, friend. Drop the shields."

He grimaced, but tapped the shields off. "Satisfied?"

"You've always been good at that. Satisfying me." She laughed and turned away.

The boy could still see her and hear a murmur of sound, but he couldn't hear what she was saying to people outside the range of the imager. She kept her head turned for several minutes, listening and speaking and listening, then came around again.

"There'll be two in the lifeboat," she said. She wasn't smiling any longer. "Watch out for the Director, I don't know what she's up to, why she wanted to get into your ship. I suspect she'll try planting a tracer of some sort, she doesn't like being beaten. Let me see him. Please."

The boy darted back to the doorway, laughing. At last he had a way to hurt her. When the thief looked at him, he shook his head vigorously. "No," he said.

The thief shrugged. "He says no."

The boy watched his mother close her eyes, press her lips together. He grinned fiercely, hot triumph exploding inside him. He watched her hurt, watched with some disappointment as her face smoothed out.

She brushed her fingertips quickly lightly across her forehead. "Open the slip, the boat's getting close."

LILIT

She sat on the steps, her hands clasped loosely in her lap. Guards and overseers clustered in small groups, sullen, silent, for the most part, a few talking in hushed tones. The Cazarits were standing by one of the open doors, talking now and then, now and then someone coming in from outside to murmur to f'Voine. Lilit looked over their heads at the few bits of sky she could see through the open doors, the green brushy slopes of the neighboring mountain, and the snow on the peaks beyond it. Her breath issued from her mouth in puffs of vapor. It was very cold now, the Cazarits couldn't shut the doors without the Aghir keys—well, they could shut them, but couldn't get them open again. Shadows were long on the slopes outside and the air was beginning to thicken. It will be sundown soon, she thought. She'd been wearing the robes for over five hours; she could feel the heat they were producing, it was getting worse, she thought, fast. They were reacting on each other, those robes, whatever it was that Acthon had given her to make them of. He should have told me what would happen, she thought. You should have told me, brother, even after I said I didn't want to know. You should have made me listen so I'd know what to expect now.

There was a whining roar outside, suddenly cut off. The Cazarits moved back a little, abruptly alert, all of them intent on the door. Lilit pulled her hands apart, flattened one of them on the cold stone beside her. The shock of the cold broke up the floating haze in her head. Her face was flushed, she could feel the heat, but the veil would hide that. Her hand was getting numb; she lifted it, set it in her lap, flattened the other on the stone. Another shock. Metis, she cried out, a silent cry, help me last. Help me.

She heard the grating of the flitter landing on the stage outside.

An ugly woman marched in. Tall, skinny, black hair, black eyes. Marched in like she owned the hall and everyone in it. And the way the Cazarits treated her it might be so; Lilit watched her, hated her, envied her.

Kalyen-tej walked in.

And Lanten-tej of Alretas, Issel-tej of Sikain, Ael-tej of Staam, Vizek-tej of Vahad.

A red-haired woman strolled in, a girl beside her no older, it seemed to Lilit, than herself. Both of them looked to be hovering between amusement and disgust, both independent, holding themselves apart from all the fuss, the girl especially was trying to hide her laughter and not succeeding very well. The two women moved behind the others toward the center of the hall, side by side in evident camaraderie. Lilit watched them, so suddenly filled with rage she thought her head would explode—she suddenly began giggling uncontrollably, exploding, exploding, her head was going to explode. She faded into one of the blurs when everything was a roaring mishmash of garbled sound and light.

She came out of it and saw the red-haired woman and the girl were standing a little apart from the ugly woman and f'Voine looking idly about the room. Lilit blinked. The blurs were coming and going at shorter intervals. She moved her fingers, her hands were hot, a little numb. She thought of pulling the tearstrip now, but the doors were still open and she wasn't sure the death she carried would be effective with them open. You should have told me, brother, you should have explained better, you should have made me listen. I don't know. . . . She blurred, blinked at the knot of people arguing in the center of the hall. It was getting dark, it was hard to turn her head, but she did and stared out a door on the far side of the hall. The sky was layered with faint rose and pale amber, a tinge of lavender. Sunset. This day's finished, she thought. She blurred again, and when she came out of it, went back to watching the group in the center of the hall. Go home, she thought. Leave us alone.

As if in answer, the group began breaking apart. Cazarits in plain dark shipsuits were fanning out. She watched them start searching the room. One of them went out and came back with a lift belt. He bounced up to the top of the walls and began poking carefully into the crack between wall and roof. Others were poking sensor tipped rods into every corner, glancing at buzzing black boxes cable-linked to the rods. Lilit watched dully as a group of three came toward her, wondering if the silver wire and beads would be enough to shield what she carried.

"Keep away from her," Lanten-tej roared, his bull voice filling the room, startling out of his sagging sloppy body. "You. Get away!" He wobbled around, spoke more quietly but as intensely to the ugly woman.

Lilit smiled behind her veil. He was having no strange males poking around his virgin bride. What a stupid creature, she thought. Poor toad, she thought, keep it up, you're my ally though you don't know it.

Kalyen-tej shrugged impatiently, said something in a low voice and came striding over to her. He took her hand. "Can you stand a moment?" he murmured.

After a minute, she said softly, "I'm stiff, a little dizzy, that's all."

Her father slipped his hand under her arm and lifted her onto her feet. He held her up until she nodded, then he led her slowly several steps from the stairs. "Do it," he called over his shoulder to the hovering Cazarits, his voice chill, disciplined. Lilit looked up at him. His face was paler than usual and his eyes had the glassy look they took on when he was suffering one of his increasingly less rare migraines. Without thinking, she patted his arm to comfort him as if he were Metis. He looked startled, then grim. He said nothing, glanced over his shoulder at the stairs. "They're finished," he said. "This will be over soon." His voice was calm, impersonal, he wore his ice mask again, the moment of weakness when he'd almost seen her disciplined away. He left her sitting on the steps again and went back to the group on the silver star. Hands clasped loosely in her lap, she watched him stand beside the ugly woman, talking easily with her, as easily as he'd talk to a man.

The search went on, some of the Cazarits going outside to poke around the base of the hall, or so she supposed. They were as suspicious as the worst of the tejed. She looked out the door and saw the sky turned to a deep violet, almost black, a few stars blooming in the velvet patch of darkness. And the Cazarits were still there, still poking about.

She blurred. She was swimming in fatigue and the poison fumes of the robes.

When her eyes focused again, the red-haired woman was standing beside her.

"You're ill," she said softly; her eyes were far too shrewd, too understanding.

Lilit stared at her. "No."

"I'm a healer, despina." She stretched out a long slim hand but didn't quite touch Lilit. "If you'll let me, I can help."

Lilit looked at the hand a long time, it was strong; she could feel life in it like electricity, the skin was smooth, soft, but the tendons and muscles beneath gave it a vigor and look of competence she found both strange and attractive. She wanted to let the hand touch her but she didn't dare. "No," she said finally. "There are reasons," she said, the words almost forced from her. She lifted her head, looked past the woman. "If you'll look around, you'll see my bridegroom," she said. "The toad looking at me out of toad eyes."

The woman glanced over her shoulder, saw Aretas watching them, turned back with a shudder. "Come with us," she said urgently. "I can get you out. I don't give a hollow damn about the fuss."

Lilit blurred. When she came back, it was a moment before she remembered what the woman had said. For another moment the temptation was almost more than she could endure; she sighed and the sigh sounded like a sob to her. "No," she said. "There are reasons," she repeated.

The woman reached out so suddenly Lilit had no chance to move or protest. Cool fingers rested briefly on her wrist then jerked away. "I see," she said. "You're sure?"

"Yes," Lilit said. She would have said more but it was suddenly too great an effort, besides she didn't think she needed to say more, the woman understood.

"May everything be as you wish," the woman said, turned and walked away to stand silent beside her young companion. The girl said something, the woman shook her head.

Get this over with, Lilit thought. Finish and leave. I'm so tired. Please. Please. Please. Please.

Several of the Cazarits gathered suddenly before the ugly woman and the cluster of the tejed. They spoke, she heard them speak, heard the words clearly enough, but she couldn't understand what they meant. She blurred out. Began to sway. Came back shaking inside her robes. She concentrated on holding herself up, getting her head clear. Go, she thought, leave us alone.

The ugly woman spoke. "Security reports the building and enclosure clear of possible danger. There should be no further difficulties. We regret the inconvenience you've suffered, but we are sure you will recognize the dispatch with which we dealt with the problem you yourselves exacerbated by your unwillingness to allow my security to patrol the island. Is there anything further you wish?"

"Your absence. Off the island." Aretas had been staring at Lilit for several minutes, a flush rising in his face. Behind her veil Lilit smiled. My co-conspirator, she thought. Boom on, my toad, my sweet stupid toad. Sweep them out for me.

"Go away," Aretas boomed. "All of you. We don't want you snooping around us."

Kalyen-tej stirred. He half-lifted a hand, let it drop.

Isn't he a lovely bridegroom, Father dear, she thought. So handsome, so intelligent. She watched with satisfaction the faint signs of disgust in her father's face. He turned to look at her. She dropped her eyes.

She blurred.

She came back to see the doors closed, the other tej on their thrones. Her father was standing alone on the silver star. Lilit couldn't be angry any more. She was only tired. Aretas was eager to get the formalities over and bed her, she knew that. She didn't care. She didn't care about anything now. Let it be over, she thought,

let it be over

let it be over

let it be over. . . .

The music started again. Soft at first, then louder as Kalyen-tej came for her. She flexed her fingers, felt them move against the satin of her robe.

Her father came for her, stretched out his hand. She took his hand, saw him frown at the burning heat in hers. For a moment she thought she wasn't going to be able to stand, but she managed it. She walked beside him, her steps slow and halting. She could feel her father's impatience, was impatient with herself, but her body was doing all it could. She kept her eyes on the stone in front of her, saying over and over to herself, let it be over, let it be over.

She saw the inlaid silver star, marred by burn marks and a

few dabs of melted plastic. Someone got it cleaned, she thought and was vaguely surprised. She didn't remember any-one cleaning up the mess of the charred and melted weapons. She stared at the star and marveled that someone in all the fuss had found time to order it cleaned.

Her father stopped her when she stood in the center of the star.

"Eamon-tej of the Lanten line," her father said. "Do you permit that I present a daughter of the Line of Kalyen?" Her father's voice was devoid of all expression.

"I do permit and with pleasure, Mannen-tej of the Kalyen Line." Aretas gabbled the words, leaning forward, his bulging eyes on Lilit.

Lilit worked her hand up under the headcloth, under the sweat-sodden hair and closed her fingers about the tear strip.

Her father stepped in front of her, unsnapped the veil, frowned down at her flushed haggard face.

She smiled at him

and jerked loose the tearstrip—

noise, sudden searing heat, her father's mouth hanging open

He stood at the window looking down at the bright spiral of Midway, playing with a smoothstone. Behind him a woman sat on the rumpled bed doing up her high boots. She had a thin rather worn face, a dancer's disciplined body, was a dancer with a troupe about to end its engagement on Caz-arit. "We're leaving tomorrow," she said. She stood, wrapped her short skirt around her and pressed the seam shut, picked up her flimsy black jersey, paused as three soft chimes sound-ed in the room. "What's that?"

"Nothing," he said. "A timer."

"Finished faster than you expected, did we?" She laughed, finished dressing, raked her fingers through her tousled hair. "See you 'round," she said.

As soon as she was gone, he moved swiftly about the room, gathering his meager belongings, packed them with quick, neat movements, not hurrying but not wasting a mo-ment.

In five minutes he left the room, a short neat dark man, went down the lift tube, whistling almost inaudibly. At the desk, he picked up a shuttle ticket, checked out and paid his bill. The plastic person at the desk—that was how he thought of the flesh and bone employees of Cazarit, he preferred the metal kind—congratulated him on getting the first shuttle up since the freeze was lifted. He smiled blandly at the youth, said with deliberate banality, "Well, isn't that a kick. Marvelous place you got here, enjoyed myself, I did. Be back next year, you wait." He strolled away from the desk, unhurried, unworried, an unobtrusive little man like so many more about, already out of the desk clerk's memory.

He eased his ship away from the parking orbit and started at a moderate speed for Teegah's Limit, letting himself go tense here where no one was watching. It seemed to him it took forever to reach the Limit, but he didn't dare call attention to himself yet by yielding to his urge to get the hell out before the lid blew off.

At the Limit, he spoke into his transmitter. "Apotheosis," he said quietly. "Apotheosis." With the howl of a Cazarit patrol in his ears, he slid into the intersplit.

Acthon stepped from the wall and walked briskly to the Weksar transmitter. A red light was burning, a signal that a message was waiting for him. He touched *playback*.

"Apotheosis." The smuggler's voice, quiet and unobtrusive like the man. "Apotheosis."

"Lilit," Acthon said softly. "So it's done, sister." For a moment he stood staring at nothing, then he got busy at the transmitter, sent the message on to the other Aghir worlds; that done, he erased the tape, walked back into the wall, out of the Hold.

Elf sat scratching the pulsing throat of the flier, amber eyes glowing. "Time?" she asked.

Acthon nodded. "Time. Tell them."

On Hadelvor:

Desperate when the thief was being goaded into throwing *Butterball* into the pot, the boy *reached* inside him and pinched off the blood flow to his brain long enough to knock him out. He had him carried back to the ship and sat beside him waiting for him to wake.

On Wolff:

Head was waiting at the landing field. "Someone got the Aghir," she said. "You covered?"

"Should be." Aleytys glanced at Tamris who raised a brow and tapped the link. "Cazarit Security searched the hall and the enclosure and certified it clean, that's in the link." While she said this she was thinking, so she brought it off, paid a price but she brought it off.

"Good. Cazar is unhappy and trying to pass it on to us."

"The ghost—they blaming it on him?"

"Trying to."

"Oh hell, I've got things I want to do this year."

"Better plan to spend most of it on Helvetia." She took Aleytys by the arm, hugged Tamris and started walking with them toward the terminal building. "Not wanting to take chances, I've got a rep from the escrow board here to take custody of the link."

"Good idea." Aleytys chuckled. "I think Mari will be quite pleased to be rid of the thing. Grey back?"

"Heard from him two days ago. He's wound it up and heading home. Should be here in about ten days."

At the edge of the metacrete, Aleytys freed her arm and turned to look across the field. Swardheld wasn't back yet, no way he could be, just as well. A bit of time for myself. I need it. Things to think about. Complications. Grey and Swardheld. Wolff. Vrithian and my mother. Where I go from here. She sighed and followed the others into the terminal building.

Presenting C. J. CHERRYH

☐ **PORT ETERNITY.** An Arthurian legend of future time and outer space. (#UE1769—$2.50)

☐ **DOWNBELOW STATION.** A blockbuster of a novel! Interstellar warfare as humanity's colonies rise in cosmic rebellion. 1982 Hugo-winner! (#UE1828—$2.75)

☐ **SERPENT'S REACH.** Two races lived in harmony in a quarantined constellation—until one person broke the truce! (#UE1682—$2.50)

☐ **THE PRIDE OF CHANUR.** "Immensely successful . . . *Tour de force . . .* This is quintessential SF. . . ."—Algis Budrys. (#UE1694—$2.95)

☐ **HUNTER OF WORLDS.** Triple fetters of the mind served to keep their human prey bondage to this city-sized starship. (#UE1872—$2.95)

☐ **THE FADED SUN: KESRITH.** Universal praise for this novel of the last members of humanity's warrior-enemies . . . and the Earthman who was fated to save them. (#UE1813—$2.95)

☐ **THE FADED SUN: SHON'JIR.** Across the untracked stars to the forgotten world of the Mri go the last of that warrior race and the man who had betrayed humanity. (#UE1753—$2.50)

☐ **THE FADED SUN: KUTATH.** The final and dramatic conclusion of this bestselling trilogy—with three worlds in militant confrontation. (#UE1856—$2.75)

☐ **HESTIA.** A single engineer faces the terrors and problems of an endangered colony planet. (#UE1680—$2.25)